Isla Gordon lives on the Jurassic Coast of England with her T. rex-sized Bernese mountain dog. Isla has been writing professionally since 2013 (and unprofessionally since she can remember). She also has five romantic comedies published under the name Lisa Dickenson. Isla can't go a day without finding dog hair in her mouth.

The Christmas Express

ISLA GORDON

SPHERE

SPHERE

First published in Great Britain in 2024 by Sphere

1 3 5 7 9 10 8 6 4 2

Copyright © 2024 by Lisa Dickenson

The moral right of the author has been asserted.

A CIP catalogue record for this book
is available from the British Library.

ISBN 978-1-4087-2895-6

Typeset in Caslon by M Rules
Printed and bound in Great Britain by
Clays Ltd, Elcograf S.p.A.

Papers used by Sphere are from well-managed forests
and other responsible sources.

Sphere
An imprint of
Little, Brown Book Group
Carmelite House
50 Victoria Embankment
London EC4Y 0DZ

An Hachette UK Company
www.hachette.co.uk

www.littlebrown.co.uk

Dedicated to
Hannah and Bec
My Dream Team ♥

Prologue

Bryn

Let me pose a question to you: if you had a scab, would you pick it? What if the scab had been there for five years and was extremely crusty? What if the scab was in the shape of five people you once called your friends, and picking at the scab could open the wound and make it all horrible and painful again? But also, what if picking it made your skin finally able to breathe?

Sorry. This is not the best opening to a tale about a snowy winter. I should have started by telling you that I'm inside a vast wooden cabin, like something out of *Architectural Digest* or maybe a Canadian Christmas movie. The only sound is coming from the crackling fireplace to my left, filled with naturally scented woods that fill the home with the most festive, fir-tree smell you could imagine. I should

1

have described how I'm sat at a desk in front of a window overlooking a glittering white winter wonderland, unusually snow-coated for November on Vancouver Island, with views of lakes and mountains and trees.

Christmastime is coming. I can feel it in the mountain air, in the frost on the window panes, in the high spirits, in the slowing down of bear sightings as they begin hibernation.

Any minute now, the cabin will come alive again with the sound of my fiancée and her family returning home. It'll be all stomping feet and shaking of hair and their non-stop chatter as they fill me in on their morning of wedding prep. It's Ruby's parents', sister's and cousins' last trip over here from their various homes across Canada before our big day just before New Year's Eve, and I've left them to it while I stay at home and ... pick my scabs.

To clarify: I do not literally have a five-year-old scab in the shape of a group of people on my body. It's a metaphorical scab. What I do have is five wedding invitations. Addressed. Stamped. All ready to be airmailed back to the UK. I've cut it fine, but that's kind of the point ... with everything arranged I've made it as hard as possible for them to say no.

I gnaw on the end of my fountain pen, turning their names over in my memories. This is a stupid idea. I don't even know if they live at these addresses any more, or work at the companies I'm posting them to in lieu of a current place of abode. I expect Cali is still in the house, the Miss Havisham that she is, but I'm pretty sure the rest of them left soon after I did.

Will they say yes? Will they come?

And will they be furious all over again when they find out what I'm planning?

There's a wallop against the window and Moglington, my cat, has leapt upon the sill, spraying snow over her grey paws.

'Come in, *madame*,' I say, opening the door. She's from Quebec so I like to speak to her in French. As I open the window, the frozen air pools in along with the sound of snow tyres pulling into the driveway.

Moglington hops down and wanders over to the fireplace, where she stretches out on the rug in front of it and shows it her belly, letting the warmth melt the snowflakes on her fur. Beyond the window, out of the car step Ruby, her sister and her mum, their identical dark hair in matching wedding rehearsal updos twinkled with snowflake-like crystals.

She's beautiful, my fiancée. I can't wait to marry her. I've only ever got close to this feeling with one other person; must have been half a decade ago now.

Right, come on, time to stop overthinking this. It's too late to back out of this plan now. Everything's paid for, everything's been put into place, my hopes are well and truly pinned on the outcome of these RSVPs.

I stack my envelopes, memories swirling like snow in a blizzard. So much changed back then, but it all led me here, to this moment.

But will it lead them here too?

Chapter 1

Cali

We know when someone likes us. Don't we? We *know*. We recognise the signs because we know we do them ourselves. The attempts to hold eye contact, the unsubtle compliments, the little excuses to come back over to see you for the fifteenth time that day. We always know, and so, if we don't feel the same, we'll often break eye contact first, bat away the compliments, ignore the fireflies you're sending into our orbit because we don't want to make things awkward. Perhaps we want to keep you as a friend.

Ah, but the blindness comes when we're the ones that like *you*. Then you're no longer a backlit book we can read, you're a mystery novel behind the dusty glass of a locked cabinet. And so, we search for signs, we scour social media for fragments of videos unpicking the way you look at us or talk to us and see if that means you're into us. We daydream, we imagine the future in a million different scenarios.

With Luke, I tried to read him for years and only cracked his coded pages when it was moments from being over between us. Now, I haven't thought about Luke in half a decade.

Except for the other week, when I saw a guy wearing a navy cable-knit jumper like the one he always used to wear.

Oh, and last month when I was on a date and the man mentioned he had a friend called Luke and I spent the rest of the meal bringing the conversation back to his friends, just in case his Luke was my Luke. He wasn't.

But before that, it had been years—

No, wait, sorry. I also had that fortnight last April where I looked after my neighbour's cat in the flat that he used to live in and ended up sat on the studio floor every day with a box of tissues, scrolling my phone for all of the photos of him and me when we used to be just friends, just those great buddies, Cali and Luke, before anything even happened. Back when the six of us lived in this townhouse, and we were as close as could be.

Now, I'm standing in the front doorway, frozen in time. I was collecting my post from the side table, about to head upstairs to my own flat and cook myself a warming bowl of pasta on this icy November evening, but one envelope begged to be opened on the spot. Something about the handwriting, familiar in a way that sent a frosty lungful of air to swoop out of my mouth. I tore into it, and now, in my gloved hand is a wedding invitation – *Bryn's* wedding invitation, of all things – and my first thought is, *will he be there*?

'Do you think Bryn invited all of us? Or just me?' I ask up to the top of the ladder, where a maintenance man is fixing something above the door frame.

He doesn't look down at me but answers, 'I don't know, love.'

'It's just ...' I turn the invitation over in my hand, the silver foil lettering glinting under the hallway spotlights. Jeeeeeeeeesus, so she hasn't forgotten me? 'She and I haven't spoken in five years. So, this is out of the blue, you know?'

'Mmm-hmm.'

'She used to live here, in the apartment that Sadie now lives in. You know Sadie?'

'Nope.' He wiggles the door back and forth on its hinges and I shuffle over an inch, my eyes glued on the invite.

'She's really nice. Keeps to herself, though. When Bryn lived here, she was always the one to organise whole-house parties and drag in a massive Christmas tree for this hallway which would stay up all winter. I don't even know her bride. Ruby.' I tested the name in my mouth. 'Bryn and Ruby. Do you think I should go?'

The maintenance man puts his screwdriver down on the top step and I can feel his sigh aimed at me from all the way down here. 'Might as well. Are you coming in or going out?'

Oops. I step in and let him close the door to the cold, hand him a sandpaper block that he didn't ask for but might need, and take a seat on the floor by the radiator. 'Did I tell you it's in Canada? The wedding?'

'You did.'

'I can't go all the way to Canada for a wedding. Over *Christmas*! I mean I have other plans to ... well ... ' Now that's stumped me. My eyes glide to the spot where Bryn's Christmas tree used to go every year. There hasn't been a communal tree in this house since they all moved out. 'Well actually, my parents are away this Christmas, visiting my brother in New Zealand. I went to see him back in the summer so I'm not going with them.'

Maintenance Man is ignoring me, but probably listening, so I carry on.

'I guess I *could* go. Theoretically. Even if she's just invited *me*, it could be a chance to reconnect. Maybe take a hike in the snow, thrash things out. She loved Christmas, so I bet the wedding will be in an amazing location. And then we could drink mulled wine by a fireplace and laugh about the wasted years.'

I glance up – did he just roll his eyes up there at the top of the ladder?

The wedding is actually set for a couple of days after Christmas, but if I did go – which I probably won't – but if I *did* go all that way, surely spending the holidays in one of the most snow-covered places on the planet would be a must?

If Luke was there, would it be better? Or would it be worse?

'It's just, there's this guy—'

Maintenance Man switches his power drill on as I begin speaking and I think it might be on purpose. But a moment later he puts it down and turns, sitting down on top of the ladder, and wipes the dust from his hands. 'Look. Weddings bring people back together, right? Good food, bit of dancing, an excuse to go to Canada; what's worth missing out on that for?'

A deeply ingrained flare of resentment flushes in my cheeks, like a match being lit under my skin. I press my lips together, lost for a moment in the past. I'm still angry at them. All of them. And they probably are with me. It's been too long, and the days where we planned who'd play what role at each other's imaginary weddings feel like a lifetime ago.

I swallow down this stubborn, scarred side of myself and change the subject. Kind of. 'You like weddings?'

'I do,' he replies, then chuckles at his vow-like reply. 'I love a wedding.'

'Are you married?'

'Twice. Loved every minute of both.'

'The weddings or the marriages?'

He pauses. 'Both.'

Hmm. I'm losing myself back into my thoughts when I hear the clonk of his ladder being folded up. 'I'm all done here, love. You'll let the other residents know they shouldn't have any problem with a sticking door any more?'

'Of course.' I nod, standing up. I'll type up a nice note and push it under each of their doors. 'Do you want a cup of tea or anything?'

He shakes his head, gathering his things.

'Some pasta? I'm not hitting on you or anything, I promise.' Way to make it awkward, Cali.

Luckily, he laughs. 'No, thanks. These evenings are getting dark early. I'm going to get home to my family.'

I wave him goodbye until he shuts the door behind him and the corridor is quiet and tidy and empty, save for the discarded wedding invitation envelope on the side table and a halo of sawdust on the carpet. Somewhere far upstairs one of my neighbours is playing a piano that I've never seen.

My phone buzzes in my pocket with an incoming notification as I make my way up the stairs to my flat. Once I've clicked my door closed behind me, I prop the invite on my small desk beside my laptop and it watches me as I make myself a tea, switch on the fairy lights that line the upper edges of my living room and change into my 'loungewear' (no bra, scraggly old pyjamas).

Bryn's name, in that loopy silver font, flickers under the fairy lights as I open my laptop. My heart shocks a little, my breath catching as her name seems to jump from the envelope to the top of my emails. One new message. Unread. Bold. From Bryn. The subject line reads, Please come.

There's a strange sensation inside me, of a hundred tiny people scrambling to build a defensive wall before my hand moves the cursor over the email. But screw them because I win, and with unblinking eyes, I open it.

Before I even read a word, my eyes settle on the 'to' line, which contains not just me, but four other names. Look at our names, all together in a row like their owners didn't spectacularly fall out on that disaster of a holiday five years previously. And right beside my name … is Luke's.

Chapter 2

Ember

It's my birthday. In this moment, I'm happy. Chilled, a little merry, a little silly. But my friend Tonia is circulating the campfire with a bottle of whisky, so we'll see how the night unfolds.

I breathe in the smoky air and the salt of the sea. Above me, the sky is cold and clear and the stars stream across it like spilled glitter on black marble. Being November, we have the beach to ourselves, me and this funny gang of friends who enveloped me when I moved here over half a decade ago, and who rarely seem to ever be out of my sight now.

'Whisky for the birthday beach bum!' Tonia pads barefoot over the sand towards me, stumbling, giggling. The flames highlight the clementine streaks in her hair and twinkle the stick-on stars she's made us all wear on our faces tonight. She flops down beside me, spraying sand onto my jeans. 'Have we hit the wall of regret yet, or do we still have time?'

Ha! I snatch the whisky out of her paws and top up my paper cup. She knows me so well.

Tonia and I have celebrated every birthday (and holiday) together since I arrived in Cornwall, and sometimes spend months staying at each other's home if we're going through hard times. I was there for her when she broke up with her high school boyfriend. She was there for me when I had long Covid. I took her in when she suffered a house fire. She took me in when my parents passed away within weeks of each other. That was a particularly tough time, and she didn't even know me very well back then.

Speaking of ... 'We still have time,' I tell Tonia. 'But let me know if you'd rather I started with the social media stalking of my ex, or the photo memories of my folks.'

Tonia chuckles softly. 'Let's wait until the end of the night to reinstall your social media apps, when we need a little light relief. Maybe we'll strike it lucky and Bryn will have posted something that gives you the ick?'

'Here's hoping,' I cheers her.

An hour or so later and the tide is creeping closer, the low waves audible even though Jack brought out a speaker and is playing birthday-themed music alongside the

13

hisses and crackles of the campfire. The eight of us have huddled in closer now, the flames glowing on our faces, a billion blankets keeping out the worst of the wintery night air.

I love it out here. I don't mind that it's cold. That it's dark. When I think that I used to live in a city, sat in an office all day, surrounded by tall buildings and hundreds of people and all those artificial lights even when I stepped outside, I can barely even remember that version of myself. Now, I work as a surf instructor when the ocean allows me to, and a coast path walking guide during any other weather, and I can't ever imagine being stuck inside a room, day after day, ever again.

'How do you feel about being the big "three-one", Ember?' calls Kim from across the other side of the fire.

'I love it,' I call back. 'You wish you were my age.'

Kim, at aged twenty-five, raises her cup in the air. 'Oh, to be as wise as you! Tell us, is there anything you're hoping to do this year?'

'More of this?' I suggest. 'Lots and lots more of this?' The group *awwws* at me but keeps staring. I think they want a real answer. Um . . . 'I don't know. I'm quite content as I am.'

Tonia snorts. 'I have a suggestion.'

'I know what your suggestion is, it's the same every year. But I don't want a girlfriend.'

'I know, you don't want a *girlfriend*,' Tonia argues. The

14

same argument I hear from her all the time. 'But just at least have—'

'Some kind of love life?' I finish for her, along with the rest of the group.

Tonia grins at her cup, scrunching her nose at me. She loves to tease me about my whopping lack of romance and I don't care. 'I just want you to be kissed, *really* well; one of those old Hollywood kisses you like to drool over in the movies you always watch.'

'I don't ... I don't *always* watch them.' Yes, I do. Especially the black and white ones. I love the happy endings. And Audrey Hepburn taught me the winged eyeliner that I always wear, even now when I can rarely be bothered to put on any other make-up. 'Hey,' I say to the group, topping up my drink again. 'Talking of love life, do we think we've reached a good time of the night to log into the socials?'

'I do not encourage this behaviour,' says Jack, edging closer to look over my shoulder as I take out my phone.

When I moved away from London, I let so much of my outer shell slip away. My clothes became looser, more comfortable. My hair less styled. My shoulders less tensed. And after a while I deleted my social media apps, just to clear my headspace a little. And I felt more like me again, even though I'd never realised I'd been anything but myself before.

But I never deleted my accounts. It's not like I stopped

15

enjoying them, I just needed some distance. So once a year I reinstall, see what's going on in the lives of people I once knew, and, after a few drinks, check up on what my ex-girlfriend is up to these days. Totally normal behaviour, right?

My friends gather around. We're a warm huddle of blankets. Whisky breath misting into the air. Limbs leaning into each other. Sand on the denim of our jeans. Orange flickers of ash drift up to join the stars above our little beach town.

'Do you know if your ex is seeing anyone?' Kim asks. She's snuck in right behind me and is resting her chin on my shoulder, watching me download the apps.

'No idea,' I reply. I've truly not checked up on Bryn since this time last year. I'm not still in love with her or anything, I'm just … curious.

She and I dated for about a year. I was Kim's age when we split, but before that we'd got pretty serious. We'd discussed moving in together, getting engaged. We used to lie on her sofa together in her flat in that house she shared in London with all her friends and plan our dream wedding. Just silly, coupley conversations, dreamy fantasies, but the kind that make you glow inside with possibility.

I know it's over now. It's been over for five years. But that doesn't mean I don't like to see her face sometimes, know she's okay.

That's why I navigate straight to her, my fingers tapping her name into the search bar as soon as I'm logged back in.

There she is. I smile, and I know Tonia's eyes are on me. 'Stop judging me, Miss T,' I say without looking away from my phone.

'I will judge you until you move on from this tradition,' replies my tough-love friend.

There's a pink circle around Bryn's face. Her profile photo has changed since last year, now it's a close-up of her pulling a silly face with a woollen hat on and a backdrop of snow. I touch my own woollen hat, and click on her face to open her story.

My screen fills with a photo of Bryn, wrapped up in a coat, a mountain behind her, a glass of something warm and steaming being held out to the camera. She's smiling, which makes me smile back at the image of her. She looks happy. I'm glad.

The story moves to the next photo, a mirror of the last one, showing another girl holding up a matching glass, the windowed doors of a café behind her revealing Bryn's reflection taking the photo, the smile still on her face.

The other woman has a long, loose plait coming out of the side of her hat. Her lips are a soft pink which matches the cold flush in her cheeks. Are they . . . ?

'Oh no,' mumbles Jack as the picture changes again to a selfie of the two of them, the other woman now sitting on Bryn's lap, while Bryn kisses her cheek. They could not look more like a happy couple, like a poster for a romantic winter movie set in the mountains.

The smoke is swirling in my eyes, the cold air suddenly making my nose run. 'It's fine,' I say to them all. 'It's cute.'

It's ridiculous that my throat is even feeling dry, or that my heart has ebbed like the tide. Of course I want her to have all the love and laughter in the world, and they look good together. I wonder how long they've been a couple?

The story moves on again, this time it's the same picture but with a text overlay, and in time with a moonlit wave, my heart crashes.

Can't wait to marry my love next month!

'Shit.' Tonia reaches over and takes my phone from me, exiting the app and stuffing it into the inside of her coat pocket. Kim pours extra whisky into my cup. Jack yanks a blanket off one of our other friends and wraps it around my shoulders, on top of the other three.

Bryn is getting married.

Okay.

'It's fine,' I say to them all again.

'Is it?' asks Tonia.

'Yes,' I reply. 'Of course. I'm happy for her.'

The whisky woozes in my head and I think I might be ready to call it a night.

I'm not sad. I'm not sad. I'm not sad.

She has every right to get married, to be happy, to be so, so loved. But did I have to find out on my birthday?

Chapter 3

Cali

'She wants us all there, the whole gang, back together again for her wedding,' I explain, holding my phone up and reading Bryn's email for the hundredth time since yesterday evening. 'She says, *"I know it's been half a decade since we all hung out, but I miss you all."* She misses us.'

The barista blinks at me and repeats her question. 'So, did you want whipped cream on top?'

'Oh – yes, please. Thank you.'

'Do you miss her?' asks the woman behind me in the queue, and I spot her boyfriend nudge her with his foot.

'Well, I guess so, of course, but . . . ' I fluster. The barista hands me my hot chocolate and I ask her, 'Would you go all the way to Canada for a wedding with a bunch of people you had a big falling out with? Including an ex?'

20

'I would,' pipes up the customer behind the couple, at the same time as someone pouring sugar into her coffee at the napkin station mumbles, 'Hell no.'

'Didn't you say she was paying for it all?' the barista asks, while raising her eyebrows at the boyfriend, signalling she was ready to take his order.

I shuffle down the counter. 'I mean, she's offered to. Which is wild because that's five flights she's saying she'll cover. And she says there's this huge lodge belonging to her fiancée's family on Vancouver Island where we can all stay over Christmas and up until after the wedding, and I googled it and it's absolutely massive.' It's so spread out that, actually, if I think about it, all six of us could probably keep a civil distance from each other if need be.

I could take some books with me, ones I've been meaning to read, and go out on hikes in the snow, and totally keep to myself if I wanted. It's not like I'd have to snuggle under a faux-fur blanket with Luke for the duration of the trip or anything. Nothing like that.

The girlfriend interrupts my thoughts. 'It sounds like, um, Bryn . . . ? really wants to make amends with you all. Be friends again, and move on. That's one hell of an olive branch.' The couple are collecting their drinks now, and the barista's stopped listening to me, angling her whole body away to serve people further down the queue.

All those things that were said, all those months and

years that have passed since, and now those friends I was once inseparable from are just . . . memories. People who used to be my neighbours. And I'm okay with that, I've been fine without them. JUST FINE.

'That's the thing though, do I actually want an olive branch—' Oh. The couple are leaving the café, arm in arm, steam rising from their drinks and drifting up into the misty morning air.

I follow them out – not in a weird way – and join the crowds cruising through the streets of London. I'm surrounded by people – commuters, tourists, joggers, dog walkers – and I fall in step with them, lost in the throng, a protective, anonymous wave for me to ride.

My walk to work takes me along the Thames, where water glints under the low winter sunshine and swooshes as boats trundle along carrying morning deliveries.

'Morning, everyone!' I say in my sunniest tone as I climb the stairs to my floor. 'Morning,' I repeat, louder. It's always boisterous in here, our PR office a constant buzz of telephone calls, stand-up meetings, break-out groups, brainstorming sessions. I love the atmosphere; never a dull moment.

Where shall I sit today? I wander the rows of hot desks, new and familiar faces flicking their eyes up at me as I pass, offering a smile or a yawn-wave combo. We're an international company, so staff from all over the world are dropping in and out all the time. It's a great way to meet new people, not so much to make any lifelong friends. I don't mind though. I'm not clingy, *or* needy.

A few hours in, I've circumnavigated all my work duties and done precisely nothing other than google information about Canada, how long it would take one to learn to snowboard, psychological tricks to make people like you again, example bucket lists and social media stalked my old friends.

I'm lost in a daydream about Luke and I getting so swept up in the romance of reuniting that Bryn invites us to have a double wedding with her under the falling snow and then we all honeymoon in that big log cabin of hers, which wouldn't be a great honeymoon for Bryn, I guess. Also, it's bloody shaky ground putting us all in one place for a holiday again, isn't it?

Anyway, I'm somewhere on the west coast of Canada in my thoughts when beside me, Nadia, a woman who pops into the office about once a month, asks, 'You wanna come for a drink with us?' Turns out, it's the end of the day already.

'I'm fine, but thank you,' I decline, automatically. I watch her head towards the door and slump my chin down on my hands. Maybe I should have gone, maybe I could have talked through some of this with her, got a fresh perspective on what I should do. 'Nadia?' I call out in my quietest voice, but lo, she does not hear me.

There's something that scares me about getting too chummy with anyone these days.

I pack up my crap, put my New York skyline mug in the communal dishwasher, and wrap myself up in my ten thousand layers again. When I emerge back onto the streets of London, darkness has fallen, and I'm embraced by the thousands of lights and the protective shield of a million different shapes and sizes of buildings. It's noisy and alive and people are everywhere and I am not alone. I am not alone.

But I do miss my friends.

Why is it that something can feel like it's working so well, that a group of people can be practically living on top of each other, in each other's pockets, know every detail of their lives, and then it's like that ball of energy suddenly becomes too much, and it implodes outward, and everything that worked now feels broken?

That holiday was supposed to be the best week ever. All six of us had been so excited – me, Luke, Bryn, brother and sister Joe and Joss, and Sara. We'd planned every detail, play-fought over who got to share a room with who, told each other daily what the predicted weather forecast was due to be in Spain.

Then, seven days before we left for Spain, Luke and I finally got together, and it was amazing and exciting and blissful, and it changed everything.

The last time I saw Bryn was one week after our

24

holiday. She was the first to move out of the townhouse, her mum owning a large home with a self-sufficient annex in Hertfordshire, and Bryn being self-employed. She nearly left without saying goodbye, but I happened to be climbing the stairs to leave some of Luke's things outside his door since I knew he'd gone out, and we crossed paths. She had a suitcase and that ridiculously huge sunhat on her head that we all made fun of her for, the one that was a gift from her ex, Ember. But there was no sun out that day.

'Are you leaving?' I'd asked her, even though it was the most obvious question on earth. There wasn't a chance in hell that hat could be packed in a box or bag. I should know. She nearly took my eye out with it boarding a plane once upon a time.

'I'm going back to Hertfordshire for a bit,' she told me, avoiding my eyes, no smile on her lips. 'For a lot, actually.'

'You're moving out?'

And that was it. She'd paused for a moment on the stairs, and then kept going. I think she said a quiet good-bye, but I never knew for sure.

Now she's getting married. My Bryn, my best friend, all grown up. Of course I want to be there . . .

About eighty-five times during my commute home, I nearly reply to Bryn's email. Sometimes I'm going to reply with a yes please, sometimes a no thank you. Sometimes just to her, sometimes a reply all.

'What do you think I should do?' I ask Mum on the phone that night. She's got me on speaker because she's repacking her suitcase into a giant backpack for New Zealand, as she's decided she and Dad and my brother are going to 'go hostelling' while they're over there and she doesn't want to look out of place.

'I think you should go.' Her voice is tinny and muffled and I can hear her shaking out her huge winter coat.

'Mum, remember it's summer in New Zealand at the moment.'

'But it's Christmastime.'

'Yes, but you don't need to take the same jacket you took to the northern lights.'

'Stop changing the subject. I think you should go; you'll regret it if you don't.'

I pick at a spot on my chin. 'Are you just saying that because you don't want me to be alone for Christmas?'

'Yes.'

'Hey! I was joking!' *Squeeeeeeze.*

Mum's voice comes on the line, louder, paying me full attention now. 'That is partly it, though, I don't want you to be alone. But Bryn was your best friend and you haven't moved forward from that friendship in several years. I think you need to go. You owe it to yourself.'

I lean towards my mirror, rounding my chin to inspect my damage, and say, 'Maybe you're right.'

'Make the decision and send your reply, tonight.

Otherwise, you'll think and think and think about it and start stress-picking at your skin again.'

Busted. 'So, you think I should go to the wedding? Even if Luke is there? What if Luke goes too and it's just me and him and Bryn, and then none of us get on, and then we come home worse? Or what if he doesn't go? What if everyone goes except for him? Should I message him first and see what he's doing?'

'Luke being there is not your deciding factor, nor is it under your control. Stop dallying about, pour yourself a hot chocolate, answer with a yes and then don't think about it any more until next month.'

We ring off and I follow her instructions, except I make peppermint tea instead, as a small hill to die on. Then, as the teabag is steeping, I open up Bryn's email, hit reply all, and write, I'll be there, Bryn – thank you x

I gulp my tea with shaking hands, and burn my tongue.

Chapter 4

Ember

Something strange is happening. I don't think I'm imagining it. And I'm not talking about the lopsided and half-dead Christmas tree Tonia is trying to erect in front of my living room window in my tiny shepherd's hut of a home. I don't remember asking her to bring me a Christmas tree, but I have been a bit distracted these past two weeks.

The light in the room diminishes further and I glance up from my phone. 'T, I need to be able to see out of the window still. It's my only big source of natural light in here.'

She shoves the tree to the left a little, and it falls over. For the third time. This time it takes my surfboard with it.

'Do you want to help me?'

'Do you want me to help you?' Thirty minutes ago, I tried to help and she yelled at me to sit down or bugger off.

'No.' She lifts the tree again and staggers it to the other side of the room, blocking the television instead.

I'm back on Bryn's social media – I know, I know, but I haven't deleted the apps again yet. To begin with, I just wanted to find out a little more about her wedding, and she's been posting pretty consistently. But I've noticed something …

Tonia steps back, pulling pine needles out of her penguin jumper. 'What are you thinking? Your forehead is all frowny and wrinkled-up.'

'Thanks.'

'What's she posted now?'

I'm so transparent. I put the phone down and sigh. 'It's just … it's the details, about her wedding, they're very familiar.'

'In what way? It's themed? Something you've seen in a movie?'

'No, closer to home.' I squirm on the sofa.

But she sits down next to me and stares at me in that teacher-way of hers until I confess.

'Look,' I say, holding my phone out to show her Bryn's recent posts. 'So, she lives in Canada, now, and she's planning to get married in Canada.'

'Makes sense. Is her fiancée Canadian?'

I shrug. I've not paid that much attention to her fiancée,

29

if I'm honest. 'I guess so. But the thing is, when Bryn and I were together, we used to plan our wedding.'

'Were you engaged?' She raises her brows at me.

I can't look Tonia in the eye, and a heat spreads over my cheeks. 'No,' I say, my voice quiet. 'It was just something we used to do. I suppose, at the time, we thought it would happen one day. Anyway, in this pretend wedding, we were getting married in Canada.'

'Ah, buddy.' Tonia pats me on the head. 'Why Canada?'

'It just looked beautiful. She always wanted to live in Vancouver and I liked the sound of the national parks. But that's not all.' I open a post of hers showing a rack of red wine-coloured floor-length gowns. 'These are her bridesmaid dresses. But she and I used to say we wanted this as our colour scheme. And I always said I liked these sweetheart necklines.'

Tonia frowns at the picture, then at me. 'Okay . . . where are you going with this?'

'Wait, there's more. Look.' I open another photo, of her in a rocking chair in front of a big, rustic cabin on the edge of a lake. 'This is her venue. *We* said we wanted to get married by a lake, specifically in a place with rocking chairs on the porch. We even joked about going back when we got old and renewing our vows in the same place, and how rocking chairs would make a great photo recreation.'

'So, you think she's just lifted the ideas you had together? That's a little lazy. I wonder if the fiancée knows.'

I stare at the wonky Christmas tree for a while. There are other things too, little things, songs she adds to her stories with lyrics about lost loves, a caption that's from my favourite old Hollywood movie. 'The very fact she's posting all these details … it's unlike her, she's usually more private with this stuff. But I just wonder if, well, she'll know that I've seen her stories. You can see who views them.'

'You think she's posting these things for you? What, to rub it in?'

I shake my head. 'No, she's not like that. I feel like it's more, trying to get my attention?'

'Why?' Tonia chuckles then tries a gentler, 'Why do you think she'd be doing that?'

'Maybe she still has feelings for me?' Ugh, I sound so big-headed. But what if I'm right?

'Mmm, that's a jump …'

'But what if it's not? What if it's, I don't know, a way of her trying to reach out, tell me she still thinks about me? She knows I only check my socials around my birthday now, so she's known I'll see the things she's posting.'

Tonia straightens the tree for the fourth time. It's only early December, so I have nearly a whole month of this thing toppling down on me. 'So, what is this?' she asks through the branches slapping her in the face. 'Are we sliding into her DMs this afternoon? Asking her what's going on?'

31

'No, no . . . ' I shake my head. 'It's nothing. It's silly and I'm just feeling lonesome, probably.' I put my phone away and set to work untangling a string of Christmas lights that Tonia brought over, dangling from her tote bag. And I forget all about Bryn, and her wedding.

As if that happens.

I shield my eyes, the December sun bright and low and glinting off the water. I'm waist deep, my wetsuit slick, my hair matted with salt, as it always is, in a straggled braid down my back.

'That's it, that's it, paddle, paddle, paddle,' I call out as my two surf newbies use every muscle in their bodies to try and catch this next wave. She catches it, her boyfriend doesn't, but both tumble into the foamy crest on the shoreline with happy chuckles that reach my ears all the way back here.

I trail my fingers through the cold ocean as they leap their way back over the breaking waves towards me, ready to jump back on and try again. 'That was awesome, you've nearly got it now.'

'It's so much fun,' the boyfriend chuckles, his rash vest riding up and making a crop top over his wetsuit.

'I can't believe we have to go back home tomorrow,' the girlfriend says with a sigh, wiping salty snot from under her nose. 'You must be so happy to live here.'

I'm about to agree with them when the perfect wave

swells towards us, not too big, not too small, just nice and chill. In several ways.

The couple take off again, both managing to stand, arms flailing a little, eyes focused on the beach, cores engaged and knees bent. This time, they make it all the way in and hop off their surfboards in unison, double-high-fiving and embracing each other in a tangle of salt and sopping neoprene.

I am lucky to live here. But ... did I give up on The One just to make this happen?

One thing about Bryn is that she always encouraged me to follow my gut, even when it ultimately took me away from her. My parents were the same, they just wanted me to be true to my heart. But now they're all gone from my life, it's like my heart doesn't know what's true any more. I mean, I think I'm happy. I think I'm okay. But am I, deep down? I don't know.

'I'm going to Canada.'

'Absolutely not.'

I'm facing off against Tonia and my other friends, who have barricaded themselves in my home while I'm trying to pack.

'Yes, I am,' I tell her.

'Nope. This is the worst idea you've ever had.'

Over by my Christmas tree, which is now practically bare because in the space of three weeks it's dropped all but about three needles, Kim pipes up. 'You should definitely, definitely just phone her if you need to know how she feels.'

I put an extra sweatshirt in my backpack with a huff. 'I need to see her. She needs to see me. This isn't something you do over the phone.'

'Yes, it is! This isn't one of your old movies; you don't fly across the globe to try and see your ex before they get married. It's not giving romance, it's giving creepy as hell.'

'Plus, nobody likes surprise visitors,' adds Kim.

I wave my hands around at them: my surprise visitors.

'This is just the birthday blues talking,' says Tonia, trying to remove things from my case without me noticing.

I snatch back my washbag. 'No, it isn't. It's my gut.'

'It's your gut that took you away from Bryn in the first place, babe. You wanted different things. And that's okay. She's happy now, and so are you.'

I shake my head. She didn't know me when I was with Bryn, and we were so good together. I've not been able to replace her, I've not even wanted to, or maybe I've not even tried. And this *is* romantic. All of December, Bryn's been sending me signs that she's been thinking about us, and our relationship. I can't spend my life wondering, what if? Because, what if she's the one, my person, my love and I just ignored it? I can't do that.

'Look, I'm going to go now so that I arrive a few days before the wedding. Then I'll see her, if it goes well have

34

Christmas together, if it doesn't, I'll find somewhere cosy and snowy to spend Christmas on my own.'

'I don't want you to be on your own,' says Tonia.

'I'm always on my own at Christmas,' I remind her.

She holds my gaze for a second, softening. 'That's not true. You might not be spending Christmas with your mum and dad any more, or a girlfriend, but we're your home at Christmas nowadays.'

She's right, in a way, they all are. I'm lucky to have them. After Bryn and I split up, I wandered around London feeling totally isolated for a few weeks, her friends – who I thought had become my friends too – having cut all ties with me. Eventually I gave up and got on with my life, with the whole reason she and I broke up in the first place, because I wanted to get out of the city and move closer to the ocean. A few months later, both of my parents passed away within weeks of each other, and I didn't hear from any of them, except for condolences from Bryn after I let her know (she'd known them well, after all).

But this group has enveloped me ever since. I know that anytime I'm having a hard day, they'll be there. If I've had a good day, I want to tell them about it.

Tonia continues, her voice calm, like you'd speak to a puppy you didn't want going berserk at an incoming parcel deliverer. 'How are you going to feel if she tells you to leave?'

I swallow. 'Maybe it'll let me move on, forget about her.'

'This marriage stuff has just thrown you, that's all; I think you *have* moved on.'

'I know you do.' I wrap my arms around Tonia's neck and hold her close for a moment. 'But . . .'

'But I'm not you?' she finishes.

'I've got to try for that Hollywood ending.' I smile, and buckle my bag closed.

Chapter 5

Cali

Jeeeeeez. My heart is thudding so loudly I can hear it even over the screech of the London Tube as it comes to a stop at Heathrow Airport. I've not been able to eat a thing all morning, and my mouth is dry, my eyes wide as I dart my gaze from face to face while I exit the carriage and follow the crowd towards the terminal. Any second now I could see one of them again. I'll recognise them all, surely? None of them are likely to have changed *that* much. Of course I'll recognise them all. Silly me. I could pick them out in the distance from any of their walks or postures alone.

I totter through the airport, my big mauve suitcase full of heavy coats and long-sleeved formal wear, dragging its wheels behind me. I am doing a good impression of a normal person, just a single gal on a solo expedition. Chin held high, eyes focused on the airline check-in desks in the distance. Nobody will guess that under this chic exterior I'm hyper-alert to the potential of hearing Joss's loud, hiccupy laugh, of Joe's squeak-squeak-squeak of that one trainer of his, of catching sight of Sara's bum-length curls among the greys of the terminal, vibrant in whatever vivid colour she's dying them these days. Of smelling Luke's aftershave – the smoky vanilla one that he didn't even used to realise was his signature scent but that made me wobbly-kneed when he'd walk into a room and cross straight over to greet me with a hug.

I join the queue to check my bag for the first flight to Toronto. Even though Bryn's wedding is in Vancouver, when she sent through our ticket info she said she'd have a surprise for us waiting in Toronto Airport for the second leg of the journey. I don't know what the surprise is, but I'm guessing either she's meeting us there, or has maybe upgraded us on our onward flight or something.

My old friends could be here in this queue. My palms leave streaks of sweat on the leather of my passport and I stand as still as a statue, eyes forward, afraid to look around me. I have the sensation that someone is staring at the back of my head – is it one of them? And if I turn, will the stare be a glare? My heart is too afraid to find out.

'HELLO,' I say a little too loudly to the pristine woman at the check-in desk when I shuffle forward. 'Hello.'

There, that was a much more airport-appropriate volume. 'Checking my bags for Toronto, please. My name's Bryn. No, it isn't!' I drop my passport in a panic and it tumbles over the counter, slapping its way past the outstretched hand of the woman.

'Excuse me?' An arched eyebrow arches higher.

'Cali, I'm Cali, not Bryn. Bryn is my friend who booked the ticket. Who the booking might be under? But probably not, I'm the passenger, you want my details, I guess. So, erm, there's my passport and look . . . ' I hold my e-ticket out on my phone screen as if it's proof I'm Very Normal.

'Yes, we just need passenger details,' says the woman, tapping hopefully only nice, positive things on her computer. She hands me back my passport and asks a few security questions as I heave my case onto the conveyer belt.

I am one hundred per cent blushing my whole face off, and my neck is hot under my hair and the woollen turtle-neck I'm cosied up in, ready for Canadian winter weather. God, I hope none of them are in the queue watching me right now.

I'm about to fill the silence with a monologue about why Bryn booked the ticket for me and how we were once friends but I haven't seen her in five years and I don't really know yet what this all means for the future, but then my case is given a sticky tag adornment and slides off into the magical suitcase tunnel of love and I'm being presented with a boarding pass and a seat number and archy-brows is wishing me a lovely flight.

'You too,' I say automatically as I move away.

I can't look back and instead shuffle my rucksack onto my back and make my way towards security. By the time I'm through, my mouth is dry from all this shallow breathing and worry-sweats, so I stroll the shops of the terminal sipping from a freshly purchased bottle of water.

Would it be weird to put my shades on inside so I can gawp at the people I'm passing, properly? I just need to see them. I need to know where they are, what they look like now, and how they'll look at *me*.

Yes, it would be strange. Or perhaps quite celebrity-like? It's worth a go.

I slip on my sunglasses and immediately feel my back straighten. Okay, this is good, it's like I'm behind a mask now. And maybe someone who works here will spot me and assume I'm somebody important and direct me into a swanky airport lounge and then I'll be escorted to the first-class cabin on the plane and draped in a satin duvet and crystal flutes of champagne will appear until I no longer even care that behind me, somewhere in economy, is the guy who whispers his name in my thoughts every single day.

'Oof, sorry,' I say, stumbling over a small child sat on the floor, sticking shiny little stickers onto the underneath of a bank of seats. I take off the sunglasses and give an apologetic smile to his parents, and something catches my eye. A splash of violet curls heading into a shop on the other side of the seats.

I back away, changing direction, diving into a travel accessories shop and engrossing myself into the minutia of plug adapters until the woman who might have been Sara is bound to have moved on. In fact, I'm there so long that by the time I emerge (empty-handed, much to the frustration of the sales assistant) the big TV screen is now displaying a boarding gate allocation for my flight.

This is it now. I walk with stiffness towards the gate like it's my personal walk of shame.

Outside the large glass windows, the skies are December-grey, made mistier by the drizzle, and it casts a gloom over the planes which seeps inside the terminal, making it seem more like late afternoon than mid-morning.

Maybe they won't even be there? Maybe they all declined the invitation in the end. Maybe it'll just be me and Bryn in that big, cosy Canadian cabin, and we can become close once again, and one day we'll laugh about the lost years and wonder whatever became of the other four and how miserable their lives must have ended up to not have found their ways back to such a beautiful friendship.

Lost in this thought, my mouth turns down along with a small sink in my heart. I guess I want them to be there, after all. All of them. Even if it's awkward, or uncomfortable, or really hard. I want them to be there.

My gate number comes into view. My tummy churns, my skin tingles, and my breath quickens as nerves mingle with excitement and fear and all three lace through my veins.

And then there he is.

He is a lighthouse, and I am a wave-beaten boat which spots him in the gloom like he's shining only for me. Just as I suspected, even from a distance, even after all this time, my eyes find him instantly.

I tuck myself behind a pillar for a moment, reaching for nothing in my bag, while I blink away my blurred vision. Luke seems to be moving in slow motion, stepping towards the gate, sipping from a takeaway coffee cup, appearing nonchalant but as he moves closer, into focus, I see his shoulders are tense.

He's right there. Only metres away from me. My heart has stopped, my breath now held. And it's just like the first time I saw him, a whole decade ago.

It had been a Sunday, in the autumn. It was mid-morning and I was expecting my new friend Bryn to pop down soon so we could try out her new roller blades over in Greenwich Park. I'd been in the middle of taping discreet kitchen sponges to my elbows under my hoodie, in lieu of proper skate protection, when I heard a key jamming into my door.

42

I'd frozen on the spot, cocking my ear to the side. Bryn? But it was a man's voice muttering outside.

Sneaking over to my door, I'd peered through my spyhole, looking straight onto a head of sandy hair. Then he'd stepped back, looking directly at me through the tiny circle of glass, making me flinch and hold my breath. But I couldn't turn away, as he looked back down and studied his keys.

Love at first sight? I don't know … But when I opened my door, giving him a fright, which turned into him unleashing the hottest and cutest chuckle I'd ever heard when he realised he was trying to move into the wrong apartment, we locked eyes and it was something, a connection.

I didn't know then if we were meant to be best friends or boyfriend and girlfriend, but I knew I wanted to be near him, as often as possible, and he was the same with me. We were like magnets, and very soon he was enveloped into the friendship group.

Then the years ticked by, and it didn't go beyond that. He never made a move. I never wanted to risk the group dynamics if he didn't feel the same.

Until one day, when it seemed the right time to risk it all, bet it all on us, and we lost.

Now, he drains the last of his coffee, licking a stray bit of foam from the lid. Damn, I wish I was that lid.

Shhhut it, Cali.

I can't look away and I watch Luke for a moment longer. His hair is a little longer than it used to be, which highlights the tousles, making them more defined. He slumps down into a seat, his teal eyes scanning the area, and I step back again, hidden further from view, until he pulls out a paperback and looks down, his eyelashes dark and blinking softly. He stifles a yawn, lifting an arm wrapped in a maroon jacket to cover his mouth.

That mouth. I used to look at his mouth all the time when he talked, back before we became 'a thing'. I couldn't keep my eyes off it. And I knew I was probably giving off huge, desperate, *I want to kiss you* signals, but so what? I did. There was something about his lips, how they always seemed to be smiling, even when he was thinking, even when he would fall asleep on my sofa during some movie marathon I'd arranged for everyone in the building.

Then during that week, that one week when everything changed for the better and just before it all changed again, for the worse, I got to know that he also smiles when he kisses, and that the way his face lit up when we broke apart could have made me smile for the rest of my life.

I swallow now, forcing myself to stop gazing at him and look away. Because I also remember the words that came out of his mouth during that group holiday. That came out of all of our mouths during that final night. I struggle to recall exactly what I said, but I know they were just as bad.

I can't think about him like I used to any more. Pull

yourself together, Cali. I walk around the chairs, quietly, trying not to draw attention, looking for an empty seat. But these naughty eyes betray me three more times, and try as a might I just keep glancing back at him, and then one time, that magnetic pull drags his head up, and he looks back.

Shit. Shitting shitting shitballs. I avert my gaze with the speed of an Olympic medallist and feel the neck sweats rush back to collide with my insta-blush.

Why did he have to lift his head at that moment? Why did I have to look back one last time?

And why did I have to like it so much when our eyes met for a millisecond?

We're all here now, all five of us, spread out on seats as far as possible from each other at the gate, like we're part of a flash mob who have no intention of getting up and dancing. There's a twinkling Christmas tree in the corner, and many of the passengers are sat beside bags with brightly wrapped gifts poking out of the top of them. And everyone is wearing their quirkiest Christmas jumper, of course.

Sara caught my attention first, confirming it was her when her violet hair pulled the gaze of everyone at our gate when she strolled in, statuesque, slick carry-on case, serene-resting face. Her eyes met mine and I gave her a stiff wave and she gave me a stiff smile, then ignored the empty seat beside me and wheeled her bag five rows

45

away, sliding her sunglasses back over her eyes. Sara is the coolest person I've ever known. If she were in a movie, she'd be the cool eighties heartthrob guy who always wears shades and a simple white T-shirt and is unfazed by life and makes everyone want to smoke. Not that Sara smokes. But she has that vibe that says, 'look at me, but I don't care if you do or not because I'm not looking at you anyway'.

Brother and sister, Joe and Joss, arrived separately and seem to have been silently squabbling from across the rows of chairs ever since they sat down, raising their brows at each other, rolling their eyes, giving each other barely concealed middle fingers. We all acknowledged each other with similar amounts of warmth. As in, not much.

Finally, I let myself catch Luke's eye again, and I tried to mouth 'hello' at him but my lips stuck together and I actually mouthed 'pillow'. He replied with a curt nod, and looked back at his book. Now I can't stop fiddling with the pieces of hair framing my face.

Is he watching me?

I do a totally casual neck stretch to see ... No.

'Passengers awaiting to depart for this morning's flight to Toronto, thank you for your patience,' an announcement comes over a speaker in the gate area and the rows of travellers hush their conversation to listen. 'We will soon begin boarding, starting with our families with young children and those needing assistance, and then our first-class fliers. We will then be calling passengers up by rows. Please remain seated until we call your row. *Please*.' The staff member puts a heavy stress on the word, which makes me smile, which makes me look back up at Luke to see if he's smiling, and this time I catch him watching me.

My heart boings with surprise and my smile slides a little bigger. I turn away quickly. Damn it. I wish I had the confidence to hold eye contact.

Over the following fifteen minutes, fellow passengers are filtered through the gate into the tunnel which leads them to the plane, and I wait for our row to be called.

I'm rehearsing some things to say to the others. I quite like, *Shall we clear the air before we get into the air?* Or maybe I should just launch into an apology, get the ball rolling, and hope they follow suit? Or how about, *Let's get plane-drunk and all ignore the tension until we get back to the UK?*

The next row is called and I spot Luke stand up. Huh? I check my ticket, moving to stand, but this definitely isn't my row – not even close. I sit back down, catching his eye again and he shrugs.

My old friends filter into the line like cards being shuffled together over the next five minutes. We aren't sitting together. I'd just assumed, but I guess I don't need to rehearse the small talk any more. I can just relax, enjoy the flight, watch a movie or two, get a little drunk on my own, enjoy not enduring the forced proximity.

A little sinking feeling, a flutter of disappointment, makes its way through my chest.

When my row is announced I join the queue, along with my soon-to-be-neighbours and those who will be sitting in the rows near me.

Is that . . . ? No. I thought I glimpsed someone else from our past for a second there, a few people ahead of me. I'm on such red alert that now I'm just seeing people I used to know everywhere.

I have a clear view of the back of Luke's head. Which makes me sound like a stalker, or a sniper, but I'm totally neither; it's just a fact, okay?

We're in the air at cruising altitude, the UK behind us and the Atlantic Ocean far, far below. Canada is somewhere in the distance, waiting for us, snow-covered and Christmassy.

Mmm. I pull up the pictures Bryn sent across of our vast log cabin again. It looks huge, such a contrast to that cramped villa the six of us had on that disastrous holiday. Each room in this cabin has its own kitchenette and bathroom, an armchair beside a huge window, some of them even have their own entrances. Really, Canada is the perfect setting for Bryn to have her dream wedding, for us to all be there, but with the ability to keep a lovely chunky distance from each other.

That's not very in the Christmas spirit though, is it?

The clouds edge by beneath my window. What do I actually want to happen by the end of this trip? Do I want to keep my distance?

My betraying eyes glide back over to Luke. God, I spent years pining over him, loving him from afar, even though we were so close, emotionally and physically. Then everything fell into place, and we fell into each other, and it was the best week ever before it all went wrong. I wish I could go back in time to when we were just friends, such good friends, all six of us.

No, I don't want to keep my distance. But I still have the scars I brought on myself and I can't let those old wounds open again. Perhaps over the next week I'll let myself be like freshly fallen snow – light, surface-level, melting away again after a few days.

The plane rumbles over a little turbulence – no big deal – but I glance at all my friends instinctively. Luke tousles his honey-coloured hair, like he always used to when he was nervous. I need a drink.

'Excuse me, 'scuse me, sorry, I'm just going to . . . Sorry.' I squeeze past knees and under loops of headphone wires out into the aisle and make my way to the back of the plane, where I convince the flight attendant to let me have a miniature bottle of vodka and some cranberry juice after I start telling her all about the fact my ex is on the plane.

Oof, it's nice to be out of my seat for a bit, though. We're only halfway to Canada but my legs are stiff and I'm really worried my feet smell because I've taken my shoes off and now everyone can see the thick ski socks I had on underneath as I pad up and down the lower end of the aisle stretching out my calves.

It's so interesting to see what everyone's watching. I feel for the woman watching a movie with a surprise sexy scene it in because she looks like she wants to be all nonchalant while at the same time scream, 'I DIDN'T MEAN TO WATCH THIS IN FRONT OF EVERYONE.'

Someone else has fallen asleep in front of the interactive flight map, their neighbour engrossed in a seat-back game, and, ahh, *It's a Wonderful Life* – I love that movie. I glance at the viewer just as she glances up at me, and I jerk to a stop, my eyes locked in hers.

'Hi,' I say.

'Hi,' says Ember.

Chapter 6

Ember

Shitting shit shit shit. As soon as my eyes connect with Bryn's friend, Cali, I curse myself for not having the discipline to just keep my head down. Maybe some part of me wanted her to see me. Wanted her to acknowledge that, yes, I am still here in the world, even after all of them cut me out.

'Hi,' she says first.

'Hi,' I reply, my mouth dry.

'Wow, I nearly didn't recognise you!'

'Yeah.' God, this is so awkward. I swallow. 'You ... having a good flight?'

'The best!' she enthuses. She looks much the same as she used to – long hair in natural curls, warm smile, casual but neat style. I must look a total mess. Which is just one of the reasons I hadn't wanted her to spot me sitting here.

51

'Well, I'd better get back to my seat. Enjoy the movie! See you in a bit!'

Cali scuttles off down the aisle like she's walking on hot dropped peanuts and I sit back and close my eyes. My heart is thumping. My lips are parched. My mind is zooming about.

Hours earlier, it was Cali I first spotted at the airport gate. She joined the queue to get on the plane a few people behind me. Goosebumps flooded my skin like a rash, and I forgot to breathe for a moment. I'd thought that flying out a week before the wedding meant I'd arrive before any of Bryn's wedding guests. I'd get to see her all on my own. But here was her best friend, who must be taking the same connecting flight as I am, otherwise that's a huge coincidence. And as I found my seat on the plane, I realised the rest of them were on board too. Not sat together, which is weird considering they're all such ram-it-down-your-throat best friends, but all there.

I kept my head down, my baseball cap on, and found my seat as quickly as I could, which luckily is near the back of the plane, and I don't think any of them saw me.

Could it have been possible to avoid them across two flights, another gate, passport control and baggage claim? Once we hit Vancouver it wouldn't have mattered, because by then it would be too late for any of them to try and talk me out of going, or to alert Bryn. Not that I wanted to ambush my ex, but I wanted to see her without any outside opinions. Just me and her. We'd always been level with each other and if Bryn was calling out for me like I think she might have been, it's between me and her.

Focus on the movie. This is one of my favourites. Focus … focus … focus …

'You okay, love?' asks the man beside me, pausing the game he's playing on his seat-back TV. 'Do you want to sit with your friend?'

'No! No, thank you. She's … we're … I'm fine.'

He raises his brows at me but I'm not about to start spilling my life story to a stranger, especially not when Cali could, technically, be in earshot.

She's fidgeting, getting her phone out. A coldness rushes over me – what if she's bought Wi-Fi access? What if she's messaging Bryn right now and telling her I'm on the plane? No. She doesn't even know I'm going to the wedding yet; perhaps I'm just a girl, heading to Toronto.

Perhaps I *should* just head to Toronto. I wish I could call Tonia right now. She'd know how to handle this.

I can't concentrate on this film any more, my attention is zipping around the cabin, a paranoid worry that they're all talking about me. Especially when Cali stands up again, and without looking back to me, races off towards Luke.

Chapter 7

Cali

I sit back down in my seat, my mind whirring. Ember and Bryn split up perhaps a month before I last saw Bryn, and before we all fell out. I remember Bryn being heartbroken and asking us all to not mention her ex after Ember moved across the country to live by the sea, shortly after their break-up. She wanted to shut down the memories and get over her as quickly as possible, so we all obliged. I can't see how Bryn went from that to being friendly enough again with her that she'd invite her to her wedding?

'Sorry, can I just squeeze out again?' I say to the man next to me, for the second time in less than twenty minutes. He sighs, and the shuffle-squeeze-shimmy dance begins again, and when I'm back in the aisle I walk briskly, my head down, until I reach Luke's row. He's in the aisle seat, and I crouch down, looking up at him.

I use the seconds it takes him to pause his movie and remove his headphones to scan his face, absorbing his skin, his lips, his brows. I haven't been this close to him in so long. Our eyes meet, his softer now in the muted dim of the aeroplane.

'Um, hello, Cali, how can I help?' Luke stumbles over the simple words, like he's reading from a script. It makes me snort out a gurgled nervous giggle, which is just great timing, thank you, me. 'You okay?' he asks me. *That voice.* Deep but with a quiet lightness, like I'm the only one who can hear him.

I find my words. 'Ember's here.'

'*Amber?*'

'*Ember*. Bryn's ex. She's on the plane.' My voice doesn't sound like my own, it's crackling and squeaky, the natural patter between us now sounding like the first table read of a pilot TV show. Between two non-actors. Who speak different languages.

'She is?' Luke llamas his neck up to try and see her but I pull on his jumper and he turns back to me.

'Don't look!'

'Are you sure it's her?'

'We said hi to each other. And yes – we knew her for like, a year. It's her.'

'Is she going to the wedding?'

'Um, I don't know. She must be, right? That would be a big coincidence otherwise?'

Luke runs a hand through his hair. His other hand, not the one attached to the arm whose jumper sleeve I'm holding onto. He hasn't moved that. 'I guess they made friends again.'

We fall into silence. I wonder if he's thinking the same as me, wondering how Ember and Bryn managed to reconcile when we couldn't.

'No.' I shake my head. 'I think it's a coincidence. She's probably just going to Toronto for work or something.' I start babbling, filling the silence with anything that comes into my head, not wanting to leave his side yet, and then there's movement beside me.

'Do you two want to keep it down so the whole plane doesn't know our business?' In a crouched position beside me, Joss has appeared, and I snap my mouth closed. Where'd she come from?

'We were just saying—' Luke starts.

'I know, I heard. You're talking about *The Ex*.'

We all fall silent, Luke pressing his lips together and, briefly, meeting my eye. My thighs are beginning to shake from squatting, and I can feel Joss's glare darting between me and Luke. I lean back a little, not wanting her to think I was being too clingy on Luke already, and subsequently topple back on my bum, which I style out by sitting cross-legged in the middle of the aisle, but I'm pretty sure I'm sat in some spilled cola.

I hope it's cola.

'Are you okay?' Luke asks, twisting and untwisting the wires of his headphones.

'Yeah, totally fine.'

Seven years tick by while we all think of something to say, and then Joss drops her voice to a whisper. 'Do you reckon she's staying in the cabin with us?'

'No.' I shake my head, an unsure chuckle escaping a little too shrilly. Christ, maybe I am a bit loud. 'I think Bryn would have told us if Ember was going to be there too.'

'Maybe Ember was the big surprise?' Luke suggests.

'Weird surprise,' mutters Joss. Then, like we aren't all in this bizarre tangle of resentment and bitterness and confusion, she reaches over and takes a swig out of Luke's drink. Even after half a decade the girl has no boundaries.

She sets it back down, slowly, as if she just realised what she did. Her cheeks glow red and she tosses her hair back, covering the embarrassment. 'Cali, find out.'

'Why me?' I hiss.

'You're good with people,' Joss replies, and we all take a short moment to process the irony of this conversation, between these people. 'Present company excluded,' she snorts. 'Sorry, too soon.'

My face is hot and my hands are all sweaty and my legs and knees are jelly from crouching, so I clamber up while whispering, 'I can't just go and ask her why she's on the plane. I'm not an air marshal.'

'Fine, I'll ask her.' Joss stands.

'*No.*' I block her. 'I'll ask her. In a while. I don't want to make it too obvious we've all just been talking about her.'

Joss shrugs and stalks back to her seat without another word. I dawdle beside Luke for a moment. I want to keep talking to him but I seem to have forgotten every word from the dictionary again. So I make a sound which is a little bit like 'bye' and stroll back to my seat.

Despite every effort to concentrate on the episode of *The Office* I've put on my TV screen, I can only focus on my interaction with Luke. I replay it again and again, tweaking myself so the imaginary version says cooler things or holds his gaze for a little longer. In some versions I'm a rock star and tell him how he hurt me and that I'm better without him and that our week together should never have happened. In other versions he leans down and kisses me and tells me he's thought about me every second of every day.

I'm lost in my thoughts and making a sultry kissy face towards Steve Carell on my screen when the man next to me waves his hand in front of my eyes. I pull off my headphones.

He sighs. 'I think this lady wants your attention. She's been saying the word "Cali" at you for a minute or two.'

'Oh!' Ember is standing beside my row, pulling on the sleeves of her sweatshirt, her eyes scanning the plane. 'Hi, Ember?'

She turns back to me and I see her properly for the first time. Her face is free of make-up, her skin lightly tanned and sprinkled with freckles like she spends most of her days outdoors, even in the winter. Now she's taken off the baseball cap, I can see that her hair is lighter, tousled, and pulled up in a messy ponytail.

Ember opens and closes her mouth a few times but I can't bear the silence so I fill it with, 'So, how are you? What's new? Your hair looks gorgeous.'

'Um, thanks. I mean, so does yours.'

'This old thing,' I say and laugh too loud, and even the man next to me shifts in his seat with second-hand embarrassment.

'Can I talk to you for a second?' Ember asks.

'Sure, go ahead.'

She looks down at the people in my row who she's talking over. 'Could we ...'

'Oh, yes, sorry.' I unclip my belt and stand up. 'Sorry, could I just? ... Thanks ... Sorry.' I follow her down to the back of the plane where we stuff ourselves into that little gap between the loo and the galley, a small window showing the first signs of white-frosted Canadian mountain peaks passing below us.

'Hi,' I say to her for the third time this flight. 'So ... what brings you to Canada? Do you know about, um—'

'About Bryn getting married? Yes.'

'Oh good. That's why you're here?' She shuffles, darting her eyes like she's working out the right answer. 'I mean, not to marry her, I know you aren't the bride,' I say, laughing. That didn't seem like a cruel laugh, did it? Oh God, I didn't mean it like that. I better clear this up. 'Not that you couldn't be. Or couldn't have been. I just mean it's not your name on the invite.'

Ember cuts me off, thank Christ. 'No, it's fine. Yes, that's why I'm here. For the wedding.'

'Are you going to be staying in the cabin with us?'

'No,' she replies. She's looking at me really closely. Is there something on my face? Did I make my spot bleed? Again? 'Actually, I didn't expect to see any guests – other guests – this side of Christmas.'

'Oh yeah, we're all connecting in Toronto and carrying on to Vancouver and staying in Bryn's fiancée's family's massive cabin for Christmas. She wanted us to spend some time together before the wedding.'

Ember presses her lips into a line. 'Cosy.'

'Well ...' A mini eye roll loop-de-loops on my face before I can stop it. 'Um, where are you going to be staying?'

'I-I don't know yet.'

'You don't have somewhere to stay? Over the holidays?'

'I'm just going to see how things pan out.' Ember is being coy as heck.

'So, you and Bryn are good friends again now?' I smile.

But Ember now won't meet my eye. Instead, she stares out of the window and mumbles, 'Not exàctly ...'

Chapter 8

Ember

'Not exactly?' Cali raises her eyebrows up at me. She looks like a puppy dog, all doe-eyed and loyal to Bryn, and I wish I hadn't opened my big mouth. 'Ember, what are you telling me?'

I don't know whether to open this particular door. Or whether to just open the emergency door we're standing beside and jump out. But if I don't tell her why I'm here, she'll tell Bryn, won't she? Before I can get there and say my piece, they'd all be messaging her, saying they're travelling with me, asking her what's going on.

'Listen.' I keep my voice low, the hum of the airplane drowning us out to any other passengers. 'Bryn doesn't know I'm coming, okay? And I'd like to keep it that way.'

'What?' she practically shouts, shifting, bumping into the toilet door, stumbling around like my words have caused another wave of turbulence. 'What do you mean she doesn't know you're coming?' She gasps. 'Are you being a wedding crasher?'

'No,' I hiss, and angle my body away from where Joss is kneeling up in her seat watching us, munching on peanuts. 'I'm not going to the wedding; I just need to see her before she gets married.'

'Why?'

'Because ... I just do.'

'Okay, but ... why?'

I press my lips together, pushing down my annoyance. 'It's between me and Bryn.'

'But it isn't,' Cali replies, refusing to let me drop my gaze. 'She doesn't know you're coming.'

Fair point. 'There're just some things we need to discuss, okay? Some things I need to say to her, and perhaps some things she needs to say to me.'

'Has she been in touch with you lately?'

'Not directly.' I can see her about to ask *why* again, so let some more words spill out before I have to go into detail. 'Please just don't tell her I'm coming, okay? Please?'

'Do you think she still has feelings for you?'

God, she is so direct sometimes. And she gets away with it because of those doe eyes.

When I hesitate for too long to answer she nods and

63

leans back against the toilet door. 'You do, don't you? Ember, she's getting married to someone else.'

'I am aware of that, and maybe in twenty-four hours I'll be back on this plane, flying back to the UK, feeling like a massive idiot. But I'm willing to take that risk.'

Cali lapses into silence, thinking, picking at a spot on her chin until it's flouro-pink. She's jolted out of her daydream when the toilet door behind her starts to open and she nearly falls backwards onto a passenger still doing up their fly.

'Haven't you ever taken a risk for romance?' I push, bringing her focus back on me.

'They don't always work out,' she mumbles.

'No, they don't. But let me take this risk. Please don't you or your friends tell her I'm coming; I just need to do this myself. I've come all this way.'

'Ember . . .'

'Cali, please?'

She looks back towards her seat, fingers trailing back to her pimple again before she appears to force her hand away. She looks me directly in the eye. 'Let me think about it.'

Cali leaves me standing beside the toilet. Beyond the window, there's bright blue sky and endless, snow-covered mountaintops. I press my nose to the glass, disappearing for a moment from the confines of the plane and pretending I'm out there, in the wild, in the open. I exhale, my breath misting the window, turning my view opaque.

Chapter 9

Cali

When the seat belt sign clicks off, I'm one of the first to leap up, my belongings already gathered in my arms, and the man next to me is so fed up with me by this point that he and his neighbour willingly scoot into the aisle to let me grab my bag from the overhead locker before them.

Ember is refusing to make eye contact with me any more, and the others are all busy getting themselves ready to disembark. Only Luke looks over his shoulder at me and I try to convey that I need to talk to him urgently, using only the power of my eyebrows.

I guess they aren't that powerful, because he puts his headphones back on and looks away.

Let's go, let's go, let's go. I don't actually push the

people in front of me shuffling off the plane, but I'd quite like to. As soon as I emerge into the tunnel, I take three seconds to let excitement wash over me at the sight of Canadian flags (I'm in Toronto!!!), and then race to catch up with Luke et al.

It's not until passport control that I get close, but Luke is too far ahead of me in the switchback queue. Joss and I, on the other hand, keep ending up side by side briefly, before we both move forward and out of sync until the next switchback.

Joss wouldn't be my first choice of initial confidante, but needs must.

'Hey,' I stage whisper to her.

She looks up at me from her phone but says nothing. I guess we haven't magically all become besties again, then.

'Ember's not here for the wedding,' I say, keeping my voice low.

'Oh. Good.' Joss goes back to her phone.

'No, I mean she is, just not in the way we thought. *Joss*?'

She taps something with a flourish and then drags her gaze back to me. 'What?'

'It's Ember. She's here to ruin the wedding.'

'No way?' The awkwardness drops for a second, and a smirk comes across Joss's face like we're just having a good gossip, but then she seems to check herself. 'No, she's not.'

'Y-yes, she is,' I stutter. I'm so bad at any kind of confrontational speaking, but we have to push aside our differences – just for the moment – until this problem gets resolved. 'In a roundabout way. She just told me – she thinks Bryn still has feelings for her so she's come out to see her, to see if they should get back together before it's too late.'

'I don't know if that's romantic or delusional.'

With that, the line moves and she shuffles forwards quickly, as if happy to be able to break up our convo as we lose our spot beside each other. By the time we're back side by side again, she says. 'I'll, um, text Joe about it.'

'Oh good.' I sigh. Joe was always a bit of a voice of reason. When he had an opinion of his own, that is. 'I'm glad you and Joe are still ... you know ... close. After everything that happened.'

'We're not close,' she replies, teeth gritted. 'I barely see him any more.'

'Ah. Sibling rivalry, eh?' I do a nervous-guffaw which is quite talented considering my foot is lodged deeply in my mouth.

She ignores me. 'Well, he reckons we should just mind our own business.'

'We can't do that, can we? Don't we have to let Bryn know? Warn her?'

Joss shrugs and we meet eyes but both quickly look away, me down at my shoes, her back at her phone. After a moment, Joss adds, 'Maybe she wouldn't want to be warned. Maybe she does still have a thing for Ember. We don't know Bryn any more, remember?'

The line moves forward again, snatching Joss with it and I do a giant sigh, ruffling the hair of the person in front of me. Somewhere too far behind me in the queue is Ember. I think I need to talk to her, urgently, but what do I even say to her at this point?

Ahead of me, Joss veers off for her turn through passport control, and I focus on looking calm rather than antsy and suspicious for a few minutes. Once I'm through too, I speed walk to baggage claim.

My phone dings with a series of messages just as I reach the carousel. I pull it from my pocket. Texts about the local phone service, one from Bryn, I'll read that in a minute. Where are the others?

I find Luke again in that strange magnetic way and zoom over to him. He's in his headphones again, but frowning at his phone. I don't get a second to signal to him to take them off before he does so without noticing me, and Sara with her long violet hair strides over, parting the sea of travellers as she goes.

'Have you seen this?' She tilts her head to the side, holding up her phone.

Hello to you, too. 'What?' I say.

She focuses on me for the first time this trip and the awkward in me wants to lob out a compliment or a smile or something, but her impassive face makes my brain blank.

68

Luke answers. 'Bryn's message.'

'I need to talk to you guys about Bryn, actually, it's urgent,' I stammer.

'What the actual—' Joss's voice rings out beside us. 'Did any of you know about this?'

'Know about what?' I ask. I give the crowd a quick scan for Ember and then open Bryn's message. 'Is this about the big surprise?'

I have to read it several times before it really registers what she's telling us. 'Wait, so we're not getting a connecting flight? We're not going to Vancouver today?'

'We're not getting to Vancouver until after Christmas,' states Sara.

'But, we're in the cabin over Christmas.' My brows furrow and I look to Luke like he might have the answers.

'We'll be in *some* cabins over Christmas,' snorts Joe. I'd nearly forgotten he was even here, and I turn to him. We exchange nods of hello but then he purposefully steps back from the group, hiding in the shadow of his sister again.

Luke's soft eyes run over my face. Does he know he makes my heart jump – still – when he does that? It's like everyone else has left the terminal and it's just me and him, once again. 'I think this is Bryn's big surprise.'

We've all received the same message, the details of the last leg of our journey spelled out, reservations attached.

We won't be flying to the west coast of Canada.

We won't be meeting Bryn here in the airport.

We won't be spending Christmas in the luxuriously large cabin covered in soft snow and sleeping under faux-fur blankets.

I read aloud from the message. '*Surprise! I know you were hoping to spend Christmas in the cabin, but you'll just have to wait a few more days. Instead, your Canadian adventure starts here. I've booked three (non-refundable!) cabins on board a cross-Canada train service which leaves Toronto tomorrow morning. The journey takes four days, and my biggest wedding wish is that when you get here, you're happy. With each other. I know that might be a lot to ask, but please leave the past in Toronto, and spend your time on the journey remembering all the things we used to love about each other. For me? Please? Sorry and love you all. Kiss kiss kiss.*

'Bloomin' heck,' I finish, looking at them in turn (but mainly at Luke). (My eyes keep betraying me!) 'So, we're spending Christmastime crossing Canada, coast-to-coast, on a train.'

I mean, in theory it actually sounds totally up my street and like a lot of fun. But, jeez Bryn. Way to try and force the reconciliation.

It's probably a sizable train, though, right? Maybe we could take a carriage each? Not even see each other until Boxing Day? 'Ember!' I cry, as she walks past us and towards the exit, her baseball cap back on her head, a backpack on her shoulder, her chin dipped.

'Ember's here?' Sara whirls around. 'Bryn's ex?'

'Ember, stop a minute,' I call.

Joss stands in my way. 'Can we focus on the train situation for a second?'

'One problem at a time,' I tell them all. 'She thinks Bryn still has feelings for her. She's on her way to crash the wedding. *Ember, WAIT.*'

My voice can be loud when I want it to be but I didn't mean to make everyone at baggage claim look at me – just one person. Thankfully, she stops, and turns, giving us all a tight smile.

'Don't go to Vancouver,' I say, desperation in my voice. I don't know how to stop her, but I know, I just *know* that Bryn wouldn't want this right before her dream wedding. At least, the Bryn I used to know wouldn't.

'Just leave it, okay? Leave me to do my thing.' Ember sighs.

'No, this isn't a good idea.' I don't know what to say, I glance around at the others, but we all share blank looks like we're strangers, not people that once could practically read each other's thoughts. They're being no help at all.

'Cali. You can't talk me out of this,' she says.

'But—'

She holds up a hand. 'No. We aren't friends any more.'

Ember starts moving again, following the direction of a sign towards connecting internal flights.

Shiiiiiiit. I have to do something. 'I know,' I call out, and

Ember stops again. 'I know we aren't friends any more. But surely we all just want to do what would make Bryn happy, right?'

'Exactly,' cries Ember. 'How do you know I'm not the one who would make her happy?'

'I don't. You're right. But ... Please just think about it a little longer.'

'I can think about it over the next five hours on my flight to Vancouver.'

I glance at the group behind me, and then back at Ember, impatient, but waiting to hear what I have to say, which is a good sign, yes?

I cling to that and throw out the only suggestion that comes to mind. 'Why don't you come with us? Travel to Vancouver with us. Turns out we're going by sleeper train.'

'How long will that take?'

I consider lying, but don't. 'Four days.'

Ember chuckles. 'Maybe I'll see you in Vancouver, if I'm still there.'

'Please?' I move towards her.

'Cali ...'

I ignore Luke trying to get my attention behind me. 'Just take a pause, come on the train with us. If you still want to see Bryn by the end of the journey, we promise we won't stand in your way.' Weird gamble I've just made on the situation, but needs must.

Ember looks at us all, which is, frankly, brave. I don't think I want to know what their faces are all saying right now. 'Why would I do that? I could go right there and be with Bryn tonight.'

'I know, but ...' I don't know what to say. She's right. What's in it for her? 'Ember?'

She looks me in the eye and I can tell she knows what I'm thinking by the way her head tilts to the side. 'Please don't say anything to Bryn. I only told you so that you wouldn't go and blab to her that I was on the plane. You know that.'

'I have to tell her.' My tummy squirms, but despite everything, Bryn is where my loyalty has to lie. 'I don't have a choice. Unless ...'

Ember narrows her eyes at me, and she has every right to because this is such a dick move I'm about to pull, but it's the only thing I can think of.

'If you come with us, I'll hold off telling her.'

Behind me, the carousel squeaks, suitcases thud to the floor, chatter drifts in and out, Joe's tummy rumbles. Eventually Ember clarifies through a sigh, 'You won't tell her?'

I shrug my shoulders. 'I can only say I won't tell her yet. We'll just have to see how things play out.'

Holding eye contact is so uncomfortable, but I don't back down, and after what feels like a hundred and fifty years, Ember mutters, 'When does the train leave?'

'First thing in the morning. Bryn's organised it all, including booking the five of us into a hotel for the night here in Toronto. I'm sure we could get you a room too.'

'We could chip in for your ticket,' Joe offers.

'You are still such an idiot.' Joss kicks him with her foot.

'I don't need you to do that, I can sort myself out.'

Ember's words come out flat, emotionless. She must be so mad at me. The yuck feeling in my stomach is still there, but also, thank gawd for that. 'You'll come with us?'

'Yep.' Ember waits while I scribble down the details of the train, from what little Bryn has given to us, then says, 'I have to go and cancel my flight. I'll see you at the train station in the morning.'

'Shall I give you details of the hotel we're going to?' I call after her.

'No thanks.'

'See you tomorrow, then?'

'I guess so.'

She walks away and I turn back to the others. 'A night in Toronto,' I say, for lack of being able to come up with anything more creative. 'Do we want to do something together?'

Joss shakes her head. 'We're about to be stuffed together inside a train for four nights. I, for one, would relish the me time.'

Joe and Sara mumble agreements, and although Luke hesitates, our eyes meeting again and that familiarity and electricity sending a tiny shock through me, even he then looks away. A sweep of sadness, perhaps weariness, crosses his face. 'I think I'll just go to the hotel and get room service.'

'Alright.' I nod.

I don't know if Luke is really spending his evening in Toronto just in his room – I kind of suspect not. But even though I keep having to blink hard to keep my eyes from drooping, and replay all the good moments of interaction today to try and replace the bad ones, I can't resist a new city.

After we've checked in, I sit in my hotel room, alone. It's too quiet. I need to get out there. I need to be surrounded by people and noise, and maybe some big guys on ice skates squashing their bloodied faces against some Plexiglas?

Mid-December in Toronto has me wrapping up in all the layers from my once-carefully packed case at the same time. I hit the streets in the dark, following the map on my phone to the Scotiabank Arena, where the Toronto Maple Leafs will be playing ice hockey tonight.

It's beautiful here, the city large and lit up for Christmas, and as I get closer to the stadium I'm surrounded by blue and white hockey jerseys, the joyous crowd sliding perfectly alongside the festive atmosphere.

75

'One, please,' I say to the lady at the ticket counter. 'Just, whatever the cheapest ticket is.'

I have a short while before the game starts, so I take a stroll in through the nearest door, and my breath immediately plumes as the cold emanates from the gigantic ice rink in the centre of the arena. The overhead lights are bright, like full moons on a frosty night above the rising bleachers of seats that tower around the rink. As well as the excited chatter from the crowd, music pumps out, and the rapid-fire whoosh of blades slicing as the skates of the team hit the rink while they warm up.

It's loud, it's crowded, it's going to keep me awake, and I can barely hear my thoughts as they try and sneak back over to Luke and my ex-friends. 'It's perfect,' I exhale, my words steaming the Plexiglas in front of me.

'First time here?' says a man with broad shoulders, stubble and a blue jersey on.

I nod. 'It's cool, huh?'

The man chuckles and bends down to lace up his boots. 'It's my home away from home.'

'My home is nothing like this. I mean, I live in London so I guess we have all the people and sports games and stuff like this. But I've never been to an ice hockey game. You just call it "hockey", right?'

'Right,' he says, straightening up and glancing towards the ice.

'In the UK, hockey is generally the grass version.'

'You in Toronto for Christmas?'

'Well . . . ' I take a deep breath and launch into a monologue about exactly how I came to be here tonight. A hundred years later, I wrap up with, 'And so now we're all about to get on this train in the morning and the distance between us all feels so weird, you know? Especially with Luke.'

Someone on the ice is waving at me, so I wave back and then refocus my attention on the burly man. 'Listen, I'm sorry to cut this short but I better find my seat, I think they want to start soon.'

'I think you're right,' he says, but instead of heading away from the rink, he starts towards it, and—oh! Those aren't boots on his feet, they're skates.

'Do you skate?' I ask, pointing down.

He chuckles in Canadian again. 'A little.'

'That's nice. So what do you think I should do? About Luke?'

'Fight for him,' says the man, and with a wave, he steps onto the ice and speeds into a sweeping curve, spraying ice crystals and waving up at the seats, causing a cheer in the crowd. His face appears on the big screen.

'You are so lucky to have talked to him,' a woman with flushed cheeks says as I find my seat. She's fanning her face with a programme, her eyes fixed on the big screen. 'I have posters of him all over my whole house. And a tattoo of his face on my ass. Do you want to see?'

Whoa. 'Sure.'

The woman is about to show me when a horn blasts and the rink comes alive as the game begins, and around me the fans rise in a wave of blue. I let myself become just a face in the crowd. Anonymous. Just how I like it.

Chapter 10

Luke

I think I'm in over my head.

My hotel room, despite its huge bed and generous floor space and big windows, feels claustrophobic tonight. I stand from where I've been slumped on my bed and move to the window, the only sound being my feet moving across the carpet. I have a great view of winter in the city, the spindle of Toronto's CN Tower poking above the other buildings, lit from within.

'Once the world's tallest freestanding structure,' I point it out to myself, pressing my fingertip against the window. I thank myself for this interesting fact, and sigh, misting the glass.

I should have just not come. I even refused Bryn at first, knowing I should keep that door closed, but she called me almost instantly, surprising me by how recognisable her voice still was to me.

'You have to come,' she'd said, by way of an argument. 'Everyone else has agreed to.'

'They have? All of them?'

She paused long enough for me to suspect that she hadn't actually had confirmation from all five of us as yet, but swiftly added, in Bryn fashion, a confident, 'Of course they're all coming, and so are you. It's my wedding. Please. Please don't be a selfish knob about this.'

Always one with a gift for persuasion, and, well, here I am. I guess if I'd really not wanted to come, I wouldn't have.

There's a wariness between us all though, and I don't know how to navigate it. I don't know how to be with these people and not be tightknit with them. I don't know how to be a stranger to them when they know everything about me. I don't know who I am to them any more, especially her.

Shutting myself in here in a stupid, lonely, protest-huff isn't doing anything to clear my mind, though. I grab my room key, my wallet, my phone, my muddled brain and head out into the night.

After wandering alone for an hour or so, I made my way towards the famous CN Tower. Some thought about the altitude keeping me from falling asleep too early.

As the glass-windowed elevator rises, the ascent taking about a minute, the lit-up city shrinks away from me. I rest my head against the wall of the lift, a weird feeling washing over me that I'm back in the plane, soaring away from here. I don't want that though, I don't really want to go home yet, do I? It's like Cali always used to say – the worst part of the holiday is the travel, but the best part is that first morning when you wake up and realise you're here and it's exciting and you have the whole trip ahead of you. Any adventure could await you . . .

We reach the top and are directed out of the lift, and the view takes my breath from me. The skyscrapers, the roads, the cars, the hum of Ontario's capital is stretched in front of me. I stroll the Main Observation Level for a while, taking in the glittering sweeps of cityscape laced with black pools where the harbour meets the land. It's relatively quiet up here, not many tourists at this time, despite the stunning sights. Just a few families, a happy couple or three, some solo viewers lost in thought, like me.

I make my way to the thick, glass-floor section of the Lower Observation Level, and, since there aren't many people around, sit down on it, as if I'm floating above the city, watching life happen down there without me.

This floor can hold the weight of thirty-five moose, apparently. I know a girl who'd love that fact.

'Beautiful, isn't it?' some guy says, hovering above me.

He's holding up a massive camera to the view. 'Especially with all the Christmas lights.'

'Beautiful,' I agree. I can't think of anything else to say.

Usually I'm good at conversation, I ask questions, I listen. But my thoughts are overtaken today, my head – literally and metaphorically – in the clouds. And as my phone starts to ring in my pocket, I think how I should be at home, spending Christmas with the important people that I love, and that are in my life now.

'A little scary though, right? Standing over it like this?'

'I think that's why I'm doing it. Keeps the mind off the jet lag.' I pull out my phone and look at the screen, but I've just missed the incoming call from the UK. Rather than ring back, I drop my head again and go back to gazing down.

I'm high, high above the city, and she's out there somewhere. Cali. Just as she's always been in London, but this feels different, she feels closer, like there's a pull to find her and to connect with her and that pull shouldn't be there, it can't be there. It's over.

Yet here we are.

Chapter 11

Ember

Why oh why oh why did I let myself get roped into this? I don't want to spend four days jammed in a train with these people. I can already feel the walls closing in on me.

They don't care about me. They don't want me there with them.

I walk through Toronto, lit up as far as the eye can see with strings of Christmas lights, though I pass them, barely noticing. My eyes are down, my stride fast, my mouth set in a line, my nose cold. I'm so stupid for agreeing to this. I just want to go home.

The city reminds me of London at Christmastime. Beautiful, lively, musical, but something I left behind. I walk past tall glass buildings and the statuesque CN

Tower. I don't slow my stride except to cross street after street. I don't know where I'm going.

I don't know where I'm going.

What the hell am I doing out here?

I sniffle into the cold. I miss my friends, my home. I miss the beach and the water. I miss my family. I miss having anyone to love me.

In front of me, the crowd parts, and the deafening noise of the city becomes dampened, just a little, and it feels like someone has tied a string to my head, lifting it, forcing me to look.

'Oh . . . ' I breathe.

My feet have led me to the harbour, to the water. I lean over a railing, letting the moonlit ripples balm me and quieten my mind.

Beside me is an ice rink, empty but for one gentleman quietly practising intricate spins, the blades of his skates slicing the ice rhythmically, softly. I watch him for a moment, and when he falls and I'm about to go and help him, he stands straight back up, dusts himself off, and starts moving forward again.

I don't believe in signs, but if I did, this feels very meaningful. Tonia will want to hear about this.

What is my gut telling me? To keep going? I think that's what it's saying. I have to do this. I can't move on unless I do this. It'll be okay, won't it?

Above me, the smallest snowflakes touch the top of my

woollen beanie. Others drift down and kiss my eyelashes, and I blink into the snow.

I don't know about my gut, but I guess I could take this as nature, at least, telling me to weather it. Whatever happens.

Tonia is chuckling down the phone at me. 'I'm sorry, I'm not laughing.'

'Yes, you are.' I laugh, towel drying my hair. It's morning here in Toronto, pretty early, and I'm decrumpling after a crappy night's sleep before I have to go and get on this train.

'I just can't quite believe you gave up a short flight on to Vancouver to spend four days on a train with a bunch of people you don't like any more. It's kind of funny.'

'Am I pushover?'

'No,' she says. Her voice is light and breezy. 'You're just a romantic.'

'Romantic would have been running straight to Bryn. I'm a scaredy-cat who gave into peer pressure to avoid having my plan scuppered.'

My phone beeps with a message from Cali, reminding me of the timing for this morning's train. As if I'd forget.

I dress warmly in a fresh sweatshirt and thick socks under my jeans, stuffing yesterday's clothes back into my bag. As I sweep on my eyeliner and chat to Tonia, I'm aware of a light breeziness to me, too, for reasons I'm

85

not quite sure of. Maybe it's that I'm always better in the morning time. Maybe it's talking with my best friend. I don't know what it is, but after I've hung up and checked out of my hotel, I make my way through the city streets towards the train station with feel-good vibes sprinkling around me like the snowfall last night.

Maybe this will be a good thing. Maybe I'll reconnect with the group, and that'll make it easier for Bryn if she is, in fact, wanting us to get back together.

A black squirrel scuttles past me, little feet jumping over the light snow that rests on the pavement. Hello, you.

As I near the station though, my nerves kick back in. I'm the odd one out. I don't belong with this group any more …

I look up at the imposing building, minutes ticking by, a battle between my head and my heart as to whether to go inside.

You agreed to this, Ember. And in return, you still get to reconnect with Bryn on your own terms. Suck it up.

Chapter 12

Cali

'Good morning,' I say to a little black squirrel who scampers past me, eyeing my Tim Hortons donut, as I take a moment outside Toronto's Union Station early the next day.

I wiggle my legs, cold despite the tights under my leggings, and step sideways to catch a little of the dawn sunshine as it slides around a tall building. The looming CN Tower is visible to my left. I would have liked to have gone up to the observation level if I'd had more time here. I bet the view is mesmerising.

I'll go into the station in a moment, just a few more minutes of soaking up this lovely new city first. I smile into the cold air, my feet crunching on hardened snow on the pavement as I shuffle.

Last night, when I got back, I sat up in my hotel bed

until jet lag got the better of me, reading everything there was to know about the cross-Canada train we'd be boarding today. The nervous flutters shimmy into my chest when I think of being stuck with the others, nonstop, for four days, but I exhale through pursed lips, creating fog, breathing out the negativity. If it wasn't for Bryn's sneaky plan, I might never have this experience. I wouldn't have got to spend the evening exploring beautiful Toronto.

I chomp the last of my donut with closed eyes and low winter sun bathing my face. Alright, it's time.

Through the doors, the station opens into a vast concourse, lit naturally from the sunlight soaking through the immense arched windows at either end.

The station is buzzing with commuters and tourists, but I spot the clock we all agreed to meet under and wheel my case towards it, immediately catching sight of Joe and Joss bickering, with one of their cases lying on the floor, open, and Joss trying to stuff as many things as possible into her backpack.

'Hi, guys.' My voice comes out timid, forced. I don't know these people any more; how do I talk to them?

Joss, in way of reply, says, 'Guess what? We have to check our luggage for the whole journey. Thanks for mentioning that, Bryn.'

'Just carry-ons allowed with us in our cabins,' explains Joe.

I nod. 'Oh, yeah, I think I saw something about that on the website.' I mean, I know I did because I got up at sunrise and repacked my whole bag, prioritising thermal undies, PJs, toiletries and my Kindle. Yes, and that fuzzy sweater I've had for years that I remember Luke liked, *okay*.

Joe and Joss glance at each other, silence filling the space between the three of us as she goes back to rearranging her belongings.

'So ... how did you both sleep?' I croak out because I can't bear it any longer. But before either of the siblings' report on their overnight slumbers, the urge to turn and look behind me sweeps over, and I do so, connecting eyes with Luke.

He walks towards us, his gait slow, like he's moving through honey and he's not sure if it would be easier to just ... not. He has bed head, small bags under his eyes, a knitted sweater the colour of red wine and a bulky grey jacket under his arm. I can't look away.

Luke holds my gaze as he gets closer. We're probably both just too sleepy to look away, but as he reaches me, he keeps going, his body stepping in close to me, into my personal space, and my breath catches.

But then his gaze drags away and he's holding out something for Joe – a phone charger, with a travel adapter dangling from it. 'Thanks, man,' Joe says, and Luke steps back, distance restoring between us. *Jesus.*

Sara is the last to arrive, moments after Luke. She greets the group with a nod. She has her signature sunglasses on her head, a coffee in gloved hands, and appears to have already checked her suitcase. Her eyes sweep our cases. 'I guess we have a train to catch.'

The five of us cart our bags over to the baggage desk, an uncomfortable silence stretching between us as long as one of the platforms, leaving Sara to drink her coffee. When we return, lighter, but still with precisely zero conversational skills between us, I scrunch my eyebrows. 'No Ember yet?'

'She's meeting us before the train?' Sara asks over her coffee cup.

'Yeah, I sent her a message. It says she read it.'

'But she didn't answer?' Joss sighs.

'No, but . . . let's give her a couple of minutes.'

Two excruciating minutes later, and the rest of them are beginning to move towards the platform. I follow, mumbling to Joe, 'You don't think she would have bailed on us and got a flight, do you?'

Joe shrugs. 'Maybe she went home.'

Where are you, Ember? I stop to scour the crowd, looking for that light-blonde hair. What colour coat was she wearing yesterday?

'Come on,' Joss barks.

She'll be here, she promised, she's just running a little late. I stop. 'I'm going to wait.'

'Cali,' Luke says, my name in his low voice a highlight and a heartbreak all in one. 'We can't miss the train.'

'We won't, I won't miss it, I just don't want her to be on her own.'

He hesitates, like he's going to wait with me, like a hundred memories are rushing through his thoughts, but clearly the bad ones win him over, because he nods and turns away towards the direction of our platform.

I watch him go. One of the things I always loved about him – even when we were 'just friends' – was that I always felt like I had someone. The two of us were always there if the other needed someone to wait with them, or to listen to a venting session. He'd always help me if I needed an extra pair of hands, I'd always come and watch reality competition shows with him so he'd have someone to discuss them with. And yes, sometimes I didn't *really* need his help, not strictly, and he didn't *really* need to curl his already-warm body under a blanket with me on his sofa, but the flirtations were all part of our closeness.

I miss the closeness, so much.

But this is probably for the best. We don't need to spend four days making love–hate eyes at each other across an aisle.

I dawdle for a few minutes, standing on tiptoes, checking my phone, and I'm about to give up when, thank God, there she is.

Ember strides with confidence that's betrayed by her face as she darts her gaze around the various electronic boards, trying to figure out where to go. I call her name and wave, and after a couple of attempts, she spots me, relief softening her features, and she comes my way.

She looks really well, you know. More rested than I do. And more herself, somehow, than when I knew her back in the day.

As she draws near, I say, 'You need to check your— Oh. You don't have a big suitcase?'

Ember shakes her head. 'No. I travelled light.'

'You came.' I couldn't help it, that just slipped out of my mouth. I didn't mean to sound so relieved.

'I said I would,' she replies, a flatness to her voice.

Why is she acting so mad at me? Because I stopped her getting on the plane? Is she wishing she was in Vancouver already, imagining that she'd be waking up beside a freshly single Bryn, ready to celebrate Christmas as a re-united couple? Maybe. But I think it's more likely that if she'd gone to Vancouver, she might have been faced with a pretty irate bride-to-be ex-girlfriend.

There's no time to imagine every potential scenario string right now, because we have to get to our train. 'This way,' I say, and she falls into step beside me as we dodge the crowds and follow the signs to our platform.

Showing our tickets, we make our way to where the rest of our group of misfits are hanging about beside one of the rows of gleaming red and gold carriages that make up our cross-Canada train. Nobody is talking to each other.

'Right, we're all here,' I declare, because sometimes stating the obvious is as good a filler as anything, when nobody else seems to want to chime in. 'Shall we say goodbye to Toronto and jump on board?'

Without a word, Joss heads up the steps and in through one of the train carriage doors before you could even say *all aboard*.

'Where's your cabin, Ember?' asks Luke.

She studies her ticket and the numbers on the carriages for a moment. 'I'm down that way.'

It'll be fine that we aren't together, won't it? I don't need to keep her under lock and key. I mean, it's not like she can jump off the train halfway and catch a flight. Well, I suppose she could. 'Shall we say we'll see you—'

'I'm sure I'll see you on board.' With a sigh, Ember turns and walks off further down the platform. I watch her for a moment, then Joe passes my vision, climbing into the train. Sara follows, and Luke steps to the side, gesturing for me to go ahead of him.

I hope he isn't looking at my bum as I climb up ahead of him.

But secretly I hope he is.

Shuffling into the carriage, I feel like I've stepped back in time. I'm now a passenger in an Agatha Christie novel (hopefully with a little less murdering. You never know

93

though, hahahaha, oh God). I'm faced with neat, soft seats on either side of me, then a series of small enclosed sections.

'What's happening?' I ask the stand-off that's occurring in the middle of the carriage corridor.

'She only booked us three cabins.' Joss's nostrils are flaring like a bull. 'Between five of us.'

'Some of us are sharing?' Luke asks from behind me. His breath tickles the hair on the back of my head, and a heat rises in me.

'I can't believe this,' Sara mutters.

'Oh my God ...' In my head that sounded a lot more convincing, but actually I already knew this was going to be the case. Bryn did say it in her message. And I did spend half the night wondering if Luke and I would end up together. Even so, nobody likes a know-it-all. 'I never even clocked we were going to have to do that,' I add. Just for good measure.

Luke leans around me to peer into one of the cabins, a light chuckle only I can hear escaping his lips. He catches me looking at them, and I turn away quickly.

Each cabin is meant for two people to share, containing two seats, a little storage unit and a fold-away loo. I look around, but can't quite figure out how it ... works. On the website I saw pictures of snuggly little bunk beds stacked on top of each other.

'So the seats fold back?' I ask.

94

'I think they convert to two berths – a bunk on top of another bunk,' says Sara.

Ah. 'Clever. Who wants to share?' Don't look at Luke. Do not look at Luke.

'I'll take the cabin on my own,' Joe offers with a shrug that suggests he just wants some peace and quiet from his sister already.

No such luck. 'Don't be so bloody selfish,' hisses Joss. 'Why should you get the solo room? Not that I'm sleeping in there on my own; what if I fall over the toilet in the night and crack my head open?'

'I *would* want to see that,' mutters Joe with a smirk, and Joss sends daggers at him via her eyeballs.

'Maybe you two should share. You are brother and sister,' I offer. I'm so curious about them. They always used to bicker, but were so close. They lived together for those years at the townhouse, after all. They started a business together. And I know it all went south, but surely, they've – of any of us – made up since then? So why the simmering rage between the two of them?

'Do we want to keep the whole train awake listening to them fight?' Luke says this to me, a hint of a smile on his lips, which I mirror.

'Well, I am more than happy to not share with any of you, and be on my own. Same old, huh?' Sara flicks her hair back, her lips pursed, and edges towards the furthest away carriage. 'Joss and Joe, and Luke and Cali.'

'Whooooa,' Luke and I say at the same time.

Sara looks at us, like, *what's the problem with sharing a room with a one-time romantic partner who you're still obsessed with*? 'Well, you have already seen each other naked.'

I splutter and stutter for a few beats. 'I've seen you naked, too. I've seen all of you naked, even Joe thanks to that night he got drunk and thought the hose behind the house was the shower.'

Joe chuckles behind me, the first genuine laugh I've heard this trip. Phew. Maybe we aren't doomed to come out of this worse than we went in? Maybe?

'Yeah, I don't know . . . I don't think that's a good idea.' Luke could not look more uncomfortable right now. Gone is the hint of a smile. And perhaps that tells me everything I need to know about where he stands. So, I am not about to try and convince him to sleep with me. I mean on top of me. I mean *in a cabin with me.*

'You and I could share?' I suggest to Sara.

'Wow. None of you want to share with me.' It's more of a statement than a question from Joss at this point, and we all make *eerrrrrm* noises until Joe steps up.

'Bunk in with me then, sis. It'll be like old times. I'll make sure you don't die in the middle of the night.'

'Thank you,' she says, sarcasm venoming her voice. The two of them lob their things into the first cabin.

'So, me and you,' Sara says. Her voice isn't cold, as such. It's not angry, like Joss, or indifferent, like Joe. Not hesitant, like Luke. Just brisk, like the air outside on the platform. Flat. Detached. 'Then Luke on his own.'

'Unless we see if Ember wants the extra bed?' I suggest.

'She has her own bed,' Joss calls out from where she's already in her cabin, facing the window, putting her headphones on. 'No.'

'Yeah, no.' Sara shakes her head, and goes into the second cabin, leaving Luke and I in the corridor just as the train lets out a long, adventurous toot, and the engine starts with a rumble under our feet.

'Let's have lunch together? As a group?' I suggest before any doors are closed.

There are grumbles of agreement, and Luke hesitates by his door, like he wants to say something to me. Then steps inside, where I hear him blow out a large exhale of air as he closes his door.

I follow Sara into our cabin, and take a seat to watch the suburbs of Toronto begin to glide past the window.

This is going to be okay, right? Surely we'll come away from this at least a little closer? Or will the vastness of Canada make us feel more alone than ever?

On our way, I text Bryn. I never removed her from my phone, so all our old texts are stored above this one, full of happy news and in-jokes and silly memes.

Ember must be lonely. The others won't be happy, but I'm inviting her to lunch.

Chapter 13

Ember

They're so cliquey. Were they always like this? Maybe not Cali, but the others. I didn't ask them to get involved in any of this. It's between Bryn and me, not them, they made it very clear a long time ago that I wasn't part of their group any more, and I've got through a hell of a lot without their help.

Still, though. I was expecting the weather to be cold but they are definitely matching that energy.

I climb aboard my carriage, a number of carriages down from the one they all went into, and recheck the number on my ticket. I'll be spending the next four nights in this very recliner seat.

The leather on the chair squeaks as I sit down, waking

up the woman in the adjoining seat, who's already tucked under a blanket, reclined, a gentle snore emitting from her open mouth.

Bet it doesn't sound so gentle at three in the morning.

She blinks at me, looks out of the window, then back at me. I smile. 'I take it these seats aren't too bad to sleep on, then?'

'Have we left Toronto?' she asks, sitting up. She's perhaps a decade older than me, with muddy walking boots on her feet and two sets of glasses atop her head.

'Just setting off now.'

'I'm Gwen.'

'Ember.'

'From England?'

'Ember from England,' I confirm.

'I'm from Arizona. Been backpacking for months now, can't get enough of it. I'm beat though.'

'I can imagine.' I like the sound of that, and want to hear more about Gwen, but she's already closed her eyes again.

Right, what do I want out of my backpack that would be worth keeping in the seat-back pocket ... I pull out a few essentials and settle in, dropping a message to my friends at home to let them know I'm on my way.

As the train picks up speed, a gentle rhythmic chug running underfoot which sways me back and forth, I let my eyelids soften. We'll be out of the city soon, making our way through the forests of Ontario, and one thing I know that'll calm my soul is the sight of endless spruce and pine trees.

Not long after we've set off, at right about the time I'm wondering if I could switch seats because Gwen is at it again with the snoring, my phone vibrates with a message from Cali.

Will you join us for lunch? Restaurant car at 1pm?

They're making an effort, at least Cali is, but I don't know if I'd rather she didn't at this point. Can't we just see each other in Vancouver?

However. What if this does turn into a second chance for Bryn and me? Then her friends will probably become my friends again. I should make an effort.

But just to be dropped again if anything goes wrong? I don't know if I can invest myself again in friendships that can all disappear overnight.

'What are you deep in thought about?' Gwen asks. Turns out, she's stopped snoring and is now regarding me over the top of her blanket.

'Whether to meet some people on the train for lunch.'

'Friends?'

'Not really. You wanna come?'

'Not really,' she replies. 'But you should go.'

'Why?'

100

'Because it's lunch. Food is good. Company is good. Just say yes.'

I'm not used to someone telling me what to do these days. I weirdly kind of like it. So, with a heart full of here-goes-nothing, I reply with a see you there.

The restaurant car has a delicious smell of rich gravy and red wine, and my stomach growls as it remembers I haven't had a proper meal since my street snacks in Toronto last night.

Sara is on her own at one of the tables of four, and I dither on the spot. Should I wait for Cali? She's the one who invited me, after all. And I don't think the others are exactly thrilled to have me along for the ride. But she looks up, puts down her phone, and her eyes flick from me to the chair opposite her.

'Hey,' I say, sitting down.

'Hi. Cali's in the toilet. The others will be here in a minute, probably.'

I'm surprised they didn't walk down the train together, but whatever. Her comment about Cali awakens a small memory in me, of Cali and Bryn doubled over with laughter about some dumb joke I told, Cali shrieking that she was going to wet herself any minute. Then I think she did a little bit. It was kind of funny.

Beyond the window, tall trees of rich, emerald green whoosh by, their branches frosted with fresh snow. I can't tell if it's warm in the carriage, if it's an illusion caused by looking at the snow, or if I'm just physically uncomfortable since I can't think of anything to say.

'Hi, how's your compartment?' Cali reappears from behind me and slots in the seat next to mine. She's chirpy, acting like there's nothing strange about me being here, or perhaps she's just plastering over the insanity of the situation the only way she knows how.

'It's, um, nice. I'm just in a recliner seat though. I'm next to a nice lady.'

'Oh. Well, that sounds nice,' she agrees, and I get that sense again that she's thinking, *Don't poke the bear, everyone remain calm.*

'Yeah.'

Joss and Joe walk in next, closely followed by Luke, who takes a seat opposite Cali and beside Sara. She just rolled her eyes. Huh.

Joe takes a seat across the aisle from Luke, Joss across the aisle from Cali. I swallow, my throat dry. I'm such a gooseberry on this trip, and now they're probably extra mad they can't all sit together because I've taken one of the prime spots.

There's a strained silence between our tables. Joss's cutlery clinks as she shoves it aside to rest her phone on the table. Luke clears his throat. Sara shifts in her seat, causing the soft leather to creak. The train glides along its tracks with a *ba-doom ba-doom, ba-doom ba-doom.*

'Welcome aboard – can I get you folks started with something to drink?'

'Oh, thank fuck,' Joss mutters across the aisle. 'Wine, please.'

'I'll have the same,' I exhale. 'Red. Thanks.'

'Make that three.'

'Four.'

Looks like we're all going straight for the wine, then.

When the server leaves to get our drinks – I hope she's quick with my wine – I wait for someone to speak. But still nobody does. I glance at each of them in turn, and all I see are stony faces, pressed together lips, eyes fixated on the view outside the window, or their phones, or the ceiling. Except Cali, she keeps taking small inhales like she's thought of something to say then scraps that idea.

Joss huffs out of the blue, and shoves her phone back in her pocket. 'Why are we even having lunch together? This is such a farce.'

'We have to eat,' mutters Luke.

Cali fiddles with the sleeve of her jumper. 'I just thought we should make an effort. We don't know anyone else on the train. I'm not being ... ' She trails off, and a blush creeps over her.

The wine arrives, big glasses of it, and we all knock back some gulps and make our orders from the menu. Like with the wine, we all order the same thing – the pasta with a starter salad – which comes as no surprise.

This group always used to end up ordering the same meal because whatever the first person chose the next would worry about getting food envy, and it was a trickle effect down until, as usual, they all ended up having the same thing. I used to find it funny. Now I find it annoying, for no real reason. But I don't want to change my order now and stick out even more.

Oh, for God's sake, I can't bear it. 'I know you're all angry at me,' I state. 'I can get off at the next station and head back to Toronto if you're going to let it ruin your Christmas.'

'No, we're not angry at you,' says Cali, shaking her head so quickly her curls ripple.

'I'm a little angry at her,' says Joss.

'Give it a rest,' Joe says with a sigh.

'It's true.' Joss leans around Cali and looks me dead in the eye. 'I'm just being truthful with you. What you're doing is messed up and I feel like we're now babysitting you.'

I shake my head and hold her gaze. 'It's not messed up. I'm sorry you feel that way, but this is between Bryn and me. And I don't need you babysitting me.'

'It's not between you and Bryn, Bryn doesn't even know you're in the country.' Joss stops talking and looks around at the others. 'And I can't decide if we should tell her, warn her, or hope "the ex" here just goes home.' She jabs a finger towards me.

I take another large gulp of my wine, steady my voice, and say, 'I hope you don't tell her. I don't want to ambush her, but I also don't think she needs the information to come via all of you. Who are a little biased.'

'You're a little deluded,' Joss mutters.

Cali let's out a sharp exhale. 'Can we just have lunch?' She holds her glass aloft in an ill-timed cheers, but she's the type of person you don't want to leave hanging, so we all reach over to clink our glasses against hers. 'Here's to ... I don't know ... being in Canada. To Christmas on a train.'

'To Bryn's wedding,' Joss says, arching a brow at me. Stupid cow.

'To a merry Christmas,' Luke says. I'm not sure if he's being facetious – I remember he always had a dry sense of humour – but we all clink our glasses again.

'It's been a while since we've done that. Doesn't feel quite as authentic as it used to, does it?' remarks Sara when we all go to put our glasses down. I pick mine up immediately, somehow feeling protected having a drink between me and them, and I shrink back into my seat to watch the conversation and get out of Joss's eyeline.

Our salads are brought over swiftly. Across from me, Luke's eyes keep flicking to Cali. It's fast, like he doesn't want to be caught. But I caught him, so I expect the others can see it too. I remember telling Bryn I thought they had a thing for each other, but she said I was imagining it.

I have a little urge to throw a grenade into the middle of the table and ask him straight-out, but I push it down.

And then Joss says . . .

'So, Cali and Luke, you're not going to suddenly confess you've been hooking up again on this trip, are you?'

Whooooooa! *Again?* My eyes widen, my lips twitch with a smile that I force away. As Cali and Luke stutter and stumble over their words, Sara snickers and Joe mutters, 'Bloody hell.'

'No,' Cali says, her voice high, and a laugh that sounds like a peacock wail comes out.

'Absolutely not,' Luke says, a little too loudly. *Alright, mate.* Funnily enough, Cali looks like she's thinking that too, her forced laughter having cut short. 'That was a long time ago. I'm sure we've both moved on.'

He won't look at Cali now, and his effort not to do so is just as obvious as when he couldn't stop looking at her. Fascinating.

Beside me, Cali does her super-fast nodding again. 'Yeah, yes, totally moved on. Very happy.'

'You seeing someone?' Sara asks.

Cali picks up her glass of wine and knocks some of it back. 'Um, yep.'

'What's their name?' I ask.

She blinks at me like she forgot I was here. 'He's called Luke.'

'He's called *Luke*?' repeats the Luke that's with us on the train.

106

'Yep. He's not you.' She does a mini version of the peacock laugh again. 'He's not some imaginary boyfriend I've named after you or anything. Haha. He's REAL.'

Oh God, poor thing. I'm sure her Luke is very real but right now Cali looks like she wants to jump out of the window, run up to the front of the train, and then just lie down in front of it. I hope she doesn't though because this is the most alive I've seen the group since I boarded the flight yesterday morning.

'How long have you been together?' this Luke asks.

'Eight months, I think. Ish.'

Eight months? And they didn't know about him? I look around at them for signs that at least some of them know this guy of hers. What's going on?

'What does he do?' I ask, when the conversation starts to dry up again.

'. . . London.'

'He does London?'

'No, sorry.' Cali shakes her head. 'I don't know why I said that. I mean he lives in London. He works in an office.'

'Doing what?'

'It's . . . a secret.'

'Like secret government work?' Joe leans forward.

'No. I can't talk about it. Mmm, this salad is delicious.' She prongs a lettuce leaf. 'So, what about the rest of you? Anyone seeing anyone at the moment?'

107

Sara shrugs. 'No one serious.'

Across the aisle, Joss shakes her head while Joe nods and says, 'Yep, my girlfriend is . . .' I somehow fade him out though as I watch Luke over my glass, who is staring at his plate, fiddling with his cutlery, and eventually nods.

'Yep,' he says in a small voice.

Cali chews her lip, like she wants to say something to him.

I'm about to ask him about his new (new?) partner, when something clicks into place for me. 'Can I take it the famous house-share is no longer? I'll be honest, this doesn't feel like a conversation between people who live in each other's pockets any more.'

Every one of them now looks as uncomfortable as I feel, so that's something. Drinks are covering lips, eyes are blinking rapidly, seats are creaking as they're shuffled in, the grate of forks on plates is the only sound over the rail lines.

Okay, I'm clearly on the right path and something's amiss. I wonder what happened.

Our main course of pasta arrives, which gives us all a reason to not feel weird about not speaking.

Until Cali swallows a massive forkful of linguine and splurts out, 'What's your girlfriend's name?'

We all look at Luke.

'Barbara,' he replies, concentrating on his pasta.

'How long have you two been an item?'

'A couple of years.'

'Ember, how's your seat?' Joss halts the conversation just as it's getting juicy by bending around Cali to look at me.

'It's fine.' Why does she suddenly care?

'Are you going to be alright sleeping there?' Cali asks, all concerned, and it twists in my tummy a little. Where was that concern when I suddenly lost all the friends I had? Where was that concern when my parents passed away only months later? At least Bryn sent flowers, but Cali and the rest of them just ignored it . . .

I don't know. Sometimes I can talk myself out of these feelings, tell myself I'm being selfish, entitled, centred on myself, but other times it flares up like a red wine blush.

'I'll sleep fine.' I nod.

Joss pipes up again, her voice both low and just-loud-enough at the same time. 'Course she will, she can escape into her deluded little Bryn-themed dreamland.'

'Christ, Joss. When did—' Cali stops herself, which makes me look at her, and she presses her lips together.

'When did what?' Joss snaps.

'Just . . . when did you get so mean?'

'I'm not mean. She's on her way to ruin our friend's wedding. And any minute now you'll no doubt be offering her a bed that Bryn herself paid for. I'm not mean, I'm just loyal. Where's your loyalty?'

Sara chuckles and mutters, 'Friend.' I don't know why, but she keeps an amused smirk on her face as she slips down her shades and sips on her wine.

'I am loyal!' Cali's voice raises a notch and at the end of the restaurant car I see the server look over.

Joss scoffs and shakes her head.

'What was that for?'

'You know.'

'Oh my God . . .'

'Excuse me,' I cut in, addressing Joss, but also the whole group. 'I don't need your loyalty, I don't need any of you to do anything for me, or to be my friends again. Just do whatever you want to do, and I'll do me.'

Enough of this bullshit. I stand and edge out past Cali, giving her a small smile as I go. At least she's being civil.

Out in the aisle I straighten my sweatshirt, my eyes down, and when they lift, there's somebody blocking my way.

'Hi,' the woman says, a smile melting out over her face like pooled honey, revealing neat teeth, dimples, dark hair pulled back in a ponytail.

'Hi,' I reply, our eyes meeting for a second. She glances down at the two tables, where the rest of them are seated in that thick, heated stillness that comes after an argument. As her head turns, her ear constellation glitters under the overhead lights like the snow outside the train.

In those seconds, I scan my eyes over her face, before clearing my throat and pointing past her. 'Excuse me, I'm just . . .'

She steps aside and I squeeze past, noticing her smell

110

(fresh, like an outdoor shower), the slight height difference (she's an inch or two taller than I am), and that her honey smile hasn't budged.

I don't look back. Sometimes you just have a moment with a hot stranger and then keep travelling in different directions.

It doesn't stop me from watching her reflection slide away when I reach the glass door dividing the carriages though. Or notice that she's watching me leave.

Chapter 14

Cali

'Uuuuugggghhhh,' I scream (quietly) into my hands as Ontario rushes by, snowy fir trees towering high above the glass-domed ceiling of the celestial carriage. Thankfully I'm alone up here at the moment, so I can merrily stew in my stupidity without any witnesses.

Why oh why oh why did I say I have a boyfriend? I could have said no, I didn't. At the very least I could have said he was called anything other than *Luke*. But when Sara asked if I was seeing anyone, and Luke had so adamantly stated that we'd both moved on, I couldn't stop myself saying yes. I just ... didn't want him to be all loved up and think I had no one. And now I've got myself stuck in an eight-month relationship with Fake Luke with the top-secret job.

Maybe it's a good thing the five of us are barely

talking, because I shouldn't have to answer too many more questions.

I shake my head and take a big gulp of Canadian, well, *train*, air, and try and pull myself back into the present. The celestial carriage has huge glass windows that curve all the way overhead, and I have a panoramic view of the forests, the snow feeling thicker the further we move away from the coast. It's so beautiful, and it's quite calming. Like I'm in the BFI IMAX in London.

He has a girlfriend. They're probably in love. They probably have sex.

And what would Fake Luke even look like? Like Real Luke, or totally different?

No, don't think about that.

An eight-month relationship sounds lovely, I have to admit. I bet Fake Luke and I would be talking about moving in together. I wonder what I would have got him for Christmas. Maybe next Christmas we'd spend it together, assuming we're still together, of course.

I rest my cheek against the train window, the cold of the glass pleasant against my still-blushing face.

Oh my God, what if Luke has a whole new set of mates and this girl was his will-they-won't-they in that friendship group, only they lasted the distance, and I'm just a really distant memory of something that was never really much more than nothing?

I should look for this 'Barbara' on Instagram.

No. I. Should. Not.

I shake the thoughts from my head, clonking my brow against the window as I do so. It's Christmas Eve the day after tomorrow, and that means Christmas Day will be our last full day on the train. It's very Bryn to decide she knows best for all of us, and to make the decision to force us together for the holidays in a mode of transport we can't just jump off without getting lost in the Canadian wilderness. I would have liked to have had Christmas in that big cabin, my own room, a window that would open out to a vista of calm, quietly twinkling snow rising up the side of a mountain.

Instead, all I have are thoughts of dear Fake Luke to keep me company.

It was already nightfall when we pulled into the station of White River, Ontario, for a short break. I haven't seen darkness like this in, I don't know, around a billion years? I kick at the terra firma, moving settled snow over the concrete, and pull my coat in closer to me using my pockets.

Now I have my back to the streak of red that is the train, running alongside the lamppost-lit track, and I'm looking outwards, past the small ticket office, and into the blackness beyond. My breath is just visible, and my nose tingles in the icy air.

Someone edges up beside me, and I half expect it to be Ember since none of the rest of them are giving her the time of day. But then he speaks.

'Hey.'

'Hello, Luke.'

He stands beside me, looking out, and it's taking all I have not to glance over, or try and fix my hair which is probably frizzing in the cold.

What shall I say? Where have all my thoughts gone?

Hello, in there?

After ten billion years, he says, 'It's cold, huh? You kind of forget when you're on the train just how cold it is outside, I mean. Are you cold?'

'No,' I lie. 'I'm fine. Are you?'

We used to talk and talk and talk, about stupid, silly things, like who did the better impression of Christopher Walken, or sometimes serious stuff, like what had someone done to make the other feel bad. We'd be able to fill silences with questions or chatter, or we'd let the silence sit, and we'd nestle into it, lean into each other, I'd rest my head on his shoulder, he'd start snoring with his arm draped around my neck.

This silence is one between strangers, and it's cold. So, yes, I am cold.

'So ...'

That was such a loaded 'so' that I brace myself.

'You don't mind being away from Luke over Christmas? The other one, I mean. Your boyfriend?'

Oh, Lord. 'No, no, he's really chilled.' I wave my hand in the air, proving that I, too, am really chill.

'Yeah? Tell me about him.'

'There's not much to tell.'

'That's a rave review,' Luke comments. I heard that smirk in his voice, and I look to him.

'What?'

He laughs, but it doesn't sound natural. 'I'm just kidding. Eight months, seriously, that's great.'

'Yeah, it is great.' I nod. 'He's really lovely, and we're thinking of moving in together in the new year.' What the fuck am I talking about?

'Sounds serious.'

'It is. Everything's great.' I look away again and nod at the dark forests I can't see. Everything is just great. 'Work is good, London life is good, my boyfriend and I are good. All is merry and bright.'

'So, you're happy.' He says it quietly, a statement rather than a question, but one that demands an answer, and when my gaze is drawn back to him like a magnet, locking into place with his, his head tilted just a little, his lips parted just a little, his brow furrowed, just a little, I forget for a moment what he even asked. Or stated. Then he says it again. 'You're happy.'

'Yes,' I answer. 'Are you?'

He shrugs. 'Sure.'

Sure is not an answer, but a whistle blows somewhere down the track and it's time to get back on board.

I want to ask him about her, about what they're like

together. Is he the type of boyfriend I always imagined? Is he tender and funny? My eyes flicker to his lips and, from the lack of vapour smoking the air, I think he's holding his breath.

Five years I've wanted to be this close to him again. That's a long time to hold onto the idea of someone.

The whistle blows again, and Luke breathes out, and only then do I realise I was holding my breath as well.

Luke stands aside and gestures for me to climb aboard before him, and he follows me down towards our cabin. I could invite him to come to the celestial carriage, talk with me, clear the air a little. Or to the restaurant car for some dinner. But when I reach my cabin door and turn back to see what his plans are for the rest of the evening, he's already halfway inside his own compartment.

Oh.

Fake Luke would never.

Chapter 15

Joe

Once upon a time, a brother and a sister, who were never very close, managed to not kill each other despite renting a flat together in the capital city, and then starting a business together. Perhaps they could be one of those loving sibling duos, like you see on TV, they thought. Then everything went tits up, and they fled to different ends of the country, for the sake of the family, and not wanting to put their mum through a double homicide trial. Now, it looks like the knives might come out again.

'Top or bottom bunk?'

My sister shrugs, and it's like we're back at primary school again and she's mad at me because I scratched my name across her metallic Westlife pencil case. I rub my aching forehead with the palm of my hand.

Joss is famous, at least in our family, for holding onto a grudge. She ekes it out, lets it lay over everything like a weighted blanket, and if you try and move from under it, she'll pin the corners down.

I'm making her sound like a monster, but it's just that her pride is her downfall. I've seen it be a strength, too. When she has a goal in mind she's determined and confident and will strive to make it happen. When she's proud of her friends or family she'll sing it from the rooftops. She doesn't take nonsense or belittling from anyone. But also, she will never, ever, admit when she might be in the wrong.

Maybe this is why it's an old habit of ours, or maybe mine, to always take her lead with decisions. It's just easier that way. I never believed I was being a doormat. Despite what the others said.

'Shall I take the bottom, then?' I prompt, gritted teeth.

'And leave me to fall out? Fuck off.' Joss steadies herself with a breath, which is something new. Perhaps she's been meditating? 'I'll take the bottom. Please.'

We study the instructions on the wall on how to convert the two seats in our compartment into a pair of beds. Joss's brow is creased when I glance at her out of the side of my eye. This trip is harder on her than me, I can tell, though she'd never admit it, or why.

My sister reaches for a lever and yanks, but the chair won't budge. She kicks at it with her foot.

'You need to—'

'I can do it,' she snaps.

After a fair amount of clonking and pulling, arguing and ignoring, we manage to make the two bunks. It's nice, actually. Cosy. For the past couple of years I've lived in Bristol, near the train station, and something about the sound brings back home. I climb up into my bunk, about ready to call it a night, even if it's only ... eight fifteen.

Beneath me, Joss potters about, grumbling. Something about Cali being stupid and Luke being smug and me not helping or having her back. I open my phone and scroll, refusing to listen, letting it play out. God, I haven't missed this side of her. Or this side of me, to be honest. I think I've come into my own living away from her, and I don't want to be her shadow again.

In fairness to my sister, she never used to ask that of me, they were roles we fell into, me being naturally more passive, her more, well, aggressive, I guess.

She climbs onto her bunk, too, and I glance at her in the mirror opposite. She's opened her phone and is looking back at photos from a night out we did for her twenty-fourth birthday. It was *Great Gatsby*-themed (even though none of us had actually read the book or seen the film). I watch her candidly for a couple of minutes, as she scrolls back through photo after photo, where we're all laughing and posing and pretending to smoke, holding martini glasses up in the air. She zooms in on one of her and Luke just as he's said something to crack her up, and a smile crosses her face as she lies there in the dim light, swaying to the movement of the train.

The worst thing about my sister is her pride when she lets it rage. The best thing is the soft moments like this, when her pride shines.

Chapter 16

Ember

My carriage is dark, save for a few, low, overhead lamps illuminating the books on people's laps. Chatter has died down, and the rhythmic sound of the train gliding along its tracks, in the darkness of the outside world, has become the soundscape in the background. That, and Gwen's snoring.

I flex my back in my reclined seat, and pull my blanket over me since it keeps sliding off and dusting the floor. Outside, the world is black, and I'm not sure if we're surrounded by trees, or just a whole lot of night-time.

Snorrrrt. Gwen wakes herself up and peers at me in the dark.

'Still awake?' she asks. 'Why?'

'Who can say?'

She's asleep again before my sarcasm soundwave even hits her.

What am I doing here? In the middle of who-knows-where in the Canadian wilderness, rushing to my ex-girlfriend who doesn't even know I'm on my way to her.

I take out my phone and turn the brightness down in the dark, scrolling back to a photo of Bryn and me on the riverbank of the Thames, Tower Bridge lit up behind us in the night sky. I don't miss city life, but I miss life with her.

I zoom in on her face, a wallowing pulling at my chest. For a while, I really, truly thought she was going to be my person, for our whole lives. Bryn had this way of making sure nobody ever felt lonely, and that day I left her flat for the last time, it was as if her warmth had been snatched away. I was cold, and alone. And all because of a little thing called wanting different things out of our lives. It was a sucky break-up, with a sea full of tears, but at the time it felt like the only way we could both move forward.

Would anyone be able to love me like she did? Will I ever want to give anyone the chance? I sigh and shuffle in my seat again, kicking my legs into the aisle and closing my eyes.

This is why I have to see her. I need to know if she still feels the same. I can't stop thinking about her walking down an aisle in a wedding dress, and my soul feels heavy at the thought of not being the one there with her.

My eyelids pop open again, much to my own annoyance.

Alright, I'm clearly not going to sleep anytime soon. I extract my shoulder from under Gwen's lolling head and step into the aisle, cricking my back. I grab my blanket, headphones and baseball cap, and make my way past sleeping passengers, avoiding eye contact with the night owls like myself.

At the celestial carriage, up the steps I climb, and before I even reach the top, I look up at a dome of stars overhead. I stop. Right on the stairs. And stare.

It's like being home again, on the beach, at night. That big wide openness that makes me feel insignificant but alive, all in good ways. I let out a long exhalation, already calmer.

Climbing the last couple of steps, I enter the near-empty viewing car. My eyebrows raise. I wasn't expecting anyone else to be up here at this time, but one person is. I hope it's not one of Bryn's friends – the thought of dealing with them right now makes me want to retreat straight back down the stairs again.

Then the person turns, and under the starlight, her eyes meet mine for the second time.

'Hello again,' I say. She's at the front of the carriage, the best seats in the house, and she rests her arm on the seat behind her to look back at me.

'Hey, you.'

Something about that phrase from her lips sounds intimate, familiar, welcoming. It's a warmth I haven't felt since leaving Cornwall, and despite my instinct to keep my distance, to sit on the opposite end of the celestial carriage, I head towards her, taking a seat across the aisle from hers.

'You couldn't sleep either?' I ask her.

'Actually, this is just my favourite time to come up here.' Her honey smile is framed by the glass that separates us from the stars. 'Nobody else around.'

Oh. 'I'll leave you to it—'

'No.' She laughs, a cute chuckle that sounds like sprinkles of stardust. 'Present company excluded. I'm Alex.'

'Hi, Alex. I'm Ember.'

'Ember . . .' She tests my name out in her mouth, like she's thinking about it for a moment. 'Nice to meet you.'

Alex's voice is salted caramel, smooth with a hint of scratch, and her accent gives away that she's Canadian. 'You've taken this train before?' I ask her.

'I actually work on this train, I'm a chief attendant.'

'Oh, you're working?'

'Not right now,' she says. 'No, this is a personal trip. How's your journey going?'

'Good,' I say. That's not a total lie.

I feel her eyes studying me. 'But you can't sleep?'

'It's not that I'm uncomfortable . . . I think I just have a lot on my mind. And probably a little jet lagged.'

When I don't elaborate, she nods and settles back in her seat, sinking down so the back of her head rests against the back and she's facing up into the night sky. I do the same. Ahhhh. That's my universe.

'I'm a good listener, if you want to tell me what's on your mind. Although I think I can guess it's something to do with the argument between you and your friends earlier.'

I roll my head to the side and find her watching me. 'No, it's not them. They aren't actually my friends; we aren't travelling together. They're just ... old acquaintances.'

'Oh. That's a coincidence.'

'Mmm ... It's not so much a coincidence as complicated.'

'Alright.'

We slip back into silence, which I'd usually feel compelled to fill, but in this low light, under the stars, with the white noise of the train trundling in the darkness, it feels easy to settle into it.

'So, if you're not with them, where is it you're going?' Alex asks me, after a while.

Where am I going?

'There's a wedding,' I start, glancing over and holding her gaze. Shall I just tell her? It might be nice to get a little unbiased perspective.

'In Vancouver.' Alex nods.

'But I'm not technically invited.' What is she going to think of me? Maybe it doesn't matter what she thinks, because she's a stranger, impartial. She's listening.

Alex is still watching me, her face lit up by the white

126

glow of the starlight, the tree tops rushing past, dark against the ink of the sky. A small frown is on her brow while she waits for me to say more.

'Don't judge me,' I begin. Always a solid way to begin a story.

Alex's frown smooths out, a smile whispering onto her face as she turns her body and rests the side of her head on her arm, on the back of her seat. 'We'll see.'

'This wedding, in Vancouver. It's my ex-girlfriend's wedding.'

'Huh.'

'Yeah. But I feel like ... you see, I think Bryn's been sending me signals.'

'Signals?' Alex's smile is growing bigger by the second.

'Yes. That she's still in love with me.'

Alex's smile drops for a moment and she lifts her head. 'What signals?'

I start to tell her about all of the things I've seen so far on social media. The venue, the menu, the honeymoon destination, the details, the décor.

'I mean, when I say them out loud, I know how I sound. And I would just like to say that I'm not normally like this.'

A soft chuckle comes out of Alex.

'I'm glad I'm amusing to you.' I laugh back.

'It's not amusing, it's just ...'

'A lot?'

'A lot,' she agrees.

'Are you judging me, Alex?'

'A little.'

I wrap the blanket around myself and look up at the sky. 'But do you not think that if my ex is getting cold feet, if she still has feelings for me, that's something we should find out?'

'Well, do you still have feelings for her?'

'I . . . ' I shrug, my shoulders hidden under my blanket. 'I don't know. But I can't get her out of my head.'

In the darkness, Alex shifts in her seat, pulling her sweater sleeves down over her hands. 'If you're not normally like this, what *are* you normally like?'

'What do you mean?'

'There must be a version of Ember without Bryn. I want to know what she's like.'

'You do?' I sneak another look at her.

'Why so surprised?'

'I just told you I'm travelling across the globe to crash the wedding of my ex-girlfriend. And I've found myself on a four-day train with a bunch of people I don't get on with. That little lot might be the most exciting thing about me, to be honest.'

'I doubt that,' she says. 'I'm not trying to pick you up or anything, I'm just curious about you.'

'I'm curious about you, too,' I reply. 'Spending your days working the railroads must be interesting?'

'You do meet some wild ones.' She laughs, and after a

second, I think she might be referring to me. 'We'll talk about me later. So, you're from the UK? London?'

I shake my head as I run my fingers through my hair and pull it up into a messy ponytail. 'I'm not a city girl, to be honest. I live by the beach, in Cornwall.'

'A country girl.'

'A coast girl,' I clarify.

'What do you like about the beach?'

I like how she pronounces beach, the last two letters sounding like a gentle wave breaking on the shoreline. 'There's something about being in nature that feels big and real and amazing and peaceful, all rolled into one. And I often think animals are better than people, so I like seeing seals and dolphins. I like that I can drive inland a couple of minutes and see sheep.' I laugh. 'There's an owl sanctuary nearby too. I don't know if I'm making sense or just sleep deprived.'

'You're making total sense,' Alex says.

'Might I see bears on this trip?'

'Bears? Not on the train.' She chuckles and adds, 'You might when you hit Vancouver Island. Although they may all be hibernating.'

I pick at a loose thread of wool on the blanket, thinking of Tonia. She likes to hibernate in winter, also.

'Do your family live in Cornwall?'

It's an innocent question, and in hundreds of similar ways I've answered this before, so I don't mind. But I'd be lying if I said it didn't still cause my heart to let out a dull throb.

'Actually, my parents both passed away, a few years back.'

'I'm sorry.'

'Thank you. It's fine. I'm fine . . . '

Alex reaches across the aisle and rests a hand on my shoulder for a breath or two. 'So now you just like to hang out with seals and owls. I get it.'

I smile. 'That's right.'

'You know,' she says, sitting up straighter, excitement flashing in her eyes like the stars have dropped out of the sky. 'If you want to see polar bears there's a great train that leaves Winnipeg tomorrow evening and travels up to Churchill. The polar bears are usually only viewable until late November but the reports are that they're around still this year.'

'You mean, get off this train? Not go to Vancouver?'

'Just an idea. If nature makes you happy, that's a pretty spectacular trip.'

But . . . leave the train? Forget about Bryn? That isn't the plan.

Alex stands up, stretching her arms out to the side, and shakes loose her dark hair. 'I'm just throwing it out there. This "Ember-without-Bryn" sounds like she's got a few things figured out, and she might just find herself having a good time. I'm going to go to bed.'

130

She looks at me, her eyes find mine again in the dark, and we lock together. My heart stumbles a little, and she lets out another little laugh, tapping me on the shoulder again.

'Goodnight.'

'But we didn't talk about you?'

'We have thousands of kilometres to cover,' she says. 'Unless you leave me for the polar bears.'

I wish her goodnight and sit back to gaze up at the stars again. I'd forgotten how nice it feels to flirt a little. But a flirtation is one thing, and I'm thinking about the one who might be the one. I can't get off the train.

Can I?

Chapter 17

Joe

I wake up in the morning having slept beautifully. The sun is streaming through a crack in the curtain, which, when I pull it an inch to the side, displays a dazzling vista of snowy forests under a blue sky.

'Close that curtain,' my darling sister croaks from the bottom bunk.

'It's incredible out there, wake up and look.'

'I've only just got to sleep.'

'I slept really well.'

'I don't give a shit.'

I pull the curtain back fully, making sure to make a racket as I do so, and she growls like a vampire caught in a sunbeam.

I smirk.

Sometimes I remember that we thought it would be a good idea to work together, and wonder why I was such a naive little twat. I'd come to live in London following a stint backpacking, and after working for a couple of years, I'd shared my idea with Joss – a website that helped people create their own travel journals. We both worked to earn more savings, before chucking in our jobs, and for months we toiled together in harmony, a proper little powerhouse family. We rented office space, bought advertising, Bryn and Sara had even both invested.

Then a week after opening, it was like the rose glasses came off and both of us suddenly realised working together meant spending all day, every day, together. And when you already share a flat, and then an office too, well, let's just say cracks in our plasterwork appeared super-fast.

We started a business together, and it failed. It's not a new story, it's not groundbreaking, but it happened. We lost money, and we lost our friends' money, and we never should have been so gung-ho because neither of us really knew what we were doing. Neither of us. And yet (thanks, pride) Joss seems to blame me. Maybe because it was my idea? And I'm guilty of blaming her, sometimes . . . maybe because it was my idea.

We haven't spent much time together since we both went our separate ways after London. The odd family gathering, sporadic holidays. We were never super-close, but it's almost like when we chose to live together in London we were both riding on a high of having that brother–sister camaraderie we'd always wanted.

'You snore,' Joss says now, out from under the arm which is dramatically slung across her face.

'You fart, like *all* night,' I retort.

We dig and snipe at each other all the way out of bed, through getting up and dressed, as we're putting the chairs back and throughout breakfast, which we eat in silence in our compartment. Silence until Joss lobs a butter pat at me.

'Can you stop chewing so loudly? Close your mouth.'

I chew wider, showing her every flake of croissant.

She shakes her head. 'I am so glad you skipped Mum's birthday dinner this year. The less time I have to spend in my life watching you eat, the better.'

'I skipped it so I wouldn't have to hear you whining, constantly, about everything.'

'I don't whine! I do not whine!'

'You haven't *stopped* whining since we left the UK, can't you see you're driving everyone wild?' My voice raises a notch.

'*Me*?' she shrieks. 'I don't whine, I get angry. You're the one who whines. Or just lets people walk all over them.'

I feel myself flush. 'Like you?'

'Like them. I'm trying to protect us from getting sucked

into what was clearly a fake, expired friendship, and you're just tiptoeing about, acting like nothing happened.'

'I'm acting like someone who just wants to let it go. It was five years ago. I don't care what they think of me any more.'

Joss tilts her head to the side, and mimics wiping her shoes on a doormat.

I grab my phone and my wallet, stuffing them in my pocket. We're pulling into Sioux Lookout shortly for a break, and I for one need some fresh air.

'That's right, run away,' my sister says in a sing-song voice.

'Grow up, for God's sake.' I sigh. 'Don't you think everyone else just wants to move on and be civil, for the sake of Bryn?'

'The problem is—'

'You are the problem!' I cry. 'I know you're embarrassed about what happened. I know you feel let down and left out by things that weren't in your control, but your ego needs to chill.'

'I am not embarrassed.'

'Really? Because everyone can see you're deflecting like a toddler midway through a tantrum. Even Luke looks fed up with you.'

Ouch. That was a stinger and I almost feel bad. Joss always had a bond with Luke, I wondered often if she saw him like the brother she always wanted. But I also felt bad for her because it was never as strong as his one with Cali, and she always seemed to be outside, waving in. Metaphorically.

She shuts up temporarily, and I take the opportunity to leave the compartment. Or am I just being the same old Joe, and passively running away?

Chapter 18

Cali

I slept fine. I slept fine! I probably snored more than Sara did, anyway. The cabin was cosy, like my flat in London, and the bunk beds made it feel like camping, and the train moving along was like being rocked to sleep.

And I only went into a spiral of resentment once as I lay there awake, thinking about how in the hell Luke had ended up getting a compartment to himself when the rest of us had to share.

None of us are really talking yet, on this trip. It's fine. It's like the past five years, really, so I guess no big deal. The corners of my mouth droop at that thought, though.

Actually, two of us are talking, in a way. Through the wall are the unmistakeable voices of Joe and Joss bickering. It's been like that for the last hour, and I could get up and go to the celestial carriage, but Sara's gone up there with her book so I'm enjoying the solitude and the view from the window.

We're still moving through the forests of Ontario today, the sunlight low in the sky and streaming through tree branches, sparkling against the white snow which seems to thicken the further we get into Canada. It's beautiful, like the glittering lights of Regent Street at Christmastime.

Click. Was that Luke's compartment door opening, behind the other wall? I sit up like a meerkat. Where's he off to? Maybe I need to take a walk too?

Don't you dare get off this seat, Cali. Glue those butt cheeks to the chair if you have to.

I wonder how he slept. Did he take the top or bottom bunk? Probably the bottom. I remember he used to sleep all drapey, arms and legs melting off the sides of the mattress, breathing slow and relaxed.

That first morning, after all those months (years?) of flirting and eye contact and imagining scenarios, when we woke up together in my bed it was summer and the sun was already up and streaming around buildings and through my window even though it was early, and I just watched him sleep like a delirious little weirdo.

The night before we'd been doing something so insignificant, so 'normal' for us, just reading books on the sofa, leaning together, him smelling of vanilla, me probably smelling of the raspberry ripple ice cream I was eating straight from the tub. Then I remember he just put down his book on his lap, lost in thought. I asked him what it was, what was happening in those pages? And he just turned in his seat, reached over, and put his fingers behind my neck. I remember sucking in my breath, my hands clasping the ice cream tub, and unable to keep the smile off my face as he came in for a kiss.

Reader, I dropped the ice cream.

We were inseparable that week in a way we'd never been before, and the icing on the cake was supposed to be the fact that at the weekend we'd be going on holiday with all our best friends and we could tell them and they'd be all supportive and we'd be like Ross and Rachel and happily ever after would begin.

'How's Luke?' Sara asks, coming back into our cabin and looking like she's too cool to care less how Luke is.

'What? I don't know. He's only just left his room, I think. I heard something, it could have been any door really. How was the celestial car?'

'Not our Luke, your Luke. Weren't you going to call him?'

Bollocks. 'Oh yeah, he's fine. Great, actually.'

'What did you get him for Christmas?' She sits down on her bed, now folded back into a chair.

'Just the usual boyfriend stuff,' I answer. Am I blushing? I'm definitely blushing. Perhaps now *would* be a good time to go for a walk around the train. 'You mentioned you were seeing someone, but nothing serious?' I deflect.

She's about to answer when an announcement comes over the speakers to say the train is about to stop at Sioux Lookout and that we all need to get off, which I don't mind because who doesn't love a lookout?

Sara and I cease conversing and busy ourselves converting our cabin back into its seats for the day and putting our belongings back in our bags. I go to clean my teeth in the shared bathroom down at the end of the carriage. She goes to make a call.

I scrub my gnashers slowly, lazily, observing my chin spots as I do so, that same heaviness coming out of me in the form of a long, frothy sigh.

Once my dramatic exhale has completed, the sound of a mumbling voice outside the bathroom door fills any quiet.

Is that Luke's voice? It sounds like Luke ... I press my ear against the door, my toothbrush dangling from my hand.

'Yep, alright. Will do. Yep. Buh-bye. Love you.'

He loves her! Well, obviously. I'm not jealous.

I lean over the sink and let the minty foam dribble from my mouth. Everything in me feels heavy.

I knew that, coming on this trip, things probably wouldn't go back to anything romantic between us. Too much time has passed. But that doesn't mean I didn't hope, if I'm honest with myself. How could I have been so stupid, all that time ago, to have finally got together with the only guy who's ever made me feel like this, only to push him away as soon as things got hard?

And now he's in love with someone else.

I stand up straight. He's in love with someone else, time to let go of the fantasy, and not be an Ember about it.

Not long after, I'm stepping down from the train, and the cold air greets me like a chilly hug, the light seeming brighter, the ground stiller. Obviously. Ahhh. I stretch my arms overhead and open my minty mouth to take a gulp of the frosty air.

We've been travelling on the train for over twenty-four hours now, and tomorrow is Christmas Eve. It's a weird thought that it'll be Boxing Day before the journey is over, and we've made it to Bryn's wedding.

I don't know if she's going to get her wish that we're all getting along like best buds again, though.

Luke steps off the train behind me and squints into the sunshine, stubble on his face, dishevelled, hunky. Who does he think he is, some kind of nineties movie star? Some kind of ... heart-throb heartbreaker from a boy band? I scrunch my nose at him, and I give him my best glare until he starts to look over and then I turn my back so he doesn't see me.

By the time we've all crunched over the thick Canadian snow, taken some photos of the surroundings, and pettily queued up separately to buy identical coffees from the kiosk, it's time to get back onboard, where we'll remain until a longer stop for refuelling in Winnipeg tonight.

But just as I'm taking my seat back by the window, a commotion outside the carriage catches my eye, and ears.

'Oh, Jesus,' I mutter, getting up again and rushing to the train door.

'I cannot spend another second with you.' Joss is seething, baring her teeth at her brother, the two of them squaring off on the platform like two duelling panthers about to strike. Beside Joss is her suitcase, which Joe keeps trying to grab.

'Joss, what are you doing?' I call from the steps.

'Leaving. Like I should have done before I ever even went along with this ridiculous plan,' she spits, without looking at me, her glare focused on her brother.

'Why are you leaving?'

'None of your business!' This time she swings around with such anger it makes me step backwards, right into Ember, who's appeared behind me. A rush of cold blood seems to race through my veins. I blink at Joss, a deer in headlights, my fingers reaching up to my chin, and for a second, I'm back in Spain, on the last day of the holiday, and even though half a decade has passed, Joss seems just as mad at me today as she did back then.

All my words have deserted me, darted into dark corners of my brain, afraid of the wrath of Joss. A whistle sounds further up the platform.

Joe lunges for her case again. 'Look. I would rather tie myself to these tracks and let the train run me over than share a compartment with you again, but if you shut up for five seconds and get back on the train then I'm sure we can figure something out for Queen Joss.'

'Nope,' she says, snatching her case out of his way. 'You can go without me. You can all go without me.'

'What, are you going to live here? Become a forest-woman? Hitchhike to Vancouver?'

'Maybe I will. I will hitchhike across all of North America before I get back on the train.'

'You are so . . . !' Joe growls in frustration.

'No, *you* are *so*, we do not work well together,' she spells out through snarly lips. 'You go your way, I'll go mine.'

'Oh my *Godddddd*.' Joe lifts his hands to his hair. 'Is this about the business, again?'

'No, it's not about the business, because if it was about the business I'd be reminding you that not only are you an awful roommate but a shitty colleague, too.'

Behind me, Ember mutters in recognition. 'Oh yeah, the failed business.'

'Fine,' Joe spits, reaching across and pushing her case over so it thumps onto the tarmac. A small crowd is forming now, people looking out of train windows, passengers pausing halfway up the steps. 'Fine! Stay here. I don't care.'

'Fine!'

Joe turns and strides towards the train. Another whistle blows, and along the platform I can hear people being shooed back inside, and carriage doors being slammed closed.

'Whoa, hold on,' I say, putting my hand up in front of

143

Joe and stopping him before he can board. 'Joss, come on, we have to go.'

Joss, suitcase handle gripped, marches away, her back to me, lifting her middle finger into the air.

'Oh my God, let her go,' Ember mumbles behind me.

'No! What?' I say, then shout back out to Joss. 'Oi, come back here this instant!'

The train conductor man is approaching our door.

'Bye, everyone, have a great life,' Joss calls back, and you know what, I don't think she means that.

'Joe, get her!' I cry as he pushes past me onto the train.

The train conductor man appears in front of me. 'Excuse me, miss, we need to close this door.'

'But our friend, she's not back on board yet.'

'The one leaving the station?'

'She's coming back, just one second, *Joss*!'

Joss doesn't turn, but down on the far end of the carriage, Luke jumps down the steps, jogging over to her.

Oh, bloody hell, now that's two of them we've lost.

In this momentary distraction, the conductor has closed my door, and now me, Ember and Joe are squeezed in the window frame, the cold air on our faces.

'Luke, leave her, mate, get back on board,' Joe shouts.

'I'm not leaving her,' Luke calls back.

'She's not going anywhere, she's just being dramatic, as usual.'

'You don't think she wants to leave?' I ask Joe.

144

'No, of course not, that case felt pretty empty to me.'

The train blows what I can only assume is a final whistle, because the train chap is now shaking his head and closing the door Luke leapt out of.

Oh my God, Luke. My heart speeds up, my lips dry. Don't go without Luke. Joss ... well, if she *really* wants to go ... 'Luke, hurry!' Then I shake my head. 'And you, Joss, come on.'

Luke's reached her and they're talking intensely. She's looking into his eyes, her forehead in a frown, and for a moment the anger seems to be replaced with sadness, and I see the old Joss again, the one who just wanted to be involved, who was a bit socially awkward but always made the effort.

Train man is at the final carriage now, with one door to close.

Come on, come on, come on.

'Hurry up!' Ember shouts in my ear, an unexpected note of genuine concern. My eyebrows dart upwards.

I know this is selfish, don't judge me, but I'm not ready for Luke to be left behind. I want to talk to him. I want to get back ... something ... of what we used to have. Even just as a friend. He has to make it back to the train.

'Joss, for crying out loud, that's enough,' Joe shouts.

'Don't talk to me like I'm a child,' she shoots, but in the same moment she angles her body back towards the train, and Luke takes her case, picking it up and then darting an amused look directly at me that makes my heart burst into a little flame (in a good way), and the two of them begin walking to the train.

Luke's walk swiftly becomes a jog and Joss tries her hardest to appear nonchalant but also speeds up a little bit. The train man throws his hands in the air, having closed the final door, as Luke pulls open the one he jumped out of again and ushers Joss inside before climbing in himself.

Seconds later, the vista begins to move, and the train drifts out of the station.

Joe and I bump our way down the carriage, meeting Luke and Joss outside Joss's compartment. She sticks her chin in the air, cheeks flushed. Her lips twitch for a moment, and then she flicks her hair back and strides to her seat, sitting down with a *humph*. 'We're switching up the sleeping arrangements,' she declares, her voice quieter, her eyes on the retreating Sioux Lookout landscape.

'Fine.' I let out a satisfied exhale, and catch Luke's eye. He grins at me, a shared humour that sparkles between us, unspoken, unmistakable. It only lasts a moment, then he remembers himself and nods at me, just a hint of a smile remaining on his lips, and turns away. But it's enough to remind me that *there he is*.

Chapter 19

Ember

I'm back in my seat, warming my hands up, a smile forcing itself onto my lips despite my best efforts. Never a dull moment with this group. There was always some kind of drama, though I don't remember it ever being vicious, but that was the classic Joss that I remembered.

Also, a small part of me respected that she was about to go off on her own into the Ontario countryside. I was almost a little envious.

I can't stop thinking about what Alex said, about getting off the train at Winnipeg and travelling north to Churchill to see the polar bears. Instead of going to Bryn.

The thought of it causes a stirring, a glimmer, deep in my soul. The wilderness is calling to me, the animals, the big sky and vast forests. More so than the city of Vancouver.

My parents saw polar bears once. They took a holiday to Greenland and said it was the most magical experience. They had matching bright white Arctic coats that they'd bought specially, and I still have one of their photos framed on my wall, because they looked like a couple of polar bears wearing them in the snow. I smile, just thinking about it.

Is this my gut telling me it's the right thing to do?

But, I can't. Not now. I have important things to do.

Speaking of … I get my phone out of my pocket and tap on it with icy fingers, bringing up Bryn's social pages. She's posting daily, nuggets of her life, excited-sounding snippets of her upcoming nuptials. I see you, Bryn.

'Hi,' a caramel, Canadian voice says beside me.

'Alex!' A smile spreads across my face, and I go to put my phone away. Then I stop. 'Look, what I was talking about last night, about my ex who's getting married. I don't want you to think I'm imagining this, and look at what she just posted.' I show her a photo of a pine cone centrepiece. She knows I love pine cones.

'Okay,' Alex says in reply, taking my phone from me for a closer look, her fingers grazing mine. She studies the photo for a moment and then hands it back, a thoughtful look on her features, then changes the subject. 'I heard your friend – sorry, non-friend – tried to escape.'

I laugh, and Alex takes an empty seat across from me. I lean forward, and she does the same. 'That's pretty typical of her, Joss, she's kind of dramatic. From what I remember.'

'Why?'

'Why's she dramatic? I don't know, that's just her, I guess. She got back on board just in time though.'

'That's good.' Alex nods, and holds my gaze.

I clear my throat. 'You're probably sick of hearing all about me and these people I've found myself travelling with. Tell me about you. What are you heading to Vancouver for?'

Alex sits back in her seat. I mirror her again. Then notice I'm doing it so move to a cross-legged position instead, tucking my thick-socked feet up under me.

After a pause, where Alex stares out of the window at the trees passing, she says, 'I'm going to see family.'

'For the holidays?' I ask.

'Yeah.'

'Where do they live?'

'Just outside Vancouver, in the countryside. I love it out there.'

'Do you normally live in Toronto?'

'Kind of,' she says. 'I rent an apartment there, sorry, a *flat*,' she teases, switching to a British accent, which makes me laugh and lean in towards her again. 'But I do love travelling, camping, heading out to the mountains when I can. But I need to have a base in the city for work.'

'Do you always work on this route?'

'Not always, but often.'

'Do you like it?'

'I do,' she answers, her smile wide and inviting, and I find myself watching her lips as she talks. Alex stands up. 'Did you think about Winnipeg?'

'About leaving the train? Yes.'

'Do you think you will? Seems like it could be perfect for you.'

'I don't know ...' How does she know what's perfect for me? I don't even know what's perfect for me. That's the whole point of this trip, isn't it? I can't abandon it now.

'Alright, I've gotta go, but I'll catch you later, right?' Alex places her hand on my shoulder as she passes, and I reach my own up to pat it before she goes. Mine is cold as snow, hers is warm as sunshine.

I haven't seen Bryn's friends all day. Not since the commotion this morning. Instead, I've been moving between my seat and the celestial carriage, watching old movies on my phone, and combing through all the information I can find about switching to the other train.

I don't know what to do. You know who would know? Bryn. But I can't really ask her, can I?

Alex is nice to talk to. Her life here in Canada, travelling the country for work, is interesting. I'm interested. In knowing more about her, I mean.

The train will be arriving in Winnipeg soon, and is

scheduled to be our longest stop yet. Man, am I looking forward to properly stretching my legs. We'll be there for around three hours, and, whatever happens, I intend to spend as much time as possible feeling the fresh, cold air on my face.

I lean out of my seat to look up and down the aisle for Alex's tall frame. Just in case she'd like a walk around Winnipeg too. I don't know where she's bunking down at the moment, but I'm guessing, being staff, she has access to a compartment somewhere. But instead of Alex, Luke is heading my way.

When I was with Bryn, I remember her pre-warning me about Luke before I came to the townhouse for the first time. (The way she spoke about them all as if I was bound to meet them the second I walked through the door, I'd assumed they were all flatmates rather than neighbours.) She'd told me he was aloof. Hard to get to know. Kept to himself. I didn't find him to be like that at all. I found him to be ... like me. He was kind of quiet, but friendly. Got lost in his imagination. He wasn't one for outbursts or gossip, but he was unfailingly warm to the people he clearly loved. Especially one person, who would make him glow from the inside out when they were in the same room. Any idiot could see that he and Cali would be like magnets drawn together, always ending up sitting beside each other on the sofa, leaning in while the other was talking, looking to catch each other's eye when one of them made a joke. It was cute. I wonder what happened?

'Hello,' he says, stopping by my seat.

I tilt my head to the side at this unexpected visit. 'Hello.'

'Just wondered if you wanted to come and explore Winnipeg with me this evening?'

I glance at my bag by my feet, which is all packed. Just in case. I don't tell him what I'm thinking of doing.

Luke continues. 'If it makes any difference, I was going to ask Joss too.' I think I curled my lip, because amusement flickers on his face from his mouth to his eyes.

'Are the others not getting off the train?'

'I expect they are, but when Joss and Joe are like this it's just better to keep them separated for twenty-four hours until they simmer down. And she's a bit of a flight risk. See you on the platform in a bit?'

I nod. The train to Churchill doesn't leave until the morning anyway. 'Okay. Thanks. Wrap up warm.'

'You too.'

Twenty minutes later I'm not just wrapped up warm, but wrapped up in almost everything I brought with me to Canada. Having left Ontario earlier that day, we're now in the providence of Manitoba, in the centre of Canada. I'm a long way from home. I'm a long way from Bryn.

It's Christmas Eve tomorrow, and the city of Winnipeg feels ready. Vast, fairy light-bedazzled decorations welcomed us to the city as the train trundled to a stop in the station. The sky is pitch-black, but the air smells of spruce trees and spices. The snow on the ground is thicker, and while I wait for Luke and Joss, people wearing bulky snow boots and long-eared hats carry shopping bags through the station, their smiles wide, a little Christmas spirit in their demeanours.

Further down the platform Cali exits the train, alone. I wait for Luke and Joss, and while doing so, I see Sara and Joe, separately, also exit the train and head away from the station. What the hell happened to this friendship group?

I shift my bag on my back, heavy with all my belongings. Where's Alex? Is she getting off the train? I would have liked to have said goodbye, just in case I don't come back aboard, but she's nowhere to be seen.

Joss appears at my side, hands in pockets, and stands like an ice sculpture, refusing to look at me. Luke, thankfully, is right behind her, zipping up his jacket.

The three of us start walking to the station exit, and I do a final glance around for Alex but can't see her anywhere.

'So I was thinking,' starts Luke. 'There's this thing called the Arctic Glacier Winter Park. It has trails that you can take, either walking or you can rent ice skates, and there are Christmas lights and ... stuff. Shall we check it out?'

'Okay,' says Joss, instantly. Little Miss Lack of

153

Enthusiasm agreed to that pretty quickly. Maybe she's an avid ice skater these days.

We walk in silence for a bit, following the way most people are going, which makes me think we're heading to quite the place to be.

Joss seems distracted this evening, at least from her annoyance towards me being there, so I dare to ask the two of them, 'So, when did you guys fall out?'

Luke starts to stutter an answer, but Joss cuts in. 'A long time ago.'

I give her a minute to elaborate, sneaking peeks at her from the corner of my eye. Okay, I guess she isn't planning to. 'Why?'

That's when I see her glance at Luke, even though he's staring down at the snow under his feet. 'A lot of reasons.'

'You don't want to talk about it?'

Joss stops and faces me. 'Nope. Do you want to talk about your plans to ruin our friend's happy day?'

'Joss.' Luke sighs.

'It's fine,' I tell him. 'I'm not going to ruin her happy day. I'd been planning to get to her nearly a week before her wedding, if you remember.'

'There aren't any eligible women wherever you're living now?'

'Probably, but I haven't been looking.'

Joss's gaze shifts away from me for a moment, looking at some Christmas lights strung through the branches of a row of trees. Her face is illuminated, a shadow in the crease of her brow. 'Have you still had feelings for her all this time?'

'No,' I answer, as honestly as I can. 'Not consciously. I've been doing well on my own, and I think I made the right decision to move away, but, I'm sure you know that sometimes there's no controlling your own heart. And right now' – I tap my chest – 'this is what she wants.'

Joss blinks at me, her eyes scanning my face, her own guarded, but with a hint of understanding. Without another word, she starts walking again, and Luke and I fall into stride beside her.

Five minutes later, as we enter the park, Joss wipes the snot dribbling from her nose due to the cold and asks, 'Are we skating?'

I'm having a nice time. Turns out, skating is something I'm not half bad at, and gently following trails through snow-covered trees, past pretty, festive illuminations, isn't the worst way to spend an evening. Even with Luke and Joss for company.

The two of them haven't been very chatty, but I'm like the go-between, the peacemaker. Or maybe there's something about me being here that's comforting to them, because I'm not part of their gang any more.

I glide around a curved path, cold air kissing my cheeks.

If this thing with Bryn is real, if I'm not imagining the

signs, and if she still has feelings for me and we give things another go, would I move to Canada? Would she move back to the UK? And if she did, would she still want to live in a city or could she come to love coastal life?

I like Canada. And I loved Bryn. So maybe I would consider coming out here. Leaving my beach house, leaving my friends.

My bag weighs on my back, pulling me towards forgetting this whole thing. I don't have to get back on the train. Bryn never needs to know I was out here. I could just take this solo expedition and return home, and continue with life. I like my life.

Ooof. I skate over a bump on the verge, tripping and slipping forwards, earning a face full of snow.

Chapter 20

Joss

It's so fucking pretty in Winnipeg. I'm furious about it. Here I am trying to make my point, not let my guard down, even taking a silent lesson from Sara on looking unbothered by everything around me, and then this place shows up looking like a winter wonderland and trying to jingle my bells.

And Ember is being nice which isn't helping me at all. I thought she was going to be the villain here, but now they're all making it seem like *I* am. I never did anything to them.

I bend my knees a little more and skate faster, leaving Luke and Ember behind me, further back on the stupid, beautiful snowy trail. I'm a good skater, I don't need them.

The path divides, two pale streaks glowing in the dark under the string lights and I hesitate, digging my toe into the ice to keep me steady. Maybe I'll wait for them after all.

I look behind me and sigh. There he is, Luke, eyes on the ground, thoughts elsewhere. One guess as to where.

'Hurry up,' I huff as they reach me.

Luke glances at me, catching my eye but barely seeing me and almost as if I'm transparent his eyes move past me and back to the path to our right. To the path the others went down.

Of course they all came here as well. This telepathic neediness we all had back in the day to be in close proximity hasn't gone away, even though some of us would like it to have.

Of course I noticed that he helped her put her boots on. Of course she let him.

Vomitttttt.

I roll my eyes so hard I think they might freeze in that position, and with a toe-kick to the ice, I take off again. We skate in silence for a while and I do my best to ignore the happy smiles of the other visitors, the cheery music, the pools of calming lights along the trails, the twinkling tunnels, the cinnamon-and-pine scents in the air, the thrill that beats in my heart when I skate fast, the flutter when I catch Luke's hand and hold him steady when he stumbles and he gives me a relieved smile.

Coming to a stop, and with pink cheeks, Luke checks the time on his phone. 'I'm done. I'm going to head back to the train,' he pants.

'Already?' Ember asks.

'Yeah.' He nods. 'Catch you both later.'

And just like that, he's skating away, and I'm hollowed out.

Ember and I lock eyes. For crying out loud. 'Maybe I'll head back too,' I say, but don't move.

'Do whatever you want to do,' she says. She seems wary of me, but not intimidated. Commendable, given the hard time I've given her.

'I don't know if the two villains should be left alone together.' I'm half joking.

Her eyebrows raise and she laughs. 'I don't know. Sounds like it could be fun?'

A smile twitches the corner of my mouth. Dammit. 'This doesn't make us friends again though,' I caution.

Ember rolls her eyes at me. 'Oh no, I'm heartbroken. The whole reason I came out here was to make friends with you again.'

'*So* funny,' I sarc her back. 'But you know you will be heartbroken if you go all the way to Vancouver. Don't say I didn't warn you.'

'I've heard you loud and clear,' she replies. 'The whole damn train probably has by now.'

We take off in a slow glide, in sync without meaning to,

the skates slicing underfoot like soft scratches. I peer at Ember from the corner of my eye, but I stop myself from preaching again.

'So. Luke and Cali finally hooked up, then.'

'What? When?' I ask, rounding a corner and accidentally (as if) spraying her shin with shaved ice.

'Back in the day. You're the one that brought it up at lunch yesterday.'

'Oh.' I thought she'd meant again, on this trip, for a moment. 'Yep. Finally.'

'What happened? Like, why aren't they together now?'

'I really don't want to talk about Luke and Cali,' I snap. 'With you, I mean. Here, I mean. Can't we just enjoy the scenery?'

Ember frowns at me and shrugs. 'Say no more.'

'It's just ... ' I stop again, my hands slamming onto my hips. 'He's gone back to the train now; do we have to talk about him? He's not the centre of the universe.'

'Totally fine.'

I blow out a plume of grumpy air. 'Why's it so cold here, anyway?'

Ember flings her arms wide, gesturing at the snow surrounding us. Patronising knob.

'Wanna race?' I ask her.

'If you want,' she chortles. 'You seem totally in a sportswoman-like frame of mind right now.'

'Were you always this sarcastic?'

'Were you always this furious with everything and everyone?'

Hmm. 'I'm not sure,' I answer, actually thinking about her question. 'I don't think so. But it suits me, no? Being a raving bitch?'

We lock eyes again and she nods, the cow, but I can see her suppressing a smile.

With that I take off, leaving her in my wake in a spray of powder, and let the icy air race over my cheeks and fill my lungs. I hunch low, tunnels of lights in the dark overhead, soaring over the snow on my blades. My heart, though heavy, lifting itself just high enough to come along for the ride.

I pick up speed, and for the final twenty minutes let the thoughts of the others, one by one, melt into the crevices left behind me.

Most of the others.

Chapter 21

Cali

This is so surreal. Here I am wandering about in another new city, in the middle of Canada, in the snow, it's Christmas Eve tomorrow. I'm on my way to a thing called the Arctic Glacier Winter Park and so far I've run into both Sara and Joe heading the same way. It could almost be like old times, like when London got heavy snowfall and we all went for a wander about and people were building snowmen outside Harrods and stuff.

Except, this time, we're all pretending we haven't seen each other.

I'm not sure what to expect from the park, but when I arrive, I shiver with excitement (and cold).

I study the sign. Looks like you can walk or skate along the trails, and I'm about to start walking because Lord knows how shit I'll be on ice skates, I've only ever done it around in circles on ice rinks that pop-up in the centre of London. Then I spot Joss, Ember and Luke in the line to get some rental skates.

Traitors!

No, that's not fair. Luke and Ember always got on well, maybe it's good they hang out; she might listen to him when he tries to talk her out of crashing the wedding. The Ember and Joss duo are puzzling to me, but from here it certainly doesn't look like they've become fast friends again.

Where have Sara and Joe gone? I look around, and see them nearby, angled away from each other, Joe on his phone and Sara ordering a mulled wine from a vendor.

'Shall we go skating?' I ask, trudging over the snow to them.

'We?' asks Sara, pulling her curls into a messy low bun before pulling her hat down over her ears.

'We don't have to stick together,' I say. We don't actually have to do this together at all, but I guess I'm feeling a little left out.

'I'm sorry, but what do you think we're doing here?'

I glance at Joe. 'We're spending the evening in Winnipeg, at the same place, so I thought we might as well spend it together.'

'But what are *we*' – she gestures at the three of us – '*doing*?'

'I guess we're reconnecting,' offers up Joe.

'Because Bryn says so?'

'Because Bryn's getting married,' I answer.

'Then what?'

She has a point. We idle beside the mulled wine cart, the sound of Christmas in the city humming around us, of snow under boots, of laughter drifting over from the skating trails. My breath is visible in the cold, lit up by the glow of Christmas lights.

'I don't know,' I say honestly. 'I think it's too early to tell.'

Sara nods. It's not exactly a yes or no, but she heads towards the queue for the skates so I totter behind her, Joe beside me.

I'm given a hefty pair of black ice-skating boots which I spend a long time trying to lace on through cold fingers. My gloves are not Canada-appropriate, the wool too thin and the fingers too loose so I keep tying the fingertips into the boot laces.

Just as I'm about to give up, someone crouches in front of me, takes my foot and yanks the laces tightly.

'Oh! Thank you—' I look up to see a head of sandy hair, and Luke's fingers working their way around the lacing.

'Remember when you broke your arm but you still wanted to wear those lace-up boots every day?' he asks. His voice is low, and not exactly warm but almost like a small cinder burning in the darkness.

164

'Yeah. You helped me.'

He places my foot down and puts his hand under my other calf, lifting it to tie that skate on too. As he does so, he glances up at me, and for a millisecond we search each other's faces in the frosty air.

As quickly as he started, he finishes, pats the top of my boot, and stands, turning away without another word, and glides off down a trail upon his own skates.

He's always there for me, even after all this time. Is it too much to think he might still care, still want to be my friend, even if he's with someone else?

I exhale, long and slow, watching the space where he'd been.

I am not very good at ice skating. And that's okay, it's fine, because it's not like I need this skill in everyday life. Did you know that there's a canal in Ottawa that freezes over every winter, so commuters skate on it to and from work? I think I would have a broken limb every week if I lived there.

I'm not terrible, but you know that satisfying *whoosh*, *whoosh*, *whoosh* that some people make as they ice skate? I don't make that noise, mine is more of a *thonk*, *thonk*, *thonk-whoops-thonk*.

I've been tottering along the trails on my own for a while, gripping trees as I pass, and sitting down when I need to pause to take a photo. During one such moment, Joe appears beside me, and helps me back to my feet.

'How's your evening?' I ask him.

'Good. This is nice. And it's nice to get away from my sister.'

'How is Joss now?'

'Still in a strop with me. As usual. It doesn't take much to set her off, really.'

'Do you two see much of each other?' I ask.

Joe shakes his head, burying his chin into his jacket neck for a moment. 'Nah. At holidays and family functions, but that's about it.'

'That's sad,' I blurt. 'You two used to be so close.'

Joe makes a noise. 'I wouldn't say that,' he says, eventually.

'You wouldn't?'

'We were close in proximity, in the townhouse. Close in that we're family and trusted each other and thought we could run a business together. But I wouldn't have said we ever were the best of siblings. Remember, before I moved to London and Joss let me become her flatmate, I hadn't seen her for over a year.'

'Do you miss her?' I ask him.

'Not really,' he says with a laugh, but there's a sadness in his smile. He misses her. He must do. 'Have *you* missed her?'

He looks like he wants to ask if anyone's missed him. And this is the thing about Joe, the reason – as bad as I feel – that people think of him as a little weak. He never stands up for himself. He never says what he wants or needs. But that's him, it's not up to us to try and change him, is it? Instead of pointing out any of this, I say, 'To be totally honest, I missed you all at the beginning, at least, after a cooling off period, but it's been so long now.'

I still miss all of you, I want to say, but I bite my lip. I don't want to be the first to admit it, I don't want to be the only one who feels this way. Instead, I say, 'Who's going to share with Joss tonight, then?'

Three hours on solid ground passed in a blur, and before you could say Merry Christmas Eve Eve I'm climbing back aboard our train, ready for our second night.

I'm just letting out a giant yawn in the space between carriages, when Ember jumps up onto the train behind me. She's out of breath, her cheeks pink, and she drops her bag down with a heavy plonk. It almost sounds like she's got all of her things in there with her.

'Good evening?' I ask.

She nods, catching her breath. 'Yeah. I think so. Yes. I nearly . . .'

'What?'

Ember stops and shakes her head. 'Nothing. I'm just really looking forward to seeing Bryn again. I know you don't want to hear that.'

I don't. But I think I'm beginning to understand it.

'Do you want to get a drink?' Ember gestures towards the other end of the train.

'Uh . . .' I look down into my carriage. 'We're switching around the sleeping arrangements because of the whole, you know, Joss refusing to be in the same space as her beloved brother. So, I'd better . . .'

'Sure.' She nods. 'Well, if you change your mind, I'll be in the bar car.'

It's one thing inviting Ember to join us for meals, but is going for a drink with her one-on-one a little strange? How would I feel if Bryn did that with one of my exes? Speaking of . . .

'Is Luke back?' I call to Ember as she's retreating. 'Just so, you know, we can do this room switch.'

'As far as I know. He left us about half an hour ago, said he was ready for bed.'

'He left you and Joss? How did that go?' Suddenly I'm more awake.

Ember nods. 'It was interesting. It was okay. Goodnight.'

With that, she walks away, and I head to my compartment. As I'm about to enter, Joe comes out of the one next door, holding his toothbrush. 'I've put my things in with Luke, and Sara's just moved her things in with Joss. You've got the place to yourself tonight.'

'Oh, great,' I said. 'Is Luke asleep?'

'He's reading.'

'Oh. Great,' I repeat.

Joe and I seem to have run out of conversation for to-night, so with a wave of his toothbrush, he squeezes past me and disappears to the communal bathroom at the end of the carriage.

In my compartment, I close the door and sit on my bunk, just as the train pulls away from the city of Winnipeg. Big city lights fade to suburban illuminations; Christmas lights around porches, street lamps, two-storey office buildings. I was so tired after walking around Winnipeg, but now I'm back on board, in the warm, in the quiet, my yawns have died right down.

I stand up and pace my compartment, all two steps of it, back and forth. If I were in London, and couldn't sleep, I could go to a show, a club, a bar, an event, meet up with friends. Not that I ever really did those things spontane-ously, but I *could*.

I guess I *could* do that here, a version of it at least. And Bryn maybe wouldn't like me hanging out with Ember, but I can't avoid her if I want to talk her out of this ridic-ulous idea of hers, can I?

Yes, tonight seems like a good night to have a good chat with her. And just one nightcap.

Three brandies later (who knew I liked brandy?!) and I'm still in the bar car, only Ember and I haven't got around to discussing anything to do with Bryn. When I arrived, Ember introduced me to a lady called Gwen who she's been sitting next to since Toronto, and who likes to talk A LOT about her backpacking adventures. It's all interesting, though.

Then this woman called Alex came along who I recognised, and Ember knew her too. In fact, the two of them practically lit up when they saw each other, kissing each other on the cheek, and Ember, who'd been tightrope-walking between stony-faced and small smiles since the plane, was now leaning forward, grinning, laughing.

This wasn't forced though; she was being herself. I remember this version of her really well. Cool, casual, fun but in a chilled way. Interesting.

Right now, Ember and Alex are bonding over a shared love of camping, something Gwen would relate to if she stayed awake, and something I cannot.

Ember throws her head back in a loud chuckle at something Alex just said. 'One of my biggest dreams would be to find myself deserted on a tropical island and never have to deal with people again.'

'Me too.' Alex touches Ember's arm. 'Maybe some people.'

'Okay, some. And I'd like to still be brought a cup of tea in the morning.'

'Ugh, tea,' replies Alex, making a barf face.

'I'm telling you, a cup of tea drunk in the doorway of a tent is perfection.'

I swirl my brandy in my mouth and look towards the

doorway of the bar. I am *ridiculous*. Luke is not about to get up from his bed and appear. And that's fine. Totally fine.

'So, who's going to tell me about Bryn?'

My attention is snapped back by Alex asking a question to the three of us, except Gwen has nodded off to sleep still holding her brandy, and Alex is really only looking at Ember.

'What do you want to know?' Ember asks.

'What's so special that after all these years you'd fly across the globe to see her?'

I was hoping she'd be having second thoughts by now, but then we have only been on the train less than forty-eight hours.

'How long were you together?' Alex presses.

'A year or so.'

'Why did you break up?'

'We wanted different things.'

'But you don't think that's still the case?'

Ember's words dry up and she takes a sip of her drink.

I chime in with a stage whisper. 'I think maybe it is still the case. What? I'm just saying. What? It's all a very complicated situation,' I end, diplomatically, before extracting my nose from their conversion.

But Ember isn't finished with me yet, and asks sweetly, 'How does your boyfriend, Luke, feel about you being here over Christmas with this Luke?'

171

'Is Luke one of the guys you're travelling with?' Alex checks.

I swear I can see mischief in Ember's eye, a hint of amusement in her smile. Does she know he's imaginary?

'He doesn't mind at all,' I say. There is no lie.

'Does he know?' Ember presses.

'No.' Again, there is no lie.

Alex and Ember chuckle, which makes me laugh into my brandy glass, flicking the liquor up into my nostrils. Then I feel bad because I shouldn't be making fun of Fake Luke. But then, he *is* fake. Maybe he's also an asshole.

Gwen snorts herself awake at that point and is completely disoriented. By the time I've helped guide her back to reality, Ember and Alex are picking up their things, saying they're going to turn in for the night. Gwen follows them, and I gulp the last of my brandy and head in the opposite direction back to my compartment.

I should have asked Ember if she wanted to bunk in with me. Last night I was resentful of Luke having his own space for the night. But now I have that myself, I'm a little lonely, lying here, the covers pulled up, the train rocking underneath me, the sound of footsteps, quiet chatter and curtains closing outside my room.

It's a little like being back home.

Chapter 22

Ember

Oof. I rub the deep ache that's settled into the right side of my neck while prising my eyes open one lid at a time. I unfurl my limbs. The last time I woke up feeling this disorientated was when my friends back home and I slept on the beach to watch the meteor shower.

Mmm. A shower would be good.

I hobble my body over to the communal bathroom and stand under the hot water, which bit by bit rinses away the brain fog.

In the steam I realise, it's Christmas Eve.

Two more sleeps until I see Bryn. Wow, that is a strange, but exciting, thought. My heart bubbles along with the suds in the shower.

Last night was actually fun. Hanging out with Alex is fun.

The last thought brings a smile to face. Nothing happened, we just chatted over drinks, flirted a little, but God, it felt good to flirt.

Out of the shower, I apply a smudgy slick of my winged eyeliner thanks to the rocking of the train, and towel-dry my hair, scrunching it into beachy waves, and spot another bruise. I peer at the small blue dot beside my elbow. Honestly, I'm knocking into things left, right and centre on this train. I don't think I'm used to being in enclosed spaces for this long any more.

As I've been doing for the last few weeks, I navigate to Bryn's social feed as I'm getting dressed, but today there's nothing new. Perhaps she's called off the wedding? Wishful thinking.

Back at my seat, Gwen is wide awake and playing Christmas music loudly from a tiny speaker she's Bluetoothed to her phone. Around us, other passengers are waking up, some enjoying the unsolicited alarm clock, some not so much.

'Happy Holidays, bunkmate!' she says to me.

'And to you. Wait, it's still only Christmas Eve, right?' I guess my brain is not quite awake yet to remember the exact day and exactly how long I've been on this train for.

'It is, but today I'm leaving you.'

'What?'

'I'm getting off tonight, in Edmonton. Seeing family, surprising them for the holidays.'

'What family?'

'My sister and her kids. Haven't seen her for six months or so and I can't wait.'

Wow. I didn't realise how attached I'd got to Gwen, but I guess when you sleep side by side with someone for two nights you can't help but feel a fondness for them. 'So, you're just going to show up? At nine p.m. on Christmas Eve?'

'Yep. They're going to be psyched.'

That's a good attitude. Positive thinking. 'I'm surprising someone too, when we get to Vancouver the day after tomorrow.'

'Who's that?'

'An ex-girlfriend. She's getting married in a few days, but ... it's a long story.'

'So, you're just going to show up? Right before the wedding?'

I nod. 'She's going to be psyched.'

Gwen laughs. 'Well tell me the story. We've got all day.'

I like talking with Gwen. She has a lovely life, travelling, living in the great outdoors for much of her time. And she's a good listener. She reminds me of my mum, but younger, which both pangs and warms my heart in equal measures.

My parents had a long and happy marriage; they were lucky. I often wonder if my mum died more of heartbreak than anything else, passing away so soon after my dad.

Did I do my own heart a disservice by tearing it away from a happy relationship?

As Gwen and I munch breakfast croissants in our seats, talking over the logistics of me arriving in Vancouver and travelling out to Bryn's and being able to speak to her without anyone else around just days before her wedding, I can tell the confidence is lessening in my voice, just a little. Like an icicle melting, dripping from a roof.

I'm doing the right thing, right? If Bryn's trying to reach out to me, which I'm still sure she is, I owe it to both of us to at least see what's happening, and see if she and I are still meant to be an us. Right?

'Alrighty,' says Gwen, wiping crumbs from her mouth. 'I got to get ready for the show.'

'The show?'

'The Christmas Eve show in the bar. You haven't seen the posters?'

My blank look tells her that no, I haven't seen any posters about a Christmas show. 'Are you in it?'

'Sure am. You can be too!'

'Nooooo, no thank you, I am not a show … girl.'

'Then come along at least. High noon. Be there or be wherever else you wanna be, it's a free country.'

High noon rolls around, at least in our current time zone which is either Mountain Time or Central Standard Time and I'm not sure which, but here we are. Since breakfast,

I've located one of the mysterious posters, and it turns out the Christmas Eve show consists of a small band that boarded in Saskatoon and will be leaving us again in Edmonton, all to play a set of festive tunes in each of the bar carriages along the train. And once their set is done, passengers (such as Gwen) are invited to stay in the bars and have their own jingle bell jam sessions.

'I'm telling you,' Gwen is saying, polishing a ukulele that she'd been storing who knows where since we first boarded. 'If you've never heard "All I Want for Christmas Is You" on the uke, you haven't lived.'

Strangely enough, I have actually. Tonia serenaded me last year when she wanted to find out if I thought posting a video of her doing exactly that on a dating app was a) cute as hell, or b) something that would go viral and end up on a BuzzFeed article about the most cringeworthy singletons at Christmastime. I told her it was definitely 'a'. And we ended up spending Christmas together anyway, so she got her wish, even if I wasn't quite what she was hoping for.

I smile at the memory. I wonder what they're all doing back home right now?

I'm about to text my bestie when the band starts up with a lively rendition of 'Holly Jolly Christmas' and I'm captivated. I've not felt particularly in the seasonal spirit thus far on this trip, but there's something about brass instruments gleaming under the spotlights of an old-fashioned train carriage, snow beyond the window, mulled wine in hand—

Wait, who put this mulled wine in my hand? Cali! She's snuck in next to me, a glass in her own paw.

'Even after all those brandies?' I chuckle after we've clapped the band and they're flipping the pages of their music. Quite the crowd is drawing in, and Cali and I have to lean into each other.

'Hair of the dog?' She laughs. 'Actually, I meant to talk to you about something yesterday evening—'

The band start up again, this time with 'Rockin' Around the Christmas Tree', which takes on a new meaning when you're actually rocking inside a train car and all the Christmas trees are outside the window. I know what she was going to say though; it's obvious, isn't it? So in the next song break I jump in quickly.

'You know, I nearly got off the train in Winnipeg. Like, permanently.'

'You did?' She straightens her face back out. 'I didn't mean to sound so . . . gleeful. Are you thinking of changing your mind though, about the wedding? Or maybe not, since you're still here?'

'I just think you have to follow your heart, you know? No matter what other people think. No offence, but this is my life, not yours, or theirs, so I have to do what's right for me.'

'And this is right for you?'

Of course 'Last Christmas' has just started. Of course Gwen is sneakily trying to join in with her ukulele from behind the back of her seat, much to the annoyed glances of a woman on a trumpet.

I half nod, half shrug, and then add to her, in a whisper over the music, 'You just do what's right for you.'

I don't know exactly how she interpreted that, but we watch the next sixty minutes of music in spiced, mulled silence, and when the open mic portion of the show comes on, Cali excuses herself, and on the way out she super-unsubtly unfurls a length of tinsel from around a picture and scampers off with it.

That girl is in her own, weird world. Shaking my head, I focus on Gwen. Who knew she was so good at mashing up ukulele Christmas songs with Tina Turner's greatest hits?

Chapter 23

Sara

Cali was on typical Cali form last night. She's out here forcing things, but the fact is, we've all grown apart. It was happening before we moved out of the house, before we even went to Spain. I'd felt it for a while, to be honest. That's just life.

I stand in the tiny shower, swaying with the rhythm of the train, and let the steam roll over my skin. I've cracked the window so cold air can rush in. In here it's just me and the countryside of Canada.

When my daughter was a baby, my shower was my little sanctuary, just a few minutes of me time with the window open and a wide view of the moors, while she was safely gurgling about with her dad. Not that I'm comparing this group to a bunch of babies, but . . . a chuckle escapes and rises with the steam nonetheless.

I moved into the townhouse in London about two years before the Spain holiday. The rest of them were solid, not quite a clique, but laughably co-dependent. However, they shined their light on me and let me in and for a while everything was great. But it was always just a temporary home, a stage in my life, plus there were little things that would happen, little memories that were discussed in front of me that I was never a part of. And that's fine! That's totally fine. But what used to get me was the, 'Sorry, Sara, it's a bit of an inside joke . . .'

They could have let me inside a little more.

I step out of the shower and take a moment to smell the clean air floating through the open glass.

No, I don't need this group back. They aren't my friends any more. But they aren't my enemies, they're just my past.

It's like my ex and me. He's a great dad, a great guy, and we had a great relationship that produced our beautiful little girl, but then we grew apart. And I'm good. My independence is my favourite thing about myself, and having him still in my life, sharing parenting responsibilities, encouraging me to take trips like this is awesome.

Wrapping myself tightly in a towel, I pad back to my cabin, which is empty, and make a call. My daughter's face fills the screen within seconds, the video feed sharp and clear, despite the distance.

'Hi, baby, happy Christmas Eve!'

'Mummyyyyyyyyy,' Dina says, all toothy smile and flour-dusted cheeks. She must be baking Christmas cookies with her dad and grandpa again – her favourite festive activity, actually her favourite activity full stop when she's spending time with him and his family. It's pretty precious.

'What are you making?'

'Nothing,' she replies, distracted by a spoon covered in chocolate-coloured dough.

'That's accurate,' her dad, Billy, says from behind her. 'She's eating more than making at this point.'

I laugh. 'Good girl.'

'How's your trip?' Billy asks, taking the phone from Dina just as I'm about to be put face-first into a mixing bowl.

'It's good. The scenery here, oh my God. You've been to Canada, right?'

'A long time ago. How are your friends getting on?'

'I'm not sure I'd call it "getting on" yet, but nobody's thrown anyone off the train so far, so that's a good sign.'

'They're still holding grudges?'

Billy knows a little about what happened between us all, but it was so far in the past, at least a year before I even met him, and who really cares at this point? I filled him in on the basics when I got the invite.

'They're still holding onto something,' I tell him. I guess I am as well, otherwise I wouldn't be here.

'What are you doing today?' he asks, as Dina comes

back into view and stares at me with a happy grin as she licks the spoon.

We chat for a while and I fill the two of them in on my Christmas Eve plans, which generally consist of enjoying the train journey, staying out of the drama, and maybe getting to know my old neighbours/friends a little more again. I've not even told them about Dina yet, and everyone should know about her, she's the best. Look at that face.

'Tell me about your Christmas plans.' I smile at my daughter through the phone as she launches into a babbly mini-monologue about singing Christmas carols for her grandparents.

I lie back on the bed in my towel, a sigh of contentment escaping from me. It pulls at my heart being so far away from her, but I love how easily she fits in with life, with changing plans, with how the world keeps on turning and she can be sad but doesn't let herself be bitter.

This crowd could learn something from her.

Chapter 24

Cali

Knock knock knock. I wait outside Luke and Joe's compartment come nightfall, my hands full of tinsel, my heart high up in my throat.

I know Joe's wandered off somewhere (I just know, okay, I wasn't spying – much) and Luke's in there alone, probably lost in whatever novel it is he keeps reading.

'Come in,' he calls.

'Can you slide the door for me?' I call back.

There's a pause, a long pause, before I hear his feet pad onto the floor and cross the small gap to the door. He opens it. He looks messy and like he's not been sleeping well, and he has a little stubble and his knitted jumper has a whole in it that his thumb is poking through. He's like a sexy, grown-up Artful Dodger.

'Hey, Cali,' he says, moving to the door frame, his book dangling from his hand. The way he's shifted his body actually puts him closer to me. We're in each other's space, that magnetic pull again, and I find my lips parting as I look at his.

'Um,' I breathe. I feel him watching me, and he shifts his weight again, my heart fluttering as it moves him even closer. I move my eyes up to his, to find him gazing down at me, emotions over every part of his face.

'Um,' I repeat, and swallow. 'It's Christmas Eve night.' I hold up the tinsel in my hands, and it reflects tiny red streaks onto his face under the overhead spotlights of the carriage.

'What are you doing with that?' His lips drift into a small, curious grin, and his hand reaches towards the tinsel I nicked from the bar car, brushing against mine when he touches it.

'You know what I'm doing with this. What *we're* doing.'

'No.' Luke shakes his head but I stand firm, edging closer to his cabin so he can't shut me out, edging closer to him.

'Please. It's tradition,' I insist. 'It's Christmas.'

It's a silly tradition, really, and I'm not going to tell Luke it's one I've carried on, on my own, for the past few years. But every Christmas Eve night, in the townhouse, he and I used to get together, stick on a Christmas movie, open some mulled wine, and make coordinating tinsel accessories for the whole gang. They were gaudy, tacky, and usually fell apart by mid-morning on Christmas Day, but it was just something fun, just between us.

He relents and stands aside, and I walk into his room, glancing up as I pass him, a spark zipping between us when we catch eyes that makes my breath catch again.

It's still there.

Inside his compartment, I take a seat on his bed, already folded out, setting the tinsel between us, along with a collection of hairclips, bobby pins and sticky tape.

Imagine if he just swept it all off onto the floor and kissed me and laid me down and we had a lovely Christmas Eve night that went into Christmas Day and merry Christmas to me.

I shake my head a fraction, barely noticeable. I don't want that, anyway. I can't just forget that we aren't each other's person any more.

Luke sits opposite me, one leg folded underneath him, the same as me, and picks up the strand of tinsel, playing with it between his fingers. My mouth is dry, and this guy I used to talk to for hours is like an outsider to me right now, and I can't think of what to say, even as small talk. Then he speaks first, in that quiet voice that used to feel like it was just for me to hear.

'This is a really weird Christmas.'

'Weird because we're on a train?'

'Weird for so many reasons.' He glances from his tinsel to me, but looks away again quickly.

'Yeah,' I agree, and it comes out like a sigh. In that word, I think my body and mind finally acknowledged this fact.

'I'm . . .' Luke starts to say something, but trails off.

I can't take the silence, my breath is short and high in my throat, and I busy my hands snipping the tinsel into sections using nail scissors, and trying to thread some of it through the claws of a hair clip, just so I don't get tempted to pick at the spot on my face. A nervous laugh escapes, and I have to fill the quiet with something. I don't think I can handle the heavy conversation that maybe we need to have.

'Where are you living these days?' My voice comes out not so much light as high and a little shaky.

'I'm still in London.'

My tinsel drops to the bed, and I look at him, my mouth hanging open. 'You still live in London?'

'Yep.'

Luke's eyes are trained on his tinsel now, which he's trimming slowly with the nail scissors, causing tiny bits of red confetti to pepper his bedsheet like shiny little blood spatter.

I stare at the top of his eyelashes, soft, dark, splayed out in a way I've always been envious of, to be honest. He still lives in London? A million thoughts are shimmering for my attention, and I want to ask him all the questions

I have. Instead, what comes out is a statement. 'I thought you moved away.'

He nods, without looking up. 'I'm the other side of the city, but that's as far as I went.'

A sadness, a longing for lost time to magically come back, seeps down me like thick tar. He's always been in my city, he never left, but he never told me, and I never asked. He's always been there, but lost in the crowd.

I swallow down the tar, and attempt my lightest voice. 'Well, I guess in a city of nine million people, it's easy to miss someone.' *I've missed you.*

Now he puts down the tinsel and looks at me, properly, his head tilted to the side, and he scans my face, my lips, like he's reminding himself, remembering. 'Actually, I was just thinking the opposite. Despite all those people, I saw you once.'

His words hit like a boulder on the railway line. 'What? Why didn't you say hi?'

'I lost all my words. And then you were gone.'

'Where was this?'

'A crossing on the Strand. It was autumn, and the ground had all these red leaves from some tree you were standing under, and you were looking down at them, waiting for the lights to change. It was sunny, and only a little cold, and it was that absolutely giant bright pink scarf of yours that first caught my eye. It was a couple of years ago.'

'I still wear that scarf all the time,' I croak out, adding precisely nothing to the conversation. He was right there, and I missed him. And it sounds like I was looking pretty cute that day, which isn't important, but, you know, nice.

I long to be brave enough to have the talk, to ask him why, all those years ago, he chose to leave rather than fight for us, at the very least for our friendship. But if he asked me in return, would I have an answer?

Outside the train window, in the dark, the shapes of the mountains are beginning to rise from the flats of the Plains we've been trundling past for the last twenty-four hours. Barely visible against the night sky, if it wasn't for the moon highlighting their white peaks.

'Are you going to take a look around Jasper in the morning?' Luke asks, forcing the conversation to more neutral ground. Probably a good thing. I don't want to mess this up before the snowflakes have even had a chance to settle again.

I push a smile back across my lips. 'Absolutely, are you?'

'Definitely, I'm looking forward to it, to be honest. The Rockies.'

'It's going to be a pretty cool way to start Christmas Day,' I say, and we each reach for some more of the decorations and set about creating our silly little accessories. The deeper stuff is still chugging underneath me, much like my own personal inner-train, but it makes my feet sweat to think about getting too intense right now, tonight, on a night that once upon a time felt like it was our special night.

'How's your family?' I ask him, always having liked his parents, and his trio of sisters.

'Good. Mel's just had a baby.'

'Another one?'

He smiles at that, like he's surprised I remembered. 'Yep, that makes two nephews now.'

'Congrats.'

'And your parents? What are they doing over Christmas?'

I tell him about them being away in New Zealand with my brother, about how I went there myself in the summertime. He talks about a holiday he took to Australia for a month the year before. I avoid any topic that might bring things around to this made-up bloody boyfriend of mine, and Luke seems to be skirting around that issue too, or maybe I'm just deluding myself that he even cares.

In too short a time we're finished with our tinsel accessories. We made six, out of habit I guess, and I lay them out in front of us on his bed in a row. 'Should we ... shall we all take a look around Jasper together? What do you think?'

'I don't know ... '

'We need to be on good, well, civil at least, terms for Bryn's wedding. It's her big day. And we arrive early Boxing Day.'

'And we need to give out these beautiful creations,'

Luke adds, straightening the row, drawing my eyes to his fingers.

'Exactly. We should ask if Ember wants to come, too. It might be our last chance to talk her out of everything.'

Luke nods. 'And we could give her one of the accessories.'

That lights me up like a little Christmas candle, that he wants to include her like that. Honestly, even though she and I have managed to have a few laughs, she still seems kind of pissed off at us, as a group, which I can only assume is because we lost touch with her. And gave her an ultimatum. But perhaps if we just keep her close, show her some love, she'll start to listen and take in our concerns, and then slip away and leave Bryn to live her happy ever after.

'What if Bryn *is* giving Ember signs, though?' I say to Luke.

He leans in towards me. 'I wondered the same thing. Ember seems convinced this is the wedding the two of them planned, even if it was only theoretical. Maybe Bryn is trying to catch her attention.'

'That doesn't seem very Bryn though. She was always kind of straightforward and direct.'

'Cold feet?' Luke asks.

'A little,' I say, and lift his bed cover to tuck my feet inside, and am just getting cosy when I realise what he meant. 'You were talking about Bryn. Getting cold feet.' A giggle pops out.

Luke laughs in return, his face softening, his eyes crinkling. I want to capture this moment, protect this little flame, because this is real, this ease between us, this laughter. I blink, just in case I suddenly have the ability to stop time, but no such luck, and as our chuckling diminishes, I hold onto my smile as long as I can.

Removing my feet from his bed, I stand up, collecting the tinsel accessories in my hands carefully, but bumping his book off the bedside table and onto the floor as I go.

'Oops, sorry,' I say, crouching down, just as he does the same.

A stone on the tracks, or maybe a little helping hand from the stars, bumps me off balance and I tip closer to Luke. He catches me, his hand gripping my upper arm and almost immediately loosening once I'm steady. But he doesn't move it. Even under my thermal sweatshirt I feel his palm open up, his fingers spreading, trailing slowly, like he's trying to cover as much area as he can without crossing any of these boundaries that haven't been broken down between us. Yet.

Luke's hand slides a centimetre further around the back of my arm. Is he pulling me into him? I'm frozen on the spot; I don't know what to do.

But I know what I want to do.

His fingertips touch my back and I lick the dryness from my lips. But then he stops, and his hand ebbs back, like he's remembered himself, and he leaves my skin to tingle without him. He picks up his book and slides his bookmark back into place.

I clear the butterflies that have lodged in my throat and check the cover. 'A Christmas murder mystery.'

He shrugs one shoulder, and smiles down at the book. 'As usual.'

'As usual,' I agree, remembering his festive reading habits. 'A gift from your girlfriend?'

Merry Christmas, Cali, here's a little torture for you.

'Uh ... yeah,' he replies, and the mood in the room changes, the distance between us widening again.

'Don't get any ideas, though,' I joke. From our place still crouched on the floor, his gaze flicks to mine. *Oh my God, get some ideas please, just not murdery ones.* 'Murdery ideas, I mean.'

No. No, this is just proximity and Christmastime and the fact my fake boyfriend can't hold a decent conversation to save his life. I did not come on this trip to pine after Luke. Yes, I did. No, I didn't! We did not work then; we will not work now. Get up, Cali.

I obey myself and push up off the floor. Luke does the same and then loads my hands up with the accessories again, and I'm not thinking about whether or not it's on purpose that his fingers are touching mine because I'm not interested anyway.

I give him a friendship nod. 'Goodnight, Luke. Merry Christmas Eve.'

'Nigh-night, Cali.' He holds open the door and I head the few steps back to my own compartment and don't give a passing thought to the way he used to say that before we fell asleep beside each other.

Chapter 25

Ember

I spent the whole afternoon listening to Christmas music, to the point where I was genuinely sad to say farewell to Gwen and her ukulele when we reached Edmonton. But the music has soaked into my soul, and I'm drawn to the celestial carriage this Christmas Eve night. I can tell myself it's because I'm not sleepy. Because I want to be under the stars. That I need some quiet time to think about what I'll say to Bryn. But the quickening of my heart is proof to my head that it's because I'm hoping she'll be there.

I ascend the stairs, listening for a certain voice among the hum of gentle chatter I can hear. When I reach the top, I see that three seats are taken, under the canopy of stars which gives the illusion of being in a planetarium, the way we move forward underneath them.

In one seat is a couple, sitting close, whispering in the darkness. In another is a man on his own, an SLR camera angled to the heavens, resting against the glass while he's mesmerised by the view. And in the other seat, turning to see me just as I see her, again, is Alex.

She smiles, a light in the dark, and doesn't say a word until I make my way over to her, at which point she slides along the seat, making room for me. I sit, our arms lightly pressed together, and smile back at her.

'I was hoping you'd come up,' she says.

'I was hoping you'd be up here,' I reply, and the two of us chuckle. 'How was your day?'

'It was good,' Alex replies, sinking into the seat and resting her head against the backrest, just like she did that first night. I do the same, my arm sliding down against hers as I go. 'I had a little admin I needed to get out of the way before the year ends, and I didn't want to do it on Christmas Day, or once I'm with my family in Vancouver.'

'Do you and your family have big plans while you're there?'

'Yeah. It's always busy when we all get together.'

'All?'

'I have a sister, and my aunt and uncle and ten billion cousins will all be there. And three dogs and a cat. It'll be chaos, but in a good way.'

I lean in, studying her as she talks about her family, feeling the warmth in her voice radiate into the carriage.

I want to hear everything about them, it's like my heart aches to be enveloped in that world, to hear tales of her mum making her a hot chocolate, her dad chopping firewood, her cousins bickering and her sister stealing her lipstick. I realise this is a strangely stereotypical family I've created in my mind for her, but before I get to find out the real story, she asks me, 'How about you? I know your parents passed, so tell me what your chosen family is like?'

I look back up at the stars (maybe at my parents?) and think of how to put this. 'Well, I'm lucky to have some really close friends. They've helped me through a lot, and it feels real. If that makes sense?'

In the darkness, Alex nods. 'Of course it does.'

'But yet, here I am, at Christmastime, away in some fantasy land,' I muse, a wry smile on my lips. 'Do you think I'm making a huge mistake?'

Alex looks down, her hair falling from behind her ear, adding a dark streak across her face.

'You can tell me,' I press.

'I think only you can answer that,' she says after a while. 'I think you should do what feels ... real ... to use your word.'

I hope she's not feeling bad about talking about her parents. I give her a small nudge, leaving my shoulder that little bit closer to her. 'I like hearing about your family, honestly, it's nice.'

She tucks her hair back behind her ear, and speaks softly, that little scratch in her voice still audible. 'I'm glad you have a great group of friends. I bet your folks would have been pleased about that too.'

My hand, the one furthest from her, moves to my chest, keeping her warm words close to my heart. I nod. 'They're much better than this bunch of miserable twats,' I joke, and the sight of Alex's honey smile reigniting on her face causes mine to do the same.

'What is with them?' she asks.

'Some kind of falling out, I don't have all the details yet. I haven't seen them since their friend and I split.'

'Bryn.'

'Bryn,' I confirm.

We both lapse into quiet for a moment, and then, and maybe I'm imagining this, it's like neither of us want to discuss Bryn again right now, because she backtracks on the conversation and says, 'That brother and sister are a piece of work.'

'Joss and Joe.' I laugh. 'She certainly is. It's interesting though, to me she seems mad at everyone, but I swear she keeps evil-eyeing Cali in particular.'

'You think? But she seems like the nicest.'

I shrug.

Alex leans in a centimetre closer. 'You have to find out and report back to me, okay? Promise.'

'I promise.' We settle back again, the silence between

us comfortable, cosy. After a while, I murmur out loud, 'These stars ... '

'I know.'

'You're probably used to seeing this all over Canada?'

'It doesn't get old, though. You must get skies like this over the beach?'

'I do,' I agree. 'It's one of the things I love the most about living away from a city.'

'Me too,' Alex says. 'And it's nice to see them with a new person.' We lock eyes briefly and chuckle again.

I like this. I feel like we could stay in this moment for hours, and that Christmas Eve night we do, not going our separate ways until soon after midnight.

'Merry Christmas,' I whisper to her at the bottom of the stairs, the first signs of the Rocky Mountains silhouetted in the night sky beyond the window.

'Merry Christmas,' she replies. There's a pause, a moment, a lingering where I realise I want to kiss her, and from the way she glances at my lips, I'd guess she's thinking the same, maybe.

But no, I can't, I shouldn't. Let's remember why I'm here. Instead, I reach for her fingertips and give them a squeeze, before turning away.

It's been a long time, but having a crush, even this small, little, delusional, can't go anywhere one, is like deep down, in some dark, hidden part of my heart that's been asleep, a tiny supernova is forming.

Chapter 26

Luke

I climb into bed, twirling the tinsel decoration Cali left me with between my fingers.

The memory of her arm under my hand lingers in my fingertips. I should have pulled back earlier; she's moved on, we both have. Haven't we?

I wish I could read her mind. I put down the tinsel, carefully, on my small side table and pick up my phone, opening social media apps and scrolling, first without really seeing, and then I dawdle on a video about how to tell if someone has a crush on you. The algorithm notices my hesitation in swiping, and soon I'm watching clip after clip and trying to tell myself it doesn't mean anything.

'Stop it,' I mutter out loud, and put my phone face down

on my chest, picking up my book instead, and reading three pages in a row without noticing a single word.

I can be her friend again. That's what she wants; her friendships are everything to her. She's happy now. I'm happy now. No more falling back into old patterns.

Flipping back a couple of pages, I manage two paragraphs before I'm back on my phone, wiling away Christmas Eve night by looking at old photographs, holding the tinsel close to my heart.

Chapter 27

Cali

'It's Christmas Day,' I whisper aloud to nobody but myself in the tiny mirror that I can see when I sit up in my bunk.

The train carriage seems quiet, the rhythmic chugging along the tracks having become white noise I barely seem to notice any more, and I open my curtain to reveal a still dark world overlooking us. But the deep blueness has been dip dyed in orange and indigo, an early morning twilight, which tells me we can't be that far away from our stop in Jasper National Park, where we're due to arrive shortly before sunrise.

I rub the sleep and crust from beside my eyes and pull on a thousand layers, leaving my cabin and creeping down silent cars to the celestial carriage.

Turns out, I'm far from the only one who had this idea.

The seats are full of passengers in various states of washed and dressed, some clutching mugs, some holding their phones up to take photos out of the domed windows. I take a stand near the back, leaning on the railing above the stairs, and wrap my arms around myself to watch the vista as the sun slowly wakes.

'Merry Christmas,' I swap softly with the people around me, as I catch their eyes. 'Happy holidays.'

The mountains I saw last night, in the dark, are now towering around us, so close it feels like I could touch them, if I had extremely long arms. Tiger stripes of grey stone cut through the thick white snow that coats the majority of the mountains, and even in this pre-dawn light that is some thick-looking snow on the ground outside the train, too.

There's a warm pink pooling in with the colours of the morning sky when somebody comes and stands beside me.

'Happy Christmas, Cali,' Ember says. She's in her woollen beanie, some fingerless mittens on her hands which hold a coffee cup in between them. Her hair is back in a messy, high ponytail and she hasn't put on her signature winged eyeliner yet, she just looks outdoorsy-fresh.

'Hey, good morning, merry Christmas,' I reply.

'I love it up here,' she remarks, sipping on her warm drink.

'See, now aren't you glad you joined us for the train

instead of just flying over all of this?' I can't help but tease, even though I'm not sure how she'll react.

But she just raises an eyebrow and chuckles. 'Are *you* glad you all took the train, now?'

Touché. 'It has some perks,' I concede.

'It has had its perks,' agrees Ember.

'Listen,' I broach. 'Being Christmas Day and all, what do you say to us putting our differences aside for one day and having some fun? For Bryn's sake?'

'Together?' She sounds doubtful that that could happen. 'I don't think the others would go for that. You're the only one who seems to want to talk to me, much.'

'They will,' I say. No bloody idea if they will, but here's hoping.

'Will you tell me why you're all fighting?'

'Uuuggghhh. Maybe later.' I don't want to ruin my mood right now. 'Will you tell me your current thoughts about Bryn?'

Ember opens her mouth to speak then stops, a wash of thoughtfulness passing behind her eyes. 'Maybe later,' she says.

'Deal. So, do you want to all explore Jasper together this morning? It's supposed to be really pretty, and we have to get off the train, apparently. And it's Christmas.' I have one more thought to convince her. 'And you could see if your friend Alex wants to come with us, too?'

204

Chapter 28

Ember

Having Alex with me is nice. I feel less like the outsider of the group. And she's not Bryn's, she's mine. In a friend way, of course.

I don't know how Cali managed it, but not only are we all trudging through the snow from the station into the small town of Jasper together, but we're all in pretty good spirits. Even Joss, who surprised all of us by laughing after Joe chucked a snowball right at her face.

Jasper National Park is bitterly cold, the sun not having quite risen over the mountains yet and the air thick with an icy mist, beyond which is some of the most spectacular scenery I've ever seen.

This is my kind of place. Big, open spaces, nature showing off her fine assets. I take a long, slow, inhale in and hold that mountain air inside me for a few beats, before breathing it out and it mists in front of me.

'Nice, huh?' Alex says beside me.

'It's stunning,' I reply.

'Thanks,' she jokes.

I laugh with her, glancing over. She's wearing her hair in a side plait, with a maroon woollen hat on her head. Tying off the end of her braid is a hairband wrapped in red tinsel, gifted from Cali, who seems to have made one for everyone (although I spotted Luke breaking his tinsel pocket-square in half and tying part of it on her wrist earlier, like they were one short). We're like a cute little gang of tourists who are all wearing something so if we get lost people know which group we're with.

Actually, maybe that's exactly what we are.

I'd happily get lost here, though. 'I wish I had more time here. Now I'm off the train I just want to head out, camp by a lake, hike to a waterfall . . . ' I trail off.

'Camp in the snow?' she asks, amused, as we pass a gigantic snow drift outside a shop, nearly as tall as me.

'Well, maybe a nice little cabin, with heating.'

'The waterfalls will all be frozen, also.'

'No way! That sounds even cooler, actually,' I marvel, and she grins, seeming pleased by my enthusiasm. She points out a group of teenagers filming themselves throwing warm water up into the air and it turning into snow before their eyes. This place is magical.

Alex stops our group as we pass the Swiss cabin-like frontage of a hotel. 'You know what? I have an idea of how we could spend our time here in Jasper this morning, if you want?'

'You're the local.' Cali shrugs, good-naturedly. 'In Canada terms.'

'As long as we can stretch our legs, it's good with me,' says Sara, and I couldn't agree more.

Alex's smile widens, and she nods, looking between the group. 'Alright. One moment.'

She disappears into the hotel, the red tinsel in her hair catching the lights of the entranceway.

While we wait, there's a quiet contentment among us. We look into the nearby shop windows that will stay closed today due to the holidays, we photograph pretty snow piled in smooth clumps upon rooftops, we point out sparkling Christmas lights on the facades of the wood-fronted buildings. Nobody is arguing, nobody is talking about arguing, everything is Christmas Day-fine. Flipping cold, but fine.

Alex emerges and I warm up from within. She's swinging a set of car keys from her gloved fingers, and beckons us over to one of the parked-up hotel shuttle buses.

'Another vehicle?' Joss moans, because if someone's going to she might as well be the one to take one for the team.

'Trust me. It's no more than a twenty-five-minute

journey each way, and we'll have over an hour to do one of the best hikes you'll ever do.'

Cali's nose crumples, giving her away, but she adds a peppy upwards inflicton when she echoes, 'A hike!' to mask her true feelings.

I, for one, love this idea. I love it! As we follow Alex to the van, I catch her arm and ask, 'Are you driving us? How did you get this van?'

'I have a friend who works here.' She looks at me sideways, a grin on her face, eye contact that feels very just for me. 'She's letting us borrow it for the morning. The hotel don't offer excursions on Christmas Day.'

We climb into the van, me sitting up front with Alex, and I try to focus on the scenery but she keeps pulling my attention as she changes gears, flicks her fingers over the indicators.

The dawn light changes to pastel tones of baby pinks and blues, the last of the stars fading for now as the drive takes us out of town and along the valley between the mountains, following the Icefields Parkway road as it winds alongside the spearmint-toned Athabasca River, which we catch glimpses of between the pine trees.

In no time at all, we turn off and Alex parks up, and we all scramble our heavily bundled-up bodies out of the van and into the even chillier mountain air, our boots crunching on the untouched snow under our feet.

'Athabasca Falls,' I read from a brown sign at the start of a trailhead. 'We're going to see waterfalls?'

'We're going to see frozen waterfalls,' she replies, and I shriek in delight. I can't tell you why this makes me so giddy, but it just does. I guess it's something about water, nature, clean air, new things to see, a cute girl . . .

The others seem pumped too, though it could be that they're just desperate to get some blood flowing and warm up, so we get going almost immediately. I snap photos along the way to shower my friends back home with in our WhatsApp group, and chit-chat with Alex along the way.

Then Sara says, 'God, if Bryn's wedding venue is as pretty as this it's going to be perfection.' Her head snaps around to me and she adds, 'Sorry. I mean, I just didn't mean to rub your face in it.'

'No, it's fine, you can talk about her wedding, of course.'

We keep walking, our footsteps creaking on the snow, and Alex pulls my sleeve so we're a few steps back from the others. 'Are you okay?'

'Yeah, of course,' I tell her. 'They're here for Bryn's wedding, I don't expect them to pretend it's not happening. Especially for my sake.' I frown and kick at the fine snow, which powders over my boot and into my sock. Damn. 'Do you . . . '

'Do I what?' Alex asks.

'Should I call her? Bryn? Just to say Merry Christmas or something.'

'Would you tell her where you are?'

'No. Just … I'm wondering if I should try and get a better sense of her frame of mind. Before I get there. Don't tell the others.'

Alex raises her brows at me. 'I don't know.'

'Sorry, I shouldn't be talking to you about this stuff.'

'Why?'

When I woke up this morning, hunkered down in my seat after the best sleep I've had since being on board the train, something happened. I didn't think of Bryn. At least, she wasn't my first thought, unlike every other morning since my birthday. I thought of Alex, I wondered how she slept, remembered star-gazing with her the night before.

Only then did I think of Bryn, and travelling all this way to see her, and a small voice that I quickly hushed asked, *but even if she does say she wants to get back together, what do you want*?

The trail takes us alongside the river, which ripples and rushes in the chasms between icy slabs, before following a pathway up to the top of the falls.

'Here we are,' says Alex at the top of the trail, to the whole group, before turning to me with hopeful, expectant eyes. 'Merry Christmas.'

I step forward to the lookout and peer over, and the view takes my breath right out of my lungs.

We're standing above a waterfall, on a platform. The

river water below is the softest mint and turquoise, and rushes down between a vast network of frozen claws.

'It looks like a foam party,' mumbles Joss, in awe.

I see what she means. The never-ending water has created icicles on icicles on icicles, all surrounding the liquid falls which rush into a teal pool at the bottom.

'It's incredible,' I exhale, and lean in against Alex, resting my cheek on her shoulder.

We all watch, mesmerised, for a while, enjoying the quiet, the only sounds being the roar of the water, the shuffling of snow under seven pairs of feet, and a chorus line of breath being blown into gloved palms.

'What's everyone's favourite Christmas memory?' Cali pipes up. 'Maybe not favourite. That's too hard. But one that makes you smile.'

This one, I think, feeling the warmth of Alex through her coat.

'A Christmas memory that makes me smile,' Joe starts immediately, leaning over the fence and staring down at the water. 'Was when Cali wanted to cook us all Christmas dinner but she burnt the turkey because she thought it had to cook overnight, not defrost overnight.'

There's a collective good-humoured groan.

'Alright, alright, it was perfectly edible,' Cali protests.

'You're the only one who ate it,' replies Joe.

'That's not true – Luke ate some.'

'Well, obviously,' I say without thinking, and see them both blush. Oops. 'Erm, a memory that makes me smile was a Christmas I spent at the beach with my parents when I was about six or seven. I'd seen a thing on TV about Australians having barbeques on the beach on Christmas Day, and begged my folks to let us do it, just once. It was freezing and drizzling but Dad stood there tending a crappy little barbeque while Mum held a brolly over the whole thing, and I kept dropping the prawns through the grates. I think we went home and had bowls of cereal, but it was still fun.' God, it was fun.

'Alex?' Cali prompts.

Beside me, she thinks. 'My first Christmas on the train. I'm super independent, but that was my first Christmas away from my family, and actually they surprised me by boarding on Christmas Eve. I was so proud to show off where I worked and so touched they'd made that effort. They live in a beautiful home that's so picture perfect at Christmastime, but they gave it up for me.'

'You're close with your family, huh?' I ask. I like that about her.

Alex gazes down at the falls. I guess she's missing them today. 'I am,' she agrees. 'You have to put family first, right?'

Joss and Joe shuffle in unison, and Joss says, 'My memory is that Christmas party of Luke's work that we all crashed and they ended up offering Sara Luke's job.'

We all laugh and Sara holds her hands up. 'To this day, I still say they weren't serious.'

'Oh, they were.' Luke grins. 'What's yours, Sara?'

She thinks for a minute. 'A happy Christmas memory was the first year I moved in, and we all went carol singing to the building next door, and that old couple gave us stollen.'

'That was nice,' the rest of them all agree. That was before Bryn and I got together.

'Luke?'

He looks at Cali for a moment, a smile twitching his lips, and she holds his gaze in that way they always did, like there was no one else in the whole world. 'I'm going to say, that Christmas at Bryn's country mansion. That whole Christmas. With the snow machine, and the games and the m-mistletoe and stuff.'

'That was awesome,' Joe agrees, painting over Cali's surprised look with his words.

'And you?' I say to Cali. 'What's a Christmas memory that makes you smile?'

'All of them. And also this,' she says, which is a bit of a cop out, but we let it slide because it's Cali.

Alex slides out from under me. 'You guys, we better head back to the bus if we want to grab a bite of breakfast in Jasper before we board the train again?'

Reluctant but grateful, we follow her towards the trail steps that lead back down to the valley path. 'Thank you

213

for this,' I say to her. 'You didn't have to be tour guide today.'

'I wanted to.' She smiles, those honey lips.

Ahead of us, Luke skids on a patch of ice at the top of the first step, grabbing the railing to steady himself. Behind him, Joss shrieks and grabs the back of his coat, steadying herself more than him.

'I knew I was going to break my head in half on this trip!' she cries, not at all over-dramatically. Coming up behind Joss is Cali, whose feet also slide out, one to each side, like she's in a cartoon.

Luke whirls around as best he can with Joss clinging onto his back, and reaches his hand back to take Cali's. Joss drops her hold, her smile from moments before fading.

When Joe collides into the back of Cali and the four of them nearly domino themselves, a snort escapes me before I can help it. 'What?' I hiss to Alex, who tilts her head at me. 'It's like watching an old slapstick movie play out in front of me.'

She chuckles, then takes charge, which is kinda hot. 'Alright, let's all walk sideways down the steps, hold onto the person in front of you, and if you feel yourself slipping on the ice just take a pause. We're not in … that much of a rush.'

The group shoot wide-eyed glances at each other, like Alex has just asked them to all form a massage circle or something.

I sigh and walk to the front. 'You're the people who used to drape yourselves over each other like you were a pile of blankets. I know you have some beef but come on, you *can* have physical contact with each other.' I take Luke's hand with my right, holding onto the railing with my left. Behind me, he lets go of Cali and takes Joss's hand, who is still standing in between the two of them. She blinks rapidly, her face set in a line.

Cali finds Joss's hand and holds it tight, and grabs Joe's with her other, who takes Sara's hand, who holds onto Alex, who really doesn't look like she needs help from a bunch of Brits getting down a few icy wooden steps at all, but is playing along so we don't feel completely useless.

We begin a shuffling descent which I imagine resembles a drunk slowworm. Halfway down, Cali starts giggling.

'Stop it, Cali,' Luke admonishes, but he can't get the words out without laughing along with her.

'It's just funny, you know? Us helping each other, like we're on a team building exercise.'

'Maybe that's all we needed, this whole time,' pipes up Sara from near the back.

This makes Cali laugh even more. 'Can you imagine? If five years ago we'd just talked everything out over a day of segwaying in a rainy forest?'

'I don't think that would have helped,' says Joss.

'Well, no,' Cali says between snickers. 'You wouldn't have made it past the first bend without falling off.'

215

'Oi!' Joss shrieks, a smile playing on her lips.

Cali is sliding all over the place now, blinking back tears of laughter.

'Just a couple more steps, Cali,' I call back. 'Hold it together!'

'I'm going to pee myself!'

And thank God we're back on flat ground because this sends everyone into giggles and now we're level again we remember that we're all still mad at each other and pull ourselves together. There's a lightness though that wasn't there before, as we trudge our way back to the bus. A camaraderie, perhaps.

Once Alex has dropped us all off outside the hotel, returning the shuttle bus, I check the time. We have about thirty minutes before we need to head back to the station.

'Does anyone want to stop for some brekkie?' I say, spotting an open diner with huge windows offering views out across the valley. All seven of us bundle inside the toasty warmth, hanging a few of our layers on a coat rack beside a large Christmas tree bedecked in red baubles and ribbons.

As we sit down to a tableful of pancakes and waffles and so much syrup we'll almost certainly spend the rest of Christmas Day on a sugar high, it's, actually, like old times. In a way. There's a comfort in that, but the best part is sitting side by side with Alex.

Too soon it's time to board the train again, and although

the others are talking about taking warm showers and calling their families once we're back on board, I plan to head straight up to the celestial carriage again. I don't want to miss a single second of this scenery.

And if anyone wants to join me, that would be okay too.

Chapter 29

Cali

All of us are energised, I can feel it as we re-board the train. We have pink cheeks, snowflakes in our hair, runny noses, cold toes and smiles on our faces. I don't want to ruin the mood by pointing this out, but, uh-oh, it's coming out anyway.

'Look at us all getting along so well!' I cry out, giddy and high from the sensation of getting back everything I'd lost, even if only for a morning, and flicking my long frost-damp curls into Luke's face as I spin around in the small space of the carriage. 'It's like that Christmas at Bryn's again, isn't it? The one you mentioned, when she hired the snow machine?'

Flickers of remembrance pass their faces, and I can't help but sneak a look back at Luke, who meets my eye,

218

and I think we might be both thinking about the same thing.

Bryn had had a huge, plush bunch of mistletoe hanging over the door of her parents' country home, and the excitement took over me when we first arrived – I'm not sure if it was the Hollywood-movie level of *White Christmas*, or the mulled wine we'd shared from a flask on the way there – but I'd slung my arms around Luke's neck and planted a big, albeit quick, kiss on his lips. He'd reciprocated, we both laughed, then I'd got self-conscious and ended up kissing all of them on the lips, but I'd played that one with him over in my mind for the rest of the holidays.

'That was a fun time,' Ember agrees, and I notice Alex looking a touch uncomfortable beside her.

Like dandelion prongs we all start to drift our separate ways, heading towards our own seats, our own compartments. 'Wait, let's ... let's do something this afternoon.'

'What like?' asks Joe.

'Um ...' I glance around, unsure what to suggest. But this is our last day on the train, tomorrow morning we arrive in Vancouver at dawn. At the start of this journey, four days seemed like a long time, now it doesn't feel enough. There's too much that hasn't been said, and I want Bryn's plan to work, for the sake of all of us. I just want my friends back. 'I don't know, but, it's Christmas, and we're together, so we should ...' *make the most of it*. I know it might not happen again.

'There's a wine tasting in the celestial carriage in a little while?' Alex suggests, and it's as if she's cracked the ice.

Nothing like a bit of alcohol to loosen the ol' tongue.

The whole gang is in agreement, especially Ember who looks glowing at the thought, and soon enough I'm showered and warmed and climbing the stairs to the celestial carriage, bedecked in my Christmas jumper and Christmas earrings and I'm ten minutes early but that's okay because it's warm and cosy up there and so am I. I think I have hope, for the first time. Hope that maybe we can all come back together, beyond this trip.

'Hi.' Ember waves from one of the seats.

'Hey!' My voice is still laced with excitement. 'Is Alex coming?'

'Yeah, definitely.'

'That's amazing, she seems really lovely.'

Ember laughs and tilts her head to the side in agreement. 'She is lovely.'

'Are you two . . . ?'

'Are you asking if I've given up on the idea of going to see Bryn?'

'Bryn? No, I hadn't even thought of her . . .'

She sighs and gazes back out of the window, where we're passing a lake of ice-blue water, surrounded by mountains blanketed in snow-topped pine trees. We only just stepped back in from that winter wonderland out there but I still can't stop staring out at it. I'm so toasty warm right now.

'I don't know,' Ember says. 'I've come all this way, Cali. But I was thinking—'

'Let's get the wine out,' says a chirpy Joss, climbing the stairs with Luke and Joe in tow.

'Sara's still on the phone to her dad, she'll be up shortly,' Luke says to me, crossing the carriage to take a seat beside me at the same time I scoot over. We're like automated moving parts, working in sync, and I don't think either of us quite registered that we were doing it until it was done.

Alex is next up the stairs, changed into a look that screams 'natural snow-bunny'. She's in thermal leggings, fleece-lined boots and a thermal waffle top bearing a Canadian ice hockey team. I catch Ember taking her in.

Luke spots it too, and beside me he holds his hand out in a 'low five' gesture, and I silently sweep my fingertips over his, a shared connection.

'Good afternoon, everyone, and happy holidays,' says a man in a Santa hat ascending the stairs, carrying four bottles of wine in his arms. Behind him is another man balancing a folder and a tray of wine glasses.

'Hey, Logan, Ned,' Alex greets them.

'Alex, good to see a familiar face at one of our wine tast-ings. Be nice,' he warns, a jokey tone to his voice. 'We've got four of these today in various carriages.'

'This is a good crowd.' She smiles, then glances at Ember. 'I think.'

'We like wine,' I say with enthusiasm.

Here's my plan. I'd like us to have a couple of drinks, get confident enough to clear the air once and for all, become best friends again, then enjoy the rest of Christmas night together with no drama and maybe some festive snogging if anyone wants to? Then tomorrow we can arrive in Vancouver bright and early and Bryn will be so pleased we've all made up (the best wedding present we could have given her, she might say?) and she'll apologise as well and we'll all cry and hug and be inseparable again forever without any more arguing. Ever. Ever. Ever.

I don't know how Ember fits into this plan yet.

The wine tasting gentlemen set about pouring measures of a juicy-looking bottle of red into the glasses. They sway in movement with the train, which is most impressive. We all watch and listen, very well behaved, like proper grown-ups at a proper posh wine tasting.

'Our first red,' says Logan, 'is a Pinot Noir from the Niagara Peninsula. Have a smell and a taste and tell me what you all think the flavours are.'

Just as the first glass is being handed out, Christmas music fades in from a speaker somewhere. Gentle festive tunes that complement the white and blue landscape beyond the domed glass of the carriage.

When we clink glasses, Joe makes a comment that

causes Ember to look confused. 'Our first cheers in years,' he quips.

'*Years*? I gathered you hadn't spoken for a while, but ... what?'

'Try five whole years,' Joss smirks, filling up her glass.

'*Five years?*' Ember and Alex cry in unison.

'What happened?' asks Alex.

I look anywhere but at Luke, my heart thumping, my cheeks blushing. 'Just something that ... pissed off everyone.'

Ember holds her hands up in the air. I reach over and put a glass of wine in one of them for her. 'Oh. Thank you. So, you all fell out not long after Bryn and I broke up?'

We all look to each other and I think back. 'Um, yeah, I guess so. Bryn was still moping and we were hoping the holiday would help, I think.'

Ember sits back in her seat. 'Huh.' She puts her wine to her lips, and turns her gaze to the window. Alex's arm, resting on the seat behind her, shifts a little to place fingertips on her shoulder.

Logan and Ned exchange a look, waiting, until Ned prompts, 'Shall we have a smell?'

We follow his lead as he swirls the glass in his hand, the wine forming dropletty legs inside the bowl. I stick my nose in. Mmm, winey. I'm about to take a gulp when Logan asks, 'What can you smell?'

'Grapes?' I offer.

'And wine,' adds Luke. I smother a laugh.

Joss takes a sniff so big I'm surprised she hasn't snorted the liquid up her nose. 'I think I can smell vanilla.'

'Interesting,' says Ned, which I think might be code for 'wrong'. He can see we're getting twitchy so he lets us take our first sip. 'Any thoughts on the taste?'

Sara sloshes it in her mouth. 'Tastes quite fruity.'

'*Trés noir*,' I add, which sounded better in my head.

Ned, unimpressed with our lack of being able to distinguish an aged oak overtone from a mellow ambience of cacao beans, decides to cut to the chase and tell us all about its origins and what we are, in fact, tasting and smelling, before moving onto wine number two.

'Next then, we have a Merlot which was produced in the Okanagan Valley in British Columbia—'

'Ooo, you had me at Merlot!' I quip. Am I drunk already? Beside me, Luke laughs, side-eyeing me and raising his glass in honour of my pun.

We sniff and we sip and we think and we drink.

'I love this one,' states Joss after she's finished knocking it back. 'Lovely and dry.'

'Like you,' snorts Joe, earning himself a death stare.

'Why do you have to ruin it?' his sister demands, and so begins a fierce little mini squabble, while Logan and Ned try and distract us by pulling out a hefty bottle of ice wine in a long, thin glass bottle.

'Now, Canada is the biggest maker of ice wine, and

most of Canada's ice wine is made in the chilly hills of Ontario,' says Logan over the raised voices.

I hold out my glass, keen to try the amber-hued ice wine, but don't take my eyes off the siblings, who are getting more heated by the second. 'You guys, let's not—' They ignore me. I'd bet there's a red wine flush on my cheeks already, and my fingers move to pick at a cheeky chin spot I can feel pulsating. 'Come on, we're having a good day.'

'Give it a rest, Cali, this isn't about you,' Joss snaps, shutting me down.

I shrink back, stuttering. 'I-I was just saying, let's just enjoy the wine tasting ...'

'Ice wine?' Ned asks us each in turn, as if nothing is happening. 'Ice wine?'

'You can't force it, you know what they're like.' Sara sighs, slumping back in her seat and getting her phone out, gulping down the ice wine and holding her glass out for a refill, without even waiting for Logan to give his spiel.

I'm stung, but I paste on a smile which I know doesn't hit my eyes and try and reel everyone back in, taking a large glug of the ice wine and following Sara's lead by holding out my glass for more. My heart is thudding, and behind my façade I feel myself shrinking, fading. We were having such a nice time ...

'What do we think of the ice wine?' Logan asks. 'Any smells hitting you? Any flavours you'd like to share with the group?'

'Sweet, isn't it?' says Luke, taking the reins on the conversation while Sara makes a mild attempt at mediation and Ember and Alex make flirty little eyes at each other over the tops of their glasses.

Right, let's get back in the game. I'm not going to let those two rain all over my snowy Christmas Day.

Using the hairband on my wrist I pull my curls back and secure them in a messy bun at the nape of my neck, shaking free a couple of tendrils, especially on the left-hand side to hide my big, picked chin spot, thank you.

I look up and Luke is watching me. 'What?' I ask.

'What?' He blinks, blushes, and looks away.

Oh my God, he was staring at me. I hope in a good way. Am I buzzed from the wine or are we science nerds because I'm feeling some chemistry?

Yeah, I might be a little buzzed from the wine. That ice wine though, mmm. Logan and Ned are facing away trying to uncork a stuck cork from a bottle of white without us noticing, so I reach over and sneak myself some more. I raise my brows at Luke and he nods, so I slosh some in his glass too.

Giving up on the white, and the group, Logan suggests they simply leave us with the remainder of the bottles and their copies of the tasting notes, and says we can come and find them in the bar car later if we have any questions.

The other passengers who'd attended have filtered off, perhaps to get some lunch, or just to get away from us.

Joss and Joe have shut up, finally, but there's a tension in the air, like we've taken a step backwards again. I swirl my latest glass of wine, watching those drippy legs and trying to remember what I once heard they indicated. Was it that the wine was good quality if it had lots of legs? Or high alcohol? Or that the glass is real crystal?

'Cali, did you speak to Luke today?' Joss asks me. It's a pleasant enough question, but coming from her, I still can't tell. There's something about her tone, the way her smile doesn't meet her eyes. I guess maybe we're still swimming in the mild confrontational part of the afternoon after all. 'Your boyfriend, I mean,' she clarifies.

Fake Luke! I nearly forgot about that guy. 'No.' I shake my head. 'He's, well, we're having a rocky patch, actually. And here I am in the Rocky Mountains, hahaha!'

Ember and Alex are kind enough to pretend to laugh, at least.

'Well, just be careful. You don't want this Luke to start thinking you're single again.'

'Doesn't she?' Sara raises an eyebrow.

Hmm, this sounds light-hearted, but I'm quite good at reading people, I think, and suddenly the red wine feels like it's dehydrated my mouth.

I'm stupid for thinking everything could be magically fixed, just like that.

Outside the train it's started to snow, fat, heavy flakes that make the mountains look like phantoms. We fall into a hushed lull, watching the snow falling, faint Christmas music in the background, the train endlessly ploughing forward. The wine is polished off. Luke and Joe go and get some more. Then a little later, I go and get another couple of bottles, and a little later again, so does Joss, and the whole time the snow doesn't let up. Then it begins to pile on the window frames.

'We should be getting into Whistler in a couple of hours,' Alex says, checking the time on her phone. 'I might call that it for this afternoon's drinking, otherwise I'll be falling asleep early. And I don't want to miss out on any of the last night fun.' She looks at Ember, who rolls her eyes, laughing.

Joe stands up and stretches. 'You're right. I might take a nap—'

I don't want it to end like this, everything was going so well, we were getting somewhere, we were getting along. 'Wait, don't go. Let's have another drink. Let's talk.'

Joss moans. 'Cali … don't be … ' She trails off.

There's silence in the group for a moment.

'Don't be what?'

'Nothing.'

'Don't be what?' I demand, hopefully sounding more confident than I feel. And why should I have to worry about feeling confident anyway? This was my friend, once. Is that really impossible to get back?

Joss looks to the others. 'I'm just saying, let whatever

happens happen. I know what you're trying to do, but you need to grow up and stop being so . . . clingy.'

I sit back, woozy in the head, and my finger runs over and over the blistered skin of my spot. 'I'm not clingy,' I say. I'm not needy, I'm not pathetic just because I need – want – my friends around. This is exactly what they said to me back in Spain. I want them to stop saying that.

'Joss,' Luke says, his tone warning, his arm coming around the back of me. 'Don't be an arsehole.'

Shaking her head, Joss sighs, breaking away her gaze. 'I don't want to get into all this again. I didn't mean to say anything.'

'But you did. You always "just have to say something".'

'Believe me, *I don't.*'

I see Alex meet Ember's eye, who shrugs.

'You do, actually,' says Sara. 'I don't think anyone needed the last word more than you on that holiday, Joss.'

'Do we have to talk about Spain again?' Joe sighs.

'But we don't talk about it,' Luke adds, speaking up, his voice cutting through the group. 'We didn't talk about it then, and we haven't talked about it now, and maybe that's the problem. Maybe that's why none of us can move forward.'

The table erupts into an argument all at once, drowning out the Christmas music.

'I have moved forward – I am just fine without you all,' stamps Joss, causing a wine glass to topple and the stem to break off.

'Don't speak for me, you all made it perfectly clear I'm not part of this gang,' says Sara, getting up to leave.

Joe groans. 'Sara, you're such a broken record.'

She turns back. 'Oh, I'm sorry, did someone say something or was it just Joss's shadow?'

I can't bear it, and I'm just plucking enough rage from deep within me, when—

Screeeeeeeeeeeech.

Like a long, slow, painful death, the train comes to a complete halt, we all still, and shut the hell up, and silence fills the carriage.

I look up, and Luke follows my gaze. The snow is quick to settle on the roof of the celestial carriage where before the airstream of the train would blow it off.

This isn't the first time the train has needed to stop in between stations on this journey. It happens. But maybe it's the new gloom caused by the snow piling overhead, the fact the sun was on its way to dipping behind the mountains already, or the way Alex, who knows everything there is to know about this route, mumbles the words, 'Oh no,' that makes this latest development cause my heart to thud.

230

Chapter 30

Ember

I'm usually wary of wine. It's a drink that makes me think of my mum, my dad, the holidays we used to take in France. Then it makes me think of Bryn. Then, before I know it, I'm lonely. But I do like red.

The tang swirls in my mouth from my latest glass when the train grinds to a stop. I'm still waiting for the heavy heart that holds hands with this particular drink for me. Waiting for those disassociated waves to rinse me of my current surroundings so I'm only pretending to listen to those around me and actually in my head. Just me and the wine.

But today my body is right here with my mind, and Alex's leg is against mine under the table, and Cali keeps catching my eye and making sure I'm included in the conversation. At least, she did before they all started screaming at each other.

However, I can't help but turn over the realisation that these people haven't seen or spoken to Bryn for nearly as long as I have. That's wild to me. I always thought they'd be best friends forever. That I was the only stranger on this trip. But in a way, we all are.

Beside me, Alex looks to the roof, watching the white duvet settle over us, a natural dimming of the lights, and I follow her gaze up, running my eyes over her neck, her face, as I do so.

'Oh no,' she says under her breath.

'What is it?' I ask her.

'I'll be right back,' she says, pulling her arm away from where it was resting behind me, taking her leg from mine. 'Wait here?' she asks, and the way she looks at me, I'm not going anywhere.

The others stand, stretch, the halting of the train having also halted them in their tracks, and agree it's time to take a break from each other.

When I'm alone, the sun behind the mountains, the now-dark sky barely visible through our heap of snow, I take out my phone. If I'm going to call Bryn, now would be the time. I'm alone. I'm a little merry.

But I'm also not sure what I would say. And at this stage, it's highly likely she'll see me get off the train in Vancouver anyway. Tomorrow morning. Wow. I guess

I'll be in a real bed tomorrow, probably in some hotel in another big city. Right?

I open Bryn's social feed, clicking on a picture of her and her fiancée. Hi, Ruby. She looks nice, they look happy.

But, what if . . . ?

Before I can scroll further, Alex slides back into the seat beside me, and I put my phone down.

'I just spoke with some of the staff, and there'll be an announcement soon, but we've hit a snowstorm, and up ahead the snow is all over the track. For miles.'

'But aren't you Canadians used to this?'

She smiles. 'We are. But sometimes Mama Nature beats us at our own game.'

'So, we're stuck? For how long?'

Alex shrugs, but there's glitter in her gaze.

My eyes flick over her face, my head tilting to the side. There's a slowing down between us and our actions, as I soak in the fact that the longer we're stuck, the more time I have to enjoy her.

It's just a crush. Fleeting, fun, it'll be over in the morning and I'll focus on real life.

Or . . . is this real life?

Two hours later we're still in the celestial carriage, our legs tangled together, slumped in the seat and talking the time away under our snow duvet. Everything about her is

233

interesting and new, and right now, Bryn is hundreds of miles away, literally and also in my thoughts.

'Ladies and gentlemen,' another announcement comes on, interrupting our conversation. 'I'm afraid we're going to be here for some time. It's not safe to clear the track in this weather so we'll be stationary until further notice.'

'Oh,' I say. 'So, what does that mean for timings?'

Alex thinks for a moment. She's cute, chewing her lip in thought. 'It means we might make up a little time, but we'll be arriving in Vancouver later than planned. Maybe ... sometime in the afternoon?'

Tomorrow is Boxing Day, the twenty-sixth of December. Bryn's getting married the day after, on the twenty-seventh. If I don't arrive until the afternoon, right before her wedding, well, why would she ever thank me for that? Is it romantic to show up that close, or is it too late?

'Did you hear that?' Cali says, coming back up the stairs. She looks bluer than she did earlier. Joss is a piece of work, huh? 'It sounds like we won't even make it to Whistler this evening.' She looks at us, tangled together. 'Did I interrupt?'

I sit up straighter, but don't answer her question directly. 'How are you all doing?' I deflect.

'I don't know about the others, but I'm alright. A little worried about how long we'll be stuck here. I don't want us to ... you know ...'

234

'Miss the wedding?' Alex chimes in. 'I don't think we will.'

'No, you're probably right.' Cali presses her nose to the window, lost in thought.

Cali looks back at us, her back straighter, a determined look on her face, the tip of her nose pink from the chilled glass. 'Nope.'

'No?' I ask.

'No. I'm not letting this be the Christmas memory from this year. We need to make the most of the situation we're in. Do something fun. Enjoy our Christmas.'

'We could have a party?' I suggest. Where did that come from? I'm not even a big fan of parties. But there's that little free version of myself zipping around inside of me right now, the one that likes late nights on the beach and bonfires and catching waves and kissing in the starlight, and she seems to want to enjoy herself. She doesn't want to say goodnight, or goodbye, anytime soon.

Cali is nodding, plotting. 'A party would be perfect. Or a disaster. But hey, it's worth a go. Could we, Alex?'

Alex laughs. 'I don't think it would ruffle any feathers to play some music and drink yet more liquor up here in the celestial carriage on Christmas night during a snowstorm.'

'Really?' I ask. 'You'd join us, right?'

'I'd love to. If I wouldn't be crashing?'

I wave my hand in the air. 'Hell, I've been crashing since I left England; don't worry about it.'

Even Cali let's out a snicker, then composes herself. 'Yes, this will be good. A bit of dancing, drinking, another go at clearing the air, even if not the tracks, am I right?' She gives Alex a high-five. 'I'm going to go and see if the others are in.'

'We should eat something first,' I call after her.

Cali's head pops back up the staircase. 'Roger that. Wear something festive! Or sexy! Or both!'

Alex stands. 'Okay. On that note, I'm going to go and check up on a few things. I'll see you in a while?'

'Looking forward to it,' I tell her, unable to keep the smile from my face.

Chapter 31

Joss

I hate seeing them together, even after all these years. The little looks between them, the flushed cheeks, the longing gazes when the other isn't watching, the body heat that radiates from them when they 'find' themselves next to each other.

It should have been me. It could have been me.

I didn't want to feel this way at Christmas. I didn't want to act this way. I'm mean and sharp and pushing everyone away all because of my stupid ego.

I'm alone in my compartment, the door pulled closed. Sara is somewhere, she didn't tell me where, and I didn't ask, after I made everyone feel shit at the wine tasting. I just had to try and take a dig, didn't I? But Joe was pushing my buttons – again – and it's infuriating. Outside the door there's still faint festive music playing, and beyond the window the snow is so plump and thick it's all I can see, even the trees are becoming obscured.

I'm so fucking lonely.

What was it I read in that self-help book, again? Something about taking responsibility for your own emotions.

There's a knock on my compartment door and I lift myself off the chair, shaking away the sadness and pasting my aloof face back on. But when I open the door, I soften.

'Hey,' says Luke.

'Hi.'

'Just wanted to check in on you?'

That's so Luke. Always checking in. Quietly observant. Kind and thoughtful. I used to fool myself into thinking it was reciprocated romantic feelings, but when he and Cali arrived for our holiday in Spain, I realised I'd had it all wrong. Like an absolute tool. I'm pretty sure I then acted like exactly that.

'I'm fine,' I say now.

'You sure?'

I study him for a moment. I've always wondered if he knew how I felt about him. Then I've let myself get mad about what the hell he thought was so special about him that he could play with two of his friends' hearts. Then I've felt bad because he did nothing wrong, really.

She did though, because Cali knew how I felt before she took the plunge and hooked up with him. And was it worth it? They didn't even last a fortnight. 'I'm fine, just a little . . . it's weird being away from home for Christmas, isn't it?'

'Everything's weird,' he says with a laugh, and it draws a smile from me, too. 'It seems everyone's going to have another crack at a cracking Christmas and throw some kind of snowed-in party up in the celestial carriage in a while. You going to come?'

I hesitate. 'I guess so.'

'Come on, it's Christmas.'

Our conversation dries up a little, but he looks relaxed, normal, comfortable and my heart pulls in on itself because any tension I feel in the silence is one-sided, and it always has been.

'How are you coping so well with all of this?' I wave my hand in the general area of the entire train.

'Alright. Kind of odd seeing Cali again. We were so close and now it's completely different. But also a little bit not.'

'Does your girlfriend know about her?' It comes out of my mouth like grit on an icy road.

He stumbles on his words and stands up straighter. 'Um, no, well, there's nothing to know, really.'

I take a breath and retreat a little into my room. 'I'll see you at the party, okay?'

He pauses, looking at me, his brow furrowed, but after a minute he nods and heads off with a wave.

I slump back down in my seat. The snowstorm is getting worse. Am I, too?

Chapter 32

Cali

I've got to hand it to my ex-group of friends. When they're called to service for a party, no matter what their mental state they've always been able to step it up. I can't believe the train hasn't started up again yet. I'd be a little nervous if I wasn't distracting myself with all this booze and sequinage.

I emerge from my compartment dolled up in my favourite gold sequin miniskirt, paired with a black thermal long-sleeve top, just as Joss is coming out in a gloriously silver pleated dress, holding a bottle of Prosecco with no stopper in.

We stare at each other for a minute, assessing each other's mood. But I can't deny what I see, no matter what she said earlier. 'You look amazing,' I admire.

She takes a long inhale, holds it for a second, and breathes out, pasting on a smile. 'So do you,' Joss answers, and when she lets me take a swig from her bottle I know it's her stubborn, prideful way of extending an alcohol-soaked olive branch. It almost feels like the friendliest she's been to me in such a long, long time. For that reason, I link her arm and hold on to her a little tighter, a little closer, only letting go when we realise we can't make it up the stairs to the celestial carriage locked together. 'This is the dress I'm wearing to the wedding,' Joss says halfway up the stairs. 'I thought, fuck it. Especially if Ember's going to run off with the bride anyway,' she guffaws.

'She won't, well maybe,' I say back, but my words are tucked in underneath the music filling the domed space of the celestial carriage. I gasp when I reach the top of the stairs. Alex is there, stringing some colourful flashing lights which reflect gem-toned blobs on the snow above us. She's popped a portable speaker in the corner, and several bottles are lining one of the tables.

'Alex, did you do all this?' I ask. When she shrugs, bashful, I add with a smile, 'Did you do this for Ember?'

'I mean, I didn't *not* do it with her in mind. But I do want all of us to have a good time too.'

'That's nice of you.'

Alex leans in. 'I actually wanted to talk to you at some point, maybe this evening? Maybe tomorrow morning.'

'You okay?' I hope this isn't about Ember. What if it

turns out she's already been in touch with Bryn? What if they've been talking all this time, plotting their runaway bride moment, and she's confessed all to Alex who now feels I need to know, but only when it's late enough I can't stop her. I reach up to pick at a spot, but she pushes my hand down.

Alex studies my face. 'You know what, it's not a big thing, and it's nothing to worry about. We'll talk about it in the morning.'

'Are you sure? It's not . . . '

'No, it's a good thing. We'll talk tomorrow.'

At that moment, Ember ascends the stairs. She's in a jade off-shoulder sweatshirt and jade bejewelled mini-skirt. She looks like the coolest mermaid ever, and I'm just background noise when she and Alex are drawn together, all big smiles and flirty, happy chemistry.

I leave them to it, and go to get myself a drink. Word must have got out, because there are a few new faces creeping up the stairs, peering at our party and when I wave them up, they're also glammed in sequins and Christmas jumpers. The more the merrier! I sway to the music, waiting for the one person I really want to be here to arrive.

Next to the party though is Joe, who hasn't changed from earlier and has one side of hair crumpled like he's been sleeping up until thirty seconds ago. I hold out a fresh glass of Prosecco to him and tears spring to my eyes as, instead of accepting it, he pulls me into a hug. A hug. Oh my God, it's been a while.

'For what it's worth, Cali,' he says into my hair, 'I just want to say I'm sorry, for everything. For whatever stupid crap I might have said in the heat of the moment, for not answering when you tried to call.'

'Oh my ... Joe ... I'm sorry too,' I say into his shoulder. 'I just want you guys back.'

Is this really happening? Did I just get a friend back?

Joe raises his glass and clinks it against mine, before heading off down the carriage, dancing on his own to the music.

I hate that I'm waiting for him to arrive. But even if I pretend I'm not, if I face away from the stairs, if I focus on the music, if I strike up a conversation with someone new, I'm still waiting for him. It's kind of agony.

Joss appears at my side again, filling up her glass. Her spaghetti-strapped dress seems, in a way, out of place when surrounded by snow, but it's actually pretty warm up here with all these bodies.

'Joss,' I start. Is there a better time to do this than now? I'm not sure there is.

But she holds out her hand. 'Can we not? Haven't we both just simmered down?'

'Don't we have to, though? What happened earlier can't keep happening, especially not once we hit Vancouver. And this is our last night before we get to Bryn.'

Underneath us, there's a grinding on the tracks, a low-pitched but loud noise letting out a series of clunks.

'It's okay,' calls out Alex. 'It's just the train powering down further to save fuel.'

'Shouldn't it be trying to move, though?' I say. Who knew train maintenance was my forte?

Alex shakes her head. 'This is normal. In this kind of circumstance. We just have to have patience and we'll start moving again when we can.'

She turns away, but I see her glance out the window down at the ground below, where the snow is blowing drifts up the side of the carriage.

I'm tallying us up. Ember is chatting with Alex. Sara and Joe are looking out of the window. Joss is hovering beside me, probably searching for something to say, like I am (how did we used to spend hours talking without even taking a breath? That feels like another life).

And finally, over her shoulder, Luke ascends the stairs.

As he reaches the top, he scans the carriage, and his gaze settles on me.

Half a second later, the lights flicker out.

I move towards the stairs, stumbling over one of the seats on my way, as nervous chatter builds around me in the dark.

'Luke?' I call out, stretching my hand forward.

Without any internal lighting, the gravity of the

snowstorm happening outside the train is magnified, and for the first time I see it for what it is. The layer of snow on top of the domed ceiling is so thick, so dense, it's making the glass creak. With the music cut, the noise of the wind howling is like a foghorn to our ears. Giant snowflakes pelt at the windows, slapping against the sides of the carriage like it's trying to get in.

A few moments later, a generator somewhere in the depths of the train kicks in, and the low-level emergency lights flicker back on. The train judders, and someone, somewhere in another carriage, screams.

Luke. I reach over the stair banister and grab for him as he stumbles back. We catch each other, hold on, his palm in mine and as he steadies himself, he loosens his grip but runs a thumb over the back of my hand.

We hold onto each other as he comes up the final stairs, and at the top, almost on an autopilot which had never been switched off, he lets go of my hand and pulls me into a hug, his arms wrapping my neck while mine wrap his waist.

I lean into his chest and we breathe against each other. 'You okay?' he whispers into my ear.

I can't speak because I think it'll come out as a weird croak, so I nod into him, and feel him brush his cheek on my hair.

'Good evening, ladies and gentlemen,' a voice crackles over the train tannoy. Luke and I break apart, but our arms stay touching, and I couldn't be more aware of it. 'We're sorry for the loss of power just now. It's nothing to worry about, but I'm sorry to confirm that we won't be moving any further until the storm outside passes, for the safety of our passengers and crew. We hope to be able to commence our journey again once the tracks have sufficiently cleared, and are currently estimating reaching Whistler sometime in the morning. We're sorry for the delay this will cause in us reaching Vancouver, the final destination for this service. Any further updates, we'll let you know.'

'We're not even going to get to Whistler until the morning,' I reiterate, to nobody in particular, but Luke stays nearby so I look up at him. 'What if we don't make it to the wedding in time?'

Chapter 33

Ember

This Christmas, I thought I'd either be curled up in a cabin, reunited with my ex-girlfriend, or on a red-eye flight back to the UK, my tail between my legs. I didn't expect to be dancing under a canopy of snow at a home-made Christmas party with a new crush who knows just how to make me smile.

Right now, I'm happy.

When she takes my hand, lacing her fingers in mine, I'm even happier.

When the lights flicker off, and the train judders, and the announcer says we won't be even reaching Vancouver until late tomorrow at the earliest, my head is demanding that I feel worried or sad or like my opportunity for reconciliation and happiness is slipping away into the snowstorm. But my gut is disagreeing.

I'm being stopped in my tracks, literally.

'Alex, what are the chances of us making it to Vancouver tomorrow night?' Cali asks, coming over to us, Luke close by, their arms touching. Sara, Joss and Joe filter over as well.

'I don't know any more than you guys.' Alex shrugs, chewing her lip. She looks nervous. 'You're worried about missing the wedding?'

Cali nods. 'We have to make it; we've come this far.'

Outside the train, somewhere high up a mountain, a rumble is heard, and we all fall silent. Listening. Alex takes my hand.

The group have separated. Only to different seats within the celestial carriage, keeping a little distance while keeping an eye on each other.

There haven't been any more scary noises, but the train is cold and still while we all await further news. Alex has taken herself off to get us an update from some of her colleagues, and I'm swirling a glass of whisky, sat beside Luke, who is staring out of the window.

I stand up and stretch, catching Cali's eye and motioning for her to follow me down the stairs.

We bundle inside our sweatshirts in the dim divider between the carriages, watching the snow swirling beyond the window.

I have to ask. 'What the hell happened in Spain?'

Cali sighs. She sounds tired. 'To be honest, you'd probably get a different answer depending on who you asked.'

'Fair enough. What's your answer?'

Cali loses herself for a moment, watching the snowfall. And just when I'm wondering if she's fallen asleep standing up, she starts.

'It all just came out of nowhere, really. Well, that's not true. It came out of me and Luke.'

I raise my eyebrows, but wait for her to continue.

'Luke and I, we'd always been close, always flirty, always chemistry bubbling about under the surface, but we were very much part of a group of six solid friends. Then, one week before we were flying to Spain, he and I, finally – I thought – got together.'

She quietens again for a moment, smiling at the memory.

'It was a good week, I take it?'

Cali laughs. 'The best. We were . . . delirious. I couldn't believe he felt the same as me. That week we cocooned ourselves, enjoyed each other away from the rest of them, figured out what we were before letting anyone else in. Then we went to Spain.

'From the moment we told the others that we were together, our protective little self-contained bubbles began bursting. Some weren't happy with this new development between him and me, and made that clear. Fault was being found in everything from the weather to the accommodation to the conversation. Arguments were breaking out and being walked away from unresolved. And then things came to a head when we were out at dinner, at a table in the centre of a restaurant, surrounded by delicious tapas that went cold as we had a blowout of an argument unlike ... anything I'd ever experienced. Things were said that weren't taken back, truths were revealed, resentments uncovered, and one by one we went home early – separately.'

'So all this because of one argument?'

'It's hard to explain, but it all just got so ... mean. You know? We were supposed to be best friends, but we were picking at each other's biggest insecurities, taking shots that are just hard to come back from.'

'And you couldn't work through it?'

Cali leans her forehead against the cold glass window, and closes her eyes. 'Everything had changed. And then they all fled, we scattered before ever giving ourselves a chance to repair. And you could say that people don't mean the things they say in the heat of an argument, but this felt like everyone did mean it. It felt like these were deep-seated, true feelings, finally bubbling over.'

'What kind of thing, if you don't mind me asking?'

'Well, Sara was stinging Joss about the failed business and the lost money, something she already felt awful about. Bryn called Joe a doormat and said none of us even really knew him after all these years because he never came out of Joss's shadow. Joss called me needy.' She stops and shakes her head. 'The list goes on. But in short, Luke and I "hooked up", and I ruined the whole dynamic, for everyone. I felt like we'd doomed the whole trip.'

'That's how you feel?'

She looks drained, but nods, then stands up straight. 'I'm going to the bathroom.'

'You okay?'

'I'm okay.'

She leaves and I climb back up the stairs, returning to my seat beside Luke, and Cali reappears a few minutes later.

I turn our conversation over in my head. These guys are living in the past and look what it's doing to them. I study Luke, who is staring out of the window still.

I follow his gaze, and realise that, actually, he's staring at the reflection of Cali on the other side of the carriage. Those two.

'Luke, how far would you go for someone that might be the one?'

'What?' he says, glancing at me like he's been caught, then drops himself in it further by flicking his gaze straight over to Cali, who has her chin on the seat in front of her like a forlorn puppy, staring forward at the blackness outside.

I shake my head and exhale. 'I think I might be making a big mistake,' I say, keeping my voice low. I don't want them all jumping all over this, but Luke, well, I think he might get it.

'In what way?' he asks, his voice just as quiet, respecting my privacy.

'I think, maybe, I might have been a bit delusional about Bryn. What the hell was I thinking, coming all the way out here? She's going to hate me for doing this to her, isn't she? So what does this mean?'

He's quiet for a while, thinking, nodding. 'I guess I think ... you have to follow your heart, but it's hard to know if your heart is telling you how you feel now, or if it's, like, muscle memory. You won't know unless you follow it and really listen, I guess.'

'Does following it all the way to Vancouver seem like a good idea to you?'

'For you? I can't answer that. But I don't think following it has to mean literally taking a physical journey to try and get the answers from someone else. You probably know the answers, whether you're on one side of Canada or the other, or back on your beach at home.'

I wriggle my nose in thought. He's not wrong. I've come this far, maybe I just plough on, see it through to the end. But Alex's face is there, and I like her, and I'm not saying she's now The One, but the fact she's made an impact on me ... maybe that's the push I needed?

'I think I want to kiss Alex,' I whisper. 'And I don't think I would be feeling like that if I was still in love with Bryn.'

253

Chapter 34

Cali

It's Christmas, for God's sake. We're in Canada. *Canada*!
And yes, we might be about to get swept away by an ava-
lanche, but shouldn't we go down dancing?

I stand up and crank the music up, filling the dimly lit
carriage with Christmas crackers.

'This is so petty,' I announce. 'This is all so unimpor-
tant when we might be about to miss our best friend's
wedding.'

Joss groans. 'Bryn isn't your best friend any more,
though, mate.'

'Stop it, it's Christmas. We are not doing this. Again.
Come on.' I pop open a bottle of Prosecco I find on one
of the tables. Probably should have asked who's that was
first. Too late now! 'Please? This is our last night on this

254

journey … maybe … let's go out with a bang? Sorry, wrong word.'

One by one they rise, accept a drink, start swaying to the music, and after a while I think they've thawed enough (or drunk enough) that we could maybe call this a party again?

'Alright,' I say, taking a shaky breath in that I try and mask. 'Sara, can I talk to you a moment? There's something I'd like to say.'

She nods, and follows me to the side of the carriage, and we take a seat together. God, this is so awkward. I'm fine with apologies – love them! – but there's something about giving one five years after the event that feels a bit rehearsed. So I've rehearsed it.

I lean in to be heard over the music. 'Sara. I wanted to say I'm sorry for treating you like an afterthought on the holiday. I know I said some things that implied you weren't as much a part of the group as the rest of us, and really, I only ever meant that you hadn't lived in the townhouse as long. But I got angry and upset and it all came out wrong.'

I cringe, thinking of how I screamed at Sara that yes, she might as well leave early because most of the time we forget she's there anyway. It was never true. 'Anyway, I know there was lots more to the arguments, not just that, but I don't want to go over every single thing said right now – but we can another time, if you want. For now, I just wanted to say I'm aware, and for my part, I'm sorry.'

Sara nods, digesting my words. 'I'm sorry too. For the names I called you. You aren't childlike, you're dreamlike, and that's actually something I've always liked about you. But, like you said, in amongst everything else that was being thrown around, it just felt like ammunition. Sorry.'

I lean in and hug her, her curls tickling my cheeks. God, I've missed hugging people. Tears leap up into my eyes and I hold her as close as I can.

'I want to get to know who you are now,' I say. 'Can we talk properly, when we're not tipsy and facing imminent death?'

'I'd like that,' she smiles in reply.

We stand after a moment, and separate, and I spot Joe, and before I can say anything, he, too, pulls me into a hug, saying into my ear, 'Thanks for pushing us all to not just ignore each other until the flight home. I always liked your determination.'

'Thanks, Joe.' I'm touched. He's not one to reveal his feelings often, and maybe it's alcohol-fuelled, but I'll take it.

'You be happy, okay? Do what makes you happy. Don't live for anyone else.'

'Same to you.'

We break away and when he moves to the side, there's Joss. We look at each other like we're facing off in a battle, and she can be so proud I can only assume this is what it is. I don't know if I have it in me.

Just as I'm about to walk away, she speaks first. 'Alright, let's talk.'

'Of course.'

We edge over to the stairs, and I wait. I think I'm waiting for an apology, to be honest. She stung me with how she reacted to me and Luke coupling up. She's never liked being the last to know about things, but this was so new that we just hadn't wanted to say anything until that moment. But whereas I expected her to smart a little because I hadn't run and told her the second we'd kissed, I couldn't believe how she actually acted. She was affronted that she didn't know sooner, said we'd treated her like a fool. She'd dripped in sarcasm when she'd congratulated us for messing up the whole group's friendship dynamic. Then we'd resorted to silly name-calling, each seeking revenge on the last thing the other said. I remember being so shocked that I was shaking, and doubting if she'd ever even liked me in the first place.

'I can't tell, even after all this time, if you don't actually know why I was so mad at you.'

Oh. That does not sound like an apology opener. 'What do you mean? Wasn't it because you didn't think Luke and I should have coupled up without telling you?'

'No,' she scoffed. 'I mean, yes, in a roundabout way. But the reason behind that was because ...' She trails off, looking back towards the staircase, as if watching for someone to come up them. She faces me again, looking me dead in the eye. 'You knew how I felt about Luke.'

'About Luke?'

'Back then. You knew.'

'What did you feel? You didn't like him?'

'No, for God's sake. I was, like, in love with him.'

Bloody hell. This would be a perfect moment to drop a glass and have it smash, but I don't think we need any more drama right now, so I clutch it tightly and take a gulp, the sparkling liquid popping and dissipating in my mouth. 'You were in love with him?' I hiss, finally, steering her further away from the stairs.

'Duh!'

'What do you mean, "duh"? I had no idea.'

'Of course you did, even I make myself cringe about how obvious I used to be about it.'

I raise my shoulders to my ears. 'I didn't know. I swear.'

Joss stares at me for a moment, her brow scrunched into a frown as she studies me, looking from one eye to the other, and I hold her gaze.

I repeat myself. 'I didn't know.'

'I'm sure you knew. I was sure.'

'So, this was all because you liked him, but thought I'd "stolen" him away from you?' I grip my glass a little harder. 'That's why you said all those horrible things to me. That's why you cut me out. Because you felt *entitled* to him.'

Joss shifts, shaking her head. 'It's not that I felt entitled. I felt betrayed.'

'Well guess what? I feel betrayed now.' I take a swig of my drink and close my eyes for a minute. 'By you. In case that wasn't clear.'

When I open my eyes, there Luke is.

Chapter 35

Ember

Alex is back, and this funny little party is complete again. The train still hasn't moved, the main lights still haven't come on, we're no closer to getting to Vancouver, but, right now, I don't care. I don't care!

'Can I show you something?' Alex says, leaning close to be heard over the music. My lips are next to her neck and I can smell her soft, outdoorsy scent, and feel her breath tickle my cheeks.

'Is that a line?' I tease.

She laughs, and pulls me towards the stairs.

As I follow, nerves buzz through my body. I don't know where we're going, but she keeps her hand in mine, and I know that wherever she's taking me, I want to go.

At the bottom of the stairs, she leads me away from the

celestial carriage, and we walk through car after car, past late-night passengers, over sleeping, outstretched legs, until we arrive at the very end of the train.

'Here,' she says, reaching to a hook beside a large, sturdy-looking door, and hands me a thick coat, lined, that reaches the ground. Interesting, we're putting *more* clothes on?

She takes a coat for herself too, and I put mine on. I want to banter, to flirt, but this feels like it, like she's going to kiss me tonight, and the thought has laid itself on top of all others, like the snow itself. And so I'm silent, trusting, and reaching for her hand again when she smiles at me and opens the door.

What she opens the door to takes my breath right out of my lungs, lifting it into the night sky, as white as the mountaintops that surround us.

We've stepped onto the platform at the back of the train. The snowfall has stopped, but it's mounded in silky ripples right across the tracks and high up the sides of the train. It looks like we're floating in the clouds.

The sky has cleared and the billion stars I saw from within the train the past few nights look like they've been polished and tripled. The moon is large tonight, and it glitters the snow and the mountains in the dark.

'This is ...' I look up, bathing in the starlight, not caring how cold my cheeks are, or that I can practically feel my eyelashes freezing on my face.

'Pretty, huh?' Alex says, interrupting my thoughts in a way I don't mind at all.

I lower my gaze to her, standing there in the dark, lit up by the moon and the stars and the snow. Suddenly, I find the only words I need to say. 'I want to kiss you.'

Her face grows serious and she steps an inch closer. 'I want to kiss you, too.'

I smile, with relief, with anticipation, with want.

Alex reaches a hand up to my face, her cold fingertips moving my hair aside, and causing a frisson to run down my back.

A hint of her honey smile crooks the side of her mouth. 'Cold?' she asks, and pulls me closer, wrapping her coat around me, too.

Her body is warm under the coat, and the fire I'm feeling tells me I'm probably the same.

I tug her by the waist, running my eyes over her lips, level with my nose, so close that if I tilt my chin up right now the kiss we both want could finally happen.

A smile forms on my own lips. A bubble rising in me that I recognise as excitement. It's so fucking nice to want someone, have someone want me, feel connected, let the Hollywood romance and the leading lady and the celestial setting sweep me away.

I lift my chin, my top lip grazing her bottom lip so lightly, testing, tasting.

Alex pauses. She pulls back a millimetre, rests her

forehead against mine, increasing the gap between our mouths.

My heart thuds, confused. Is she coming back in?

'Ember,' she whispers, her voice nearly lost in the dark, it's that quiet.

'What?' I take a step back too, moving my forehead from hers, but she stays looking down. 'Is it the Bryn thing? You ... you don't have to worry about that any more. I think you know that you've changed how I felt when I first started this trip?'

'It's not that,' she says, and her shoulders slump. She won't look at me.

'Can you tell me what it is back inside, later, once we've kissed? It can't be that important.' I'm half joking, half covering the worry which is threading its way into my happiness. Despite the worry, though, I'm still pulling myself towards her, longing for the kiss, for the moment, to keep going. I think I might need this, for some reason.

Alex looks up at me then, pain in her eyes, her head tilted, and she scans my face like it might be the last time she sees me.

'What is it?' I ask, a little more forcefully this time, the cold creeping under my coat now.

She swallows, taking her time, stretching out the moment, looking at me like she wants to take me somewhere where we can forget about the rest of the world. Finally, she licks her lips, and says, 'I need to tell you something.'

Chapter 36

Luke

'Joe? Mate? Can I talk to you about something?'

My old friend stops what he's doing and gives me all his attention. 'Always.'

The wine has made us all break down the walls we've built a little, for better or worse, and Joe, for one, seems tired of holding onto any past animosity. So despite the sway, which we can't put down to the train any more, he feels like one of the most level-headed among us to talk through what's on my mind.

We're huddled in one corner of the celestial carriage, the lights low and the storm howling outside, an undercurrent to the festive music. The snow is still pummelling outside, settling over everything from near to far.

The two of us haven't talked much this trip, about

anything deeper than a light dusting of surface conversation at least. 'How are you finding all this?' I ask him.

'This trip?' Joe laughs and puts his phone down on the side. 'It's . . . a good thing? I think?'

'I think so, too. We're a stubborn bunch though, aren't we?'

Joe nods, yawning. 'We really are. Can we move on?'

'We can.' I smile. 'Sorry for everything.'

'Ditto. What do you want to talk about? As if I don't know – should I say "who"?'

I groan. 'I'm so transparent.'

Joe nods. 'What do you want to do? What do you think she wants to do? You've both grown from the people you were, don't you want to know if things have changed or stayed the same?'

I think about his words, watching Cali from across the carriage as she talks with Joss. I can't keep away from her. We're fused together somehow, bonded, and I can't tell what the future looks like but I know I need her in it, in some way.

When she walks by me, she lights everything up like sunshine.

When I talk to her, I can be myself.

When she goes off on her random tangents and catches herself, it feels like the greatest story ever told.

When I saw her in the airport, walking up to the gate, it was as if no time had passed and I had to force myself not to get up and go over there and fit myself around her like I always used to. Because what if she didn't want that any more? Where would that have left us? A memory, abandoned on the tarmac?

That time I saw her in London, standing among the autumn leaves, I wanted to stop the traffic just so she'd have to keep waiting for the lights to change.

And now, I don't want the train to start moving again. I want to have another week with her, like that week before Spain, to tell her how I've always felt. I want to see her first thing in the morning, and last thing at night.

I sigh, an ache in my heart as my mind fills with thoughts of her that never really went away. I look back at Joe. 'She's trying to rebuild these friendships. Her friends mean everything to her. It broke her when everything fell apart, and I think it was my fault.'

'You do? Why?'

'I don't know. I just think if I hadn't pushed things, if I hadn't initiated the kiss, nothing would have changed. I can't risk everything again. She needs to feel safe to get her friends back.'

Joe lets out a snarf.

'What?' I ask him.

'You talk about change like it's a bad thing, but it's just life, right? You can't stop anything from ever changing.' He pauses. 'I know people think I'm passive and just walk away from problems, but that's why. I know I can't change people or change what's going to happen, so I just let it go. I don't know. It's just how I am.'

I think he's right. 'I like how you are,' I tell him.

'Thanks, bud. So, do you regret it?' Joe asks.

'Regret what?'

'Kissing her? Back then?'

'No.' I shake my head. 'Not at all. I would have regretted not kissing her.'

He holds his hands in the air. 'You just gave yourself a good talking to, and I think you talked yourself into a new plan.'

Joe's right. I stand up, steadying myself on the backrest, and make my way down past the other seats, past our other friends and the strangers who have joined us. My eyes are on Cali, who is frowning at Joss, and I want to kiss that frown away. I get closer, my heart thumping, my palms sweating, my mind, though full of thoughts of her, as clear as mountain air.

Chapter 37

Cali

It's been five years since I've seen this guy, and now I struggle to focus on anything else when he's out of sight again.

I don't think I like that feeling for me.

So when he appears in front of me now, and his eyes immediately seek me out, I force my feet to stick to the ground rather than run straight over.

I've been fine on my own, actually. I swallow down my shallow breath. Yes, I've been lonely. Yes, it's been a long time since I felt the comfort of a close friend or a confidant. But I've survived, right? I've carried on without him in my life just fine, thank you.

Haven't I?

Luke pauses on the spot, reading me from a metre away, sensing, perhaps, the conflicts I'm feeling right now.

Beside me, Joss sighs and moves away. Good, I don't want to talk to her any more.

Luke steps towards me, the colourful lights lighting up his skin as he moves, and I start to melt. Before anything else, before we fell into bed together all those years ago, before the disastrous holiday, before the years of silence, he was my friend, and I think I need him back.

He doesn't say a word when he reaches me, just wraps his arms around my head in that hug that has always made me weak, and I push my face into his chest, smelling the woodsmoke and vanilla on his sweater, feeling his breath tousling my curls.

I put my arms around his torso, and the muscles of his back relax in my hold, like they always did.

One morning, all those years ago, our first morning waking up beside each other, the sun was streaming through my flat window. I slept with the curtains and windows open in the summertime, and a warm breeze was coming inside to say hello. Luke was asleep, face down, and I traced my fingers over the skin of his back. In that moment, everything felt right.

And now, as we stay pressed together, swaying to the Christmas music under the lights, he whispers to me, 'I'm sorry, Cali.'

I pull my head back a little and meet his eyes. 'I'm sorry too.'

'I didn't mean any of the things I said back then. It was never "nothing".'

That word stabs at my heart the same way it did back then, in the Spanish rain, as we stood outside the tapas restaurant. The skies were as grey as our moods, three days into the holiday. Ever since that first night, when, on arrival, Luke and I announced that actually, we'd like to share a room, please, things had gone downhill. I'd thought everyone would be happy for us, but instead it was the catalyst for everything that happened after that. And following the blowout argument, I'd walked out into the rain, and Luke had followed me.

There have been times over the years that I've wished I could remember the exact order of what we said to each other. The changes in tone, body language, but it blurred together, pooling into a puddle that we stood in. But would that have helped make me feel any better?

I know I felt this was our fault, I know I suggested he and I should never have got together if it would have saved our group friendship. I remember him agreeing with me, but instead of being what I wanted to hear, I remember being crushed that he felt that way, wanting him to take it back. And I remember a long stretch where we said nothing, just listened to the rain, and then Luke told me that what we had was, in fact, nothing.

Now, it's Christmas, and we've grown up, and apart,

but his arms are back around me and it doesn't feel like nothing, at least not to me.

'Why did you say it?' I ask him, over the music.

Luke's hands move down over my arms, his head tilted down, his lips by my ear. I look at his eyelashes, willing his eyes to meet mine again. 'I thought it was the only way you could be happy.'

'What do you mean?'

'Our group of friends was everything to you, and seeing you so sad as it fractured . . . it killed me, Cali.'

I swallow down the emotions blocking my throat. It killed me, too.

Luke finally meets my eye and instinctively we move closer, like the other's heart is our only source of warmth. Above him, the lights glow like the comfort of Christmas in the city.

'Then what?' The question leaves my lips and I see him glance down at them, like he'd be able to see the words in the space between us.

'You were regretting what we'd done, and I regretted it too, because of how it made you feel. I acted like you weren't as important to me as you really were. I thought I had to let you go for you to be happy.'

I extract an arm from under his and reach up, moving my hair, rubbing my face, and he looks back down. He seems tired, sad, lonely. 'But that wasn't your decision to make for me.'

'I know. I'm sorry.'

My hand moves to his face and I force him to meet my eyes again. 'Why didn't you call me? When the group stayed fractured anyway? Why didn't you come back for me?'

'I got stuck in that moment in our lives. I don't think I've ever really moved forward or grown up or done the right thing. I didn't realise you were feeling the same. Especially after I saw you in London that day, and you looked so well and healthy and happy.'

'You saw me for one second,' I argue. How could he know any of that about me?

'Maybe I just saw what I wanted to, then. I only wanted you to be happy, Cali. By that point I'd pushed you away and I didn't want to make you sad again, ever.'

One of his hands runs through the end of my curls, causing tingles to journey up the back of my neck. I rest my elbow on his shoulder, and move my hand to his hair. 'I'm sorry too,' I whisper.

We're the only two people on this train, frozen in time, the music is just for us, and everything and everyone and the past is melting away. Luke is focused on me, his lips parted, his nose brushes against mine, and I stroke my thumb on the side of his neck.

'What do you want now?' I ask him.

'You,' he breathes against me. 'This. What about you?'

'You,' I answer.

'But I want you to be happy.' He swallows. 'I think you already have a happy life, without me.'

'Stop it,' I say, shaking my head, increasing the space between us a little. 'Don't do this again, don't you make the decision for me.'

'Does he not make you happy?'

'Who?'

'Luke.'

For a second I'm thrown. Is he talking about himself in the third person all of a sudden? Is he actually sloshed? Oh God, he's not even going to remember this in the morning, is he? I'm going to wake up in his bunk with him and he'll be like, *whoa, what are you doing here, stalker?*

'I don't want to get in the way of you and your boyfriend if this is just, you know, the lights and the stars and Christmastime.'

Oh bloody hell, my 'boyfriend'. And he has a girlfriend! I shake my head, and a small laugh escapes which I smother into his shoulder. 'I have a confession. There is no Other Luke. I . . . I made him up.' How embarrassing.

His chest vibrates with a chuckle, and his arms tighten around me. 'Well, maybe your fake boyfriend could date my fake girlfriend?'

'*What?!* There's no Barbara? Also, why was the first name you thought of "Barbara"?'

'Yeah, I made her up too. Good old Barbara. You know I've always had a crush on Barbra Streisand.'

273

Oh my God, *that's right!* I'd forgotten that about him.

Luke blushes, just a touch. 'I'm so stupid when it comes to you, you know that by now.'

He doesn't have a girlfriend … Could we, maybe …?

Luke is still chuckling. 'You made him up? And still called him Luke?'

'It was … I wasn't thinking. I just didn't want to feel like the only one who hasn't moved on.'

'Well then,' he says, his voice dropping low, and I lift my chin, and here we are again.

'Well then …' I echo.

It would feel so good to kiss Luke again, the memory tingles my lips like it left an imprint. But … I glance around us.

Joe and Sara are dancing on the other side of the room. Joss is by the stairs, watching us, pain on her face. Bryn is waiting for us in Vancouver.

Everything is so delicate right now, like a snowflake I'm holding in my hand that could melt or blow away at any moment. Doubt creeps up my neck, under his gaze. We're just all coming back together, what if Luke and I move too fast, and ruin everything again?

Luke steps back, my hesitation glaring like the lights being switched on at the end of a night at a club.

'Luke—' I start, needing his proximity.

'Listen.' He smiles at me, soft eyes, all heart. 'The ball is in your court. I'm not going to make this decision for you this time, but I don't want you to have regrets. I'm going to bed.'

Holy crap, did he just proposition me? No, no, he probably meant that he was literally going to bed, and we could talk in the morning.

As he walks away from me, I lean against the wall, cooling my back against the steel, propping myself up to stop myself being torn in half.

Chapter 38

Sara

You have to laugh. This group can swing from love to hate to love again quicker than you could shake a candy cane at.

But I am strangely fond of the weirdos. We had some good times, even when I felt like a bit of an outsider, even when it seemed I was the only replaceable one in the house. Was that really their fault, or my own insecurities because they weren't my forever people, just my people for that time in my life?

It's this fondness that makes me walk away from Joe and his wild dancing and cross the carriage to his sister, who for once doesn't look like thunder but like rain. Her face is washed with sadness, her eyes downcast, her shoulders slumped.

I put my arm around her shoulders, and she leans into me.

'He's only a guy, you know,' I joke, my voice light.

'A stupid guy who's never looked at me like he looks at her.'

'Good. Because that means you now get to find the one who does.'

'I don't think there is a "one",' she grumbles.

'Maybe not,' I agree. 'But love comes in all sorts of forms.' I dig my phone from my pocket and hold the screen up for her. 'Joss, meet Dina.'

'Who's this?' Joss asks, her eyebrows rising as she takes my phone.

I hesitate. 'My daughter.'

Surprise coats her from head to toe and she blinks at me, shaking her head. 'You have a daughter?'

I nod. 'She's a little sweetheart.'

'Sara ...' Joss looks back at my phone, holding it tenderly in her hand, and keeps tapping the screen so the wallpaper photo of Dina stays bright and lit. 'Congratulations. She's amazing. She's you. Why didn't you tell us?'

'I was scared of being too open with you all about the things that are most important to me, in case it all went away again. But I think we've all grown a bit, right? We can be friends without being in each other's faces every day?'

Joss gazes back down at my phone, and I watch my friend, her face soft with love for this little person she doesn't even know. 'Can we meet her, though, one day? When you're ready?'

My heart glitters. 'I'd like that. Maybe you should come and visit me once this whole trip is out of the way?'

A smile crosses Joss's face. 'You'd let me?'

'Of course. Besides, I like to try my hand at new business ideas and I'd love some input from someone who has some experience.'

Joss scoffs. 'You don't want to talk to me then.'

'Yes, I do. You have experience. I can learn what not to do,' I joke.

Chapter 39

Ember

Six words. Six words that rarely seem to indicate something you want to hear is on its way.

'I need to tell you something,' Alex says to me in front of a sky heavy with stars and a vista of deep snow and tall mountains.

'What?'

'Do you want to go inside?'

'No,' I cry. 'I want to know what's happening. Are you married? Do you not like me like that? Are you worried I'm going to try and move to Canada to be with you because I like you, but I just wanted to enjoy tonight and enjoy you and not think about the future.'

'It's none of those things.'

I raise my eyebrows at her. 'If you don't want to kiss me,

just say so and I'll go back in and warm up and tomorrow we don't have to see each other ever again—'

'I told you I was travelling to Vancouver to see family,' she interrupts me.

'Yes?'

'I told you I have a sister. But I never told you her name.' Alex shuffles, her mouth twitching. She breaks eye contact and looks away, out towards the mountains. 'Her name is Ruby.'

'Okay.' I shrug. 'What, is she made up or something?'

It's only when she looks back at me, sadness shrouding her, that I realise what she's saying.

'Oh my God. Bryn's fiancée?'

She doesn't have to say anything else; I can read it all over her face.

'Your sister is Bryn's fiancée,' I repeat to myself, and face the dark. I swallow through a dry mouth, try to steady my breathing, push down the sickness feeling. I have to hold the railing to stop myself from the weight of this pushing me to the ground. This must be why they call it a crush, because the emotions can be crushing.

'Em, I don't want you to think—' Alex puts a hand on my back but I move away.

'You know Bryn. You're going to her wedding. You were ...' Oh, God. 'You were just trying to ... to distract me.'

'No.'

280

'Yes.' A weird little laugh escapes, quickly swallowed up by a fresh wave of mortification. I look at her again. 'Did you know who I was from the start?'

'No. I knew a group of Bryn's friends would be on the same train as me, and she sent me an old photo of them. I was going to introduce myself but that first time we met you were all in the middle of an argument. Then the second time, it was just you and me, and then you told me you were coming to stop the wedding.'

'I wasn't going to stop the wedding!' I growl, fed up with this narrative. 'I was never going to crash the wedding; I was just going to talk to Bryn. If the wedding then got stopped it would have been because she wanted it stopped.'

'Okay,' Alex says, lapsing into silence for a minute while I stand with my face in my icy hands.

'So, then what, you just decided to manipulate me with all that stuff about the polar bear trip, the "Ember without Bryn is someone that sounds cool", to try and get me to leave?'

'No ...'

'And then you pretended you were into me? So I'd change my mind about her?'

'Yes, alright, at first I did think that. It was my sister's wedding—'

'But you could have just told me.'

'I should have. I wasn't expecting us to have this much, you know, of a draw to each other, to be honest.'

I nod, hearing her loud and clear, and now wanting to be far away from her. 'I'm going inside,' I say.

'Let's go and warm up,' Alex agrees, opening the door and letting me through first. I take the coat off. 'Keep that for a while if you like, until you're thawed out?'

'No thanks.' I hand her back the coat. 'I told you so much, about me, about my relationship with Bryn.'

'I'm not going to tell anyone. It was all between me and you. I know you won't believe this now, but it turned into something real for me, it still is. You were always safe with me.'

I give her one more long look. 'I can't talk to you right now, not about any of it, Alex. So, I'll just say, Merry Christmas. To you and your beautiful family.'

My feet take me back through the never-ending carriages. I am numb.

Chapter 40

Cali

It's been a long day, and it's not late but I think I'm ready to put Christmas Day to bed. I think. Or am I?

I leave the party and the music and the lights behind me and descend the stairs, taking it slow, dawdling, straightening things in the bar area, wasting time while I decide if I'm going to my compartment, or his.

Like a mini, blonde tornado, Ember storms into the bar car and, before she even sees me, grabs a bottle from behind the counter and takes a swig.

'Hello,' I say. 'You okay?'

She turns and focuses on me, seeing me suddenly. 'Did you know?'

'Did I know what?' Shit, what have I done? Does she mean did I know about Joss liking Luke? 'No, I swear I

283

didn't know she liked him. But she can't hold this against me forever, right, nobody can stake a claim over another person.'

Ember shakes her head, and shakes the bottle towards me. 'I don't know what – this – is about but sounds like you might be in need of this.'

'Actually, I was just going to … no, fuck it, give it to me.' I take a big gulp before realising its neat vodka. I splutter. Mmm, quite nice though. 'So, what are you talking about?'

'Did you know that Alex is about to be Bryn's sister-in-law?'

I blink at Ember. 'Why?'

'Because Ruby, Bryn's fiancée, is Alex's sister.'

'Alex's SISTER?' I boom. 'Whoa. No, I didn't know. Why didn't she tell us?'

Ember takes another vodka gulp. 'Oh she did, just now, right before we were about to kiss.'

'Oh my God, you guys nearly kissed?' I squeak. 'Sorry, not important right now.'

'I'm so tired,' Ember says, flopping onto one of the seats and rubbing her forehead with her free hand, the vodka bottle dangling perilously from the other. 'And confused.'

'Me too,' I agree, and then get an idea. 'Hey, do you want to sleep in a proper bed tonight? You can bunk in with me; I'm in a cabin on my own. I would have asked you sooner but kept missing the opportunity.'

'And I'm "The Enemy".'

'You were never the enemy, Ember, never.' I sit beside her and extract the bottle from her fingers, taking a sip before setting it down on the floor.

Ember looks so sad right now, so alone. She sits in silence for a while, but her lips keep opening like she's forming some string of words to let out into the world. Eventually, they're released. 'You were my friends, too,' she says, her voice barely louder than a whisper. 'I know you knew Bryn first, but when she and I split up I lost all of you. I didn't have any other friends in the city, nobody to talk to. And it was a sucky break-up that wasn't because of cheating or hating, it was just about wanting different things. I didn't do anything to make you all drop me like that.'

I stare at Ember. What do I say? Oh my God, she's right.

'We hung out every day for, like, a year. And then nothing,' she continues.

My palms sweat and pulse along with the beat of my heart. 'I'm so sorry.'

'You don't need to apologise, it was a long time ago, I don't even know why I'm bringing it up again now.'

'I think I do need to apologise. I want to. And I want to explain. Bryn was broken after the two of you split. I know it was mutual, I know you wanted different things, but she thought the two of you were going to be forever.'

'We both did.'

'I know.' I nod. 'I guess we stepped back from you as a way to protect her, and just didn't think. And we knew you were planning to start a new life by the beach. And then just as Bryn was beginning to heal, everything went to shit, and within a fortnight we'd all stopped contact with each other.'

Ember doesn't say anything, just stares down at the ground, but I watch her eyelashes twitch as she thinks over what I've said.

'I'm not trying to make excuses,' I add. 'We shouldn't have deserted you.'

'No, I get it,' Ember interjects. 'But I have to ask one thing – did you know I lost my parents, both of them, a couple of months after the break-up?'

My hand jumps to my heart. 'You lost your parents? Ember . . . I can't, I wish, I'm so sorry.'

To my surprise, she looks up at me with a mist of a smile on her mouth. 'Thank you. That actually makes me feel an iota better, if you can believe it.'

'In what way?'

'After it happened, I contacted Bryn to let her know. The six of you shared everything with each other, so the fact that she was the only one to check in on me afterwards hurt. I knew we all weren't friends any more, but I thought we were still *something* to each other. Now I know it was after she'd moved away, after you'd all stopped talking.'

'I wish she'd told me though,' I murmur.

'But you never knew my parents. It probably didn't cross her mind to tell you all my business at that point. I don't think she did anything wrong.'

We drop to silence, heavy shoulders, aching brains, and after a while I ask, 'Want a sleepover at mine, then, friend? Or should I say frenemy? Just kidding. Too soon?'

Twenty minutes later, Ember's lying in the bottom bunk, me in the top bunk, and we're chatting quietly.

'How are you feeling about tomorrow?' I ask her.

'I feel . . . like I'm going to have a headache in the morning. And like it's going to be really humiliating if I show up to see Bryn and Alex is already there with her sister.'

I make an agreeable noise and stare up at the ceiling. 'Wouldn't it be totally weird if you and Alex got married and her sister was married to your ex? Would that make you . . . sister wives?'

'No.' Ember laughs. 'It would make us exes-in-law, I think?'

'Oh. I'd watch that TV show. If you promised to bring the drama.'

She yawns. 'I don't think I have enough drama in me.'

Hmm. 'I wonder if the train will start moving again during the night.' I lean over the bunk. 'Look, maybe we won't even make it to Vancouver for this stupid wedding anyway. Then in a way, problem solved. Do you think Bryn would delay the wedding if we don't make it?'

Ember chuckles, swiftly followed by a groan. 'I don't know what to do any more.'

'Well, do you still want to see Bryn or not?'

'I don't know. I think so. But maybe that's not enough, now.'

'How will you feel if you don't see her? Will you regret it?'

She opens her eyes and looks up at me. 'Aren't you supposed to be talking me out of it?'

Resting my chin on the bed, I gaze down at the floor. 'You know how sometimes doing nothing can make you feel lethargic? I think I'm just shattered, and am just all for moving forward, somehow, whatever that looks like. I also think I'll have a hangover in the morning.'

'You're not going to puke on me, are you?'

'I don't think so. I'll let you know if that changes.'

She's quiet for a time and then moans, 'I feel used.'

'You think Alex used you?'

'I think she might have done. She says she didn't, that she truly liked me and just felt she couldn't tell me, but I still feel like a prize knob.'

'Well ... that is the best type of knob to be.' I pad down the bunk steps to retrieve my water bottle, pull a sweatshirt over my PJs, and sit on the edge of her bed while I sip. 'So, you don't believe what Alex said, about liking you?'

'I mean, I think I believe her.'

288

'Did you go into this thinking it would be more than a holiday romance?'

'I didn't go into it thinking anything, really. I was talking to her about Bryn. But she's cute and we had chemistry and . . . it's been a long time since I've felt that. It was nice, even if it wasn't serious.'

'That's a lot of past tense,' I comment. 'Considering you got something positive from it.'

'Positive? I'm more confused than ever. And what about you?' Ember asks. 'Why are you sitting in here with me when behind that wall is the guy everybody knows you're meant to be with. You know, apart from your boyfriend.' She smirks at me.

'So . . . there is no "Boyfriend Luke". I made him up.'

'Shocker.'

I laugh, and take another gulp of water before offering the bottle to her. 'I am too afraid of rocking the boat. Or the train. And I mean that metaphorically, not like, *if it's rocking, don't come knocking.*'

'Is that why you stayed in London, even after all the others left?'

'Partly. I know it, like a comfort blanket. But I love the city like you've always loved the countryside and the coast.'

'What do you love about it?'

What don't I love about it? 'You can be exactly who you want to be. There're always possibilities and opportunities and people to meet and things to go and see. In a big city I feel like I could make anything happen.'

'Do you? Make things happen? Explore lots of new opportunities?'

'No . . .'

'You don't want to see what happens?'

Hmm. 'I do want to see what happens, but I'm afraid.'

'That doesn't sound like someone with Big City Energy to me. If I can offer *you* some advice, I think you should take more risks, starting with getting yourself next door.'

'This is completely the opposite advice I'm trying to make you take.'

'Well, we are completely different people.'

Ember yawns again then, and flutters her eyes closed. 'I have to go to sleep, man, I can't think any more with this vodka-head.'

'Alright, night night,' I say, but she's already zonked, and so I tiptoe out through the door to go and fill my water from the tap beside the shared bathroom.

The carriage is quiet but not silent, what with it being Christmas Day still, and not particularly late. I pause outside Sara and Joss's room, and don't hear anything.

I stop outside Luke and Joe's room ... nothing. I wonder if Joe is still up at the party?

Not that it matters, I'm not going to do anything tonight. I need a clear head. We need to talk properly, without the influence of mood lighting and music.

I pad back and forth along the corridor a couple more times. It'll probably help with the hangover tomorrow if I get a little exercise now.

Just going to top my water bottle up a little more, then I'll go back to my compartment, get a good night's sleep.

I'll sleep better if I stretch my legs out a bit more first. Ten laps of the carriage should do it.

The ball is in my court with Luke, that's what he said.

'Luke?' I whisper, so quietly that even I don't hear myself.

I listen at the door, but it's still silent. Phew, he didn't hear me either, that's that then, off I go to sleep. 'Luke?' I say louder, tingling with excited defiance at myself.

The sound of a footstep on the floor comes from behind the door, and my heart and nerves skitter. I take two steps towards my door, as if I might have time to get back in before he comes out, then stop myself.

I should not go into his compartment. But I'm going to!

'Hey,' Luke says, opening the door. He's in boxers and no T-shirt, the sly dog, and I try my hardest to look him dead in the eyes, and the eyes alone. 'You came.'

A million thoughts twirl about, so fast I can't keep up, but one important one pops out. 'I wish you'd said hi, that day, in London.'

Luke exhales. 'So do I,' he breathes the words out and I fall into him, my hands cupping his neck, trailing on his skin, my arms around his neck, resting on his shoulders.

We pause for second, just a second, with our lips close to each other, and when he smiles, I'm reminded of the best part of kissing him, and I'm not scared any more.

I kiss him, and it's just how I remembered it, but it also feels new and real, because we came back to each other. I murmur his name and he chuckles, saying mine back to me, printing it onto my lips with his own,

Luke pulls me into him, and into his room.

Chapter 41

Ember

The train judders. A screech sounds somewhere underneath me. For a moment I'm disoriented by the fact I'm lying down flat.

Ah, yes. I'm in Cali's compartment. And ah, yes, I drank a lot last night.

I stand up on shaking legs and open the curtain a crack, scrunching up my face against the blinding white of the snow, the sun risen and beaming, the sky blue, and the trees moving.

Oh my God, we're moving! We're moving forward again!

'Cali,' I say, not expecting the rasping wheeze of a voice to come out of my mouth. Ugh, I haven't felt this bad since the morning after my birthday party at the beach. I try again. 'Cali, the train's moving.' I pat her bunk, but it's flat, and that's when I look over.

There's not even a hint of warmth on those sheets. I smile. That naughty girl crept next door after all. Well, good for her.

Damn, that makes me remember what might have been with Alex.

Which makes me remember that I'm supposed to be reuniting with Bryn today.

Bryn doesn't deserve to be an afterthought. She deserves to be happy. I know what I need to do.

Not long after the tracks are cleared and the train has resumed its journey, Cali comes thumping back into her room. Her hair is a mess and her cheeks are pink and her sweatshirt is on backwards.

'Good morning, sunshine,' I say.

'Why did we drink vodka? We were on our way to bed.'

'And did you sleep well?'

She closes the door behind her and sits down on the bottom bunk, holding her forehead with one hand and picking at a spot on her chin with the other. 'I don't know if I did something really stupid last night.'

'I wouldn't call Luke *really* stupid,' I quip, which makes her laugh and then wince, rubbing her forehead.

'I don't know if it was a good idea. I mean it was definitely *good*. But what if I should have just left it as friendship this time? What if I've messed it up again? What if everyone's mad at me, and then Bryn accuses me of sabotaging her wedding, and then they call the whole thing off? I mean, sorry, I know that wouldn't be the worst thing for you.'

'Actually ... ' I gesture to my bag, which I've just finished packing.

Cali looks at it. 'You can hang out in here today. I don't think we'll get to Vancouver until tonight.'

'I've decided not to go to Vancouver.'

She drops both her hands to her lap and looks at me, wide-eyed. 'You have?'

'I have. I'm going to get off when the train reaches Whistler.'

'Is there an airport there?'

'No, I'm going to catch another train, back to Jasper, spend a little time in the National Park before I head home.'

'Won't you be lonely?'

'No, I think I'm going to be just fine.'

Cali is quiet for a minute, nodding. 'Okay, so when do we get to Whistler?'

I look at my phone. 'In about fifteen minutes.'

'Fifteen minutes!' Cali cries. 'Have you told the others? I need to get dressed. Am I going to be sick ... ? No, I'm fine. What do you want me to tell Bryn?'

I sit beside her and put my arm around her shoulders. 'I

don't need you to tell Bryn anything, but if you want to, or feel you should, just go ahead, it's fine. You don't need to get dressed. You need to take a lovely shower, stop picking at that spot, drink some tea, and then spend the day looking at this amazing scenery happening right outside our window.' I gesture to where the Rocky Mountains, shining in the morning sun, are silently drifting by beyond the frost-speckled glass. 'And I'm not going to tell the others, I'm just going to slip away.'

'You don't want to say goodbye?'

I shake my head. 'Not this time. I feel like we've made our peace, now it's time for me to step away, go back to my real life, which is actually pretty wonderful.'

'It is? You're okay without Bryn? Your beach friends treat you well?'

'I'm more than okay. I've moved on, and now the best thing for me, I think, is to let the past go.' Her face crumples back to worry and I laugh, in a way I hope is gentle both to her soul and her poor head. 'But that's what's right for me. My version of moving forward has to be to forget. I think you can only move forward if you forgive, and get your friends back.'

'What if they don't want me back?'

'They want you back. You just have hangxiety.'

'Oh.'

I stand up and pick up my bag, then hold my arms out, inviting her for a hug, if she wants one.

'Will you stay in touch?' Cali asks, standing, delicately.

'I'd like that,' I say, and she totters into my arms. 'If you don't throw up on me . . .'

When we pull away, I move towards the door.

Cali stops me. 'You'll tell Alex you're getting off the train though, won't you?'

I check the time again. I have ten minutes before we arrive at Whistler station. 'If I find her.'

Ten minutes is about enough time to walk the length of the train looking for Alex, but I think I know where she's likely to be.

I ascend the stairs to the celestial carriage. It's Boxing Day today, and the scenery is stunning, the snow having cleared itself in the breeze from the domed glass. Most seats are full of other passengers, gazing, photographing, relaxing under the filtered sunshine.

Alex's dark hair is loose, shiny but tousled, and she leans her head against the window. She doesn't spot me, lost in the view, or in thought, or in both, until I'm standing beside her seat.

'Oh hi, is that Bryn's sister-in-law?' I say. I don't know why I'm making a joke of it, but I give her a small smile to let her know it's just that.

Alex whips her head around, pushing her hair back, looking up at me with big eyes that have sleepy bags under them, which she still manages to pull off. She scrambles upright, scooting over, and I slide into the seat next to her.

'Ember, I can't even begin, I'm so sorry, please know that I wish I could go back to the start and tell you who I was, who I am, and it wouldn't change anything because I really have liked getting to know you and hanging out with you.'

I nod, and swallow down any words that might muddle this. 'I'm getting off the train when we get to Whistler.'

'What?' she says. 'But that's in a few minutes!'

'I wanted to say goodbye.'

Alex drops her eyes. 'You must hate me.'

'I don't hate you one bit. And this is a good thing, for your sister's wedding, and for me.' I mean it. I don't want to hold any resentment in me any longer. I just want to remember the good times, and drift back to the life I love.

I stand up, and she stands with me. 'Can I give you a hug?' she asks.

'Yes please.'

When Alex put her arms around me, a part of me vows to keep the memory of her safe in my heart. 'I'm sorry,' she says again, but I shake my head.

'No more sorrys. I'm not sorry.'

'No?'

'No.' An announcement comes over the speaker; we're pulling into Whistler, and I give her one last embrace. As I pull back, our lips hesitate near each other, breathing each other in for the final time, willing things to be just a little different.

But they aren't. 'Goodbye, Alex,' I say, and I slide out from her arms, pick up my bag, and step off the train.

I've wandered out of the station while I wait for the train that'll take me back to Jasper. I don't want to see any of my old friends again if they get onto the platform to stretch their legs during the short rest stop.

I'm just studying the opening hours on the small café, when footsteps running catch my attention. The sun is low and bright, and I have to squint into it to see her dark hair billowing out behind her.

'Wait, Ember, wait,' says Alex. She's carrying a bag.

'What are you doing?'

'I'm getting off, I'm staying with you. I'll miss the wedding.'

'No, you won't.'

'Yes, I will, I need you to know this wasn't all a lie, I wasn't just trying to make you forget about Bryn.'

'I don't think that. Alex, get back on the train. If this one leaves without you, I think you'll get there too late.'

'It doesn't matter. I really like you.'

'Of course it does. I really like you, too. But … but it couldn't work between us.'

She hesitates, like she knows I'm right, but she takes

my hands, running her fingers down my arms, and steps in close. 'Why not?' she asks with a sigh.

'Well, you live in Canada. And I don't. And your sister is marrying my ex.'

'That is a little awkward, I guess.' A hint of her honey smile returns.

'One day we'll find it funny. And just because it can't be forever doesn't mean I didn't have the best time, and it doesn't mean I won't hold onto it as one of my favourite memories.'

'I will to,' Alex says, meeting my eyes, then glancing down at my lips.

'So, you're going to get back on the train?'

'You don't want to be a plus one or anything?'

I laugh at that. 'You know that awkward thing we were just talking about . . . ?'

'Oh yeah, that.' She chuckles.

This is hard to let her go; we never even really got started. But though my heart aches, it's nice to feel it again. 'Good memories,' I state, my voice firm.

'Good memories.' She holds my gaze.

On the platform, the train whistles. She has to go. She drops her hands, steps back and turns towards the station.

'Wait,' she says. 'One more good memory.'

Alex reaches for my hand and pulls me back towards her, and her lips kiss mine like sweet honey. Everything about her is warm, and she kisses me for as long as she can until the second whistle goes.

We break apart, but in the best possible way.

One hour later, the café has opened, and as I wait in line, I snap a photo on my phone of the sign. 'Open for Business' it says.

Shortly after, coffee in hand, I board the train, ready for a long journey back to Jasper. In my seat, I take a sip of my warm coffee, topped with cream as white as the snow, and tip my head back to lean it against the rest.

Last night, after Alex confessed, I thought I'd made the worst decision of my life by coming to Canada. I was wrong.

And not *just* because of that amazing kiss which I'll never forget.

I pick up my phone and navigate to the photos, pulling up the one of the 'Open for Business' sign. Then I do something cheesy, mushy, and a little bit old Hollywood romance, and I text it to Alex along with the message, My heart, thanks to you.

Chapter 42

Bryn

Moglington dislikes my friends already, and they haven't even made it here yet.

I hold her in my arms and pace the porch, as if they're going to appear around the corner any minute, while around me a blizzard of activity is occurring.

Ruby, fresh flowers in one hand and a candelabra in the other, stops on her way into the cabin. 'They'll be here.' She smiles. 'You can put the cat down.'

'But what if it stops again? What if they don't make it, after all this?'

'They're going to make it. Alex told me, clear tracks ahead, all the way to Vancouver. Do you want me to drive you to the station?'

I shake my head, my shoulders loosening a little at her

reassuring tone, and Moglington uses this opportunity of weakness to make a break for it, leaping free into the snow, four deep little paw holes forming, and skitters indoors after the wedding cake maker.

'Did Alex meet them? Did she like them? Did she say if they're all still mad at each other, and at me?'

Ruby considers my questions, head tilted to the side, dark hair glistening under the low, winter afternoon sunshine. 'Yes she met them, yes she likes them, no she hasn't said anything about them other than that they'll all be there this evening.' She hands the flowers and candelabra to one of her cousins walking by. 'How are you doing?'

'Super nervous,' I answer. I have swirls of anxiety rolling in my stomach, worst-case-scenarios playing out like pilot TV shows with bad scripts in my mind. 'Wait, do you mean about seeing them or getting married?'

'Seeing them.' Ruby laughs.

'Yes then, super nervous. Getting married in the morning will be a breeze.' I check my watch. 'I'd better get going soon. Are you sure you don't mind me leaving the rest of this to you?'

I'm getting married tomorrow, and all my friends are coming to witness it, just like I always imagined. The forecast is for half rain, half sun, which is just fine with me. The decorations are up, the food is in the fridge, the cake is here, the guests are nestling into nearby lodges

303

and hotels. One bride is cool and calm, even if the other is a garter full of nerves.

'Of course not, we've got this. Go, get your friends, feed them, hug them, then get back here and marry me.'

'Yes, boss,' I tell her, and give her a final squeeze before grabbing my bag and jumping in the chauffeured van I've hired to collect my friends and bring them back here. I think they're going to love Ruby, even if they still hate me. She's great. And I always love having her sister to stay as well.

This is it.

The van boards the ferry and I climb out, grabbing a coffee from the kiosk inside and taking a seat beside one of the big windows. It's overcast and cold and perfect out here on the water, and I let my thoughts drift about with the rocking of the boat.

That's when I realise something. I am nervous, but I'm excited, thrilled even. Like that feeling you get when you finally pick that big scab just to see what happens, haha. At least now I'll know what happens. And it's already going to be a big, beautiful wedding so why not throw a few old friends and foes into the mix? Hell, maybe I should have flown some exes out too?

No, maybe not. A smile is crossing my mouth though, which I cover with the lip of my coffee cup.

I bet they were so mad when they got to Toronto Airport. I bet Joss, in particular, was furious and stomping her feet about. I bet Cali was trying to shine sunshine all over the plan. But Alex has done that trip enough times that I know it's an incredible journey; they'd struggle not to fall for the beauty in their surroundings, even if they're just admiring it between clawing at each other's eyeballs. But I don't think it will have come to that, not really. Because they came. They could have said no (some of them tried) but they came which means something is still there, something still makes the six of us *us*.

I can't wait to hear all about it. I can't wait to see them.

Chapter 43

Cali

'We will shortly be arriving in Pacific Central Station, Vancouver. This is the final destination for this service. Please take all your belongings, family, friends and memories with you.'

The announcement was expected, of course, but I can't help but feel a weird little flake of sadness that it's over. This train has been my home for the past five days, the place where – yes, Bryn – we've come back together and are stronger and better for it. I think.

Be it due to hangovers, sleepiness or stubbornness, I've not seen much of the others today. We've all kept mostly quiet, to ourselves, watching the Canadian landscape drift by. We've rolled without drama – outside or inside the train – through the district of British Columbia, alongside rippling rivers, cutting through canyons, and, eventually, into the suburbs of the city.

My friends and I have greeted each other with minor-hangover friendliness. I've told them about Ember leaving and nobody scoffed or whooped or anything. Alex is picking up a hire car at the train station and making her own way over to Vancouver Island.

I've told Luke I need a little time. It's cowardly to care what the others think, but I do. And, of course, I know they all know. Joe came back to his room last night when (thankfully) we were fast asleep, but there was no missing the fact we were snuggled together like a couple of Arctic foxes in Luke's bunk. And Joss is being a little softer today. But I can't help it . . . there's still this horrid feeling deep in my stomach, like the ice our group friendship is on is so thin that he and I becoming a duo might just cause it to crack. Again.

I stand, and gather up all my crap – my bag, my coat, my tinsel bracelet, and go to meet the others at the exit nearest our cabins.

The station appears outside the window, benches and signs and waiting passengers coming into view.

'Is anyone else nervous to see Bryn?' Joss asks, chewing on her fingernails.

'No more so than I was seeing the rest of you,' Sara admits.

'You never seemed nervous,' I say, surprised.

307

'I was bricking it,' she says, laughing. 'I thought you all hated me.'

'Me too,' says Luke.

'Me too,' chorus Joe and Joss.

'Me too.' I laugh.

The train grinds to a slow stop, drowning out our nervous laughter, and Luke reaches through the window to open the door. We bundle outside, weary, relieved, happy, and not too late for the wedding in the morning.

I look up and down the platform for that final, familiar face that's been missing up until now. 'There she is!'

Bryn is standing on the platform, holding up a sign that says 'I'M SORRY!' and looking for us. Her hair is shorter, it looks freshly coloured, her skin is more tanned than she ever achieved living in London. She still dresses like one of those rich people who aim to look casual but end up looking like they've just come from buying a country club, and still sports an impressive fuchsia lipstick.

'Bryn!' I call, my voice loud and high-pitched and drawing the attention of several people who aren't even Bryn, and I wave until I'm the first one to catch her eye. She lowers her sign, puts her hand on her heart, smiles, and then starts running towards us. It's very movie-like. Well done, Bryn.

She stops short though, and studies us, and for a moment we're back at that place of awkwardness and silence, and nobody quite knowing if we can call each other friends again or not.

But then it's Joss, *Joss*, who steps out of the crowd and hugs Bryn first, and that's all it takes.

We envelop ourselves into the group hug I've needed for a long time, all arms and hot breath and talking over each other and rushed compliments.

Afterwards Bryn steps back and takes us all in. 'You came.'

'Of course we did,' I reply.

'And you didn't kill each other on the train. Are you all very angry about the train?'

'No.' I wave her away, and can't help but sneak a subtle glance at Luke.

Bryn sees and gasps, pointing at me and then him and then back at me. 'Did you two hook up again?'

I stutter a non-reply, looking from the others to her, and, thank God she's smiling. 'We had sex on the train!' I blurt out, and slap my hand across my mouth. 'It was awesome!' *Shut up, Cali!* 'Are you mad?'

'Why the hell would I be mad? I feel like a match-maker!' She laughs in delight and slings an arm around my shoulders. 'Listen, we have some catching up to do, but it's also the night before my wedding so I don't want to catch a cold from hanging around a freezing train platform for too long. Who wants something to eat?'

In the warmth of a large pub with mahogany tables and gigantic burgers, Bryn chats about her wedding the next day, and even as she's stuffing cheese-topped chips into her mouth she's grinning with infectious happiness.

'You are going to love Ruby. She's so creative and funny and we're into the same things and she's Canadian so has the hottest accent. And she's so organised, which you know I love; she's almost single-handedly planned this whole wedding.'

'She has? In what way?' I ask, Ember and her social media stalking coming to mind.

'Well, the venue is her family's cabin, and she wanted red bridesmaids' dresses because it's her mum's favourite colour, hence the name Ruby, and … oh God, everything really. But we have similar taste, so it's all good with me.' Bryn is glowing, giddy, totally and utterly in love with the right person, and it's the loveliest thing to witness. Thank God we're all here.

I nod along, listening, and I sink back into the seat with secret relief. I wish Ember all the happiness in the world, and later I'll check in with her, make sure she's made it back to Jasper and is doing okay. But I don't think Bryn's had any thought to luring her out here or rekindling what they once had, I think Ember just saw what she wanted, maybe needed, to see. And Bryn is just a happy bride, completely in love.

'Listen,' Bryn says, growing serious for a moment. 'My big plan was that we would have had the whole day today to talk everything out, wipe the slate clean, as it were, but I'm sure you're all tired now. I wanted to show you Vancouver Island, all the things I love about it, introduce you to my second family. But that'll all have to wait. So, none of you need to say anything, but can I just tell you all how sorry *I* am for how everything went down on that holiday? I never wanted to lose you all. And if there's anything I can do to make it up to you, please let me know. Maybe after the wedding, though.'

'Yeah, I'm annoyed you aren't putting us first since we've come all this way, but it sounds like you have a pretty full day tomorrow,' Joss says, and she flashes a grin at Bryn. 'But just to add, I'm sorry too.'

We all parrot each other, apologising, expressing regret, vowing to take back everything we said, and I'm definitely not crying, it's just that my burger has chillies in it or something.

By the last bite, I know I'm not the only one stifling a yawn.

'Come on, sleepyheads,' Bryn says, standing and gesturing for us all to bundle back into our big winter coats. 'Ready for one last leg of the journey out to that beautiful cabin I promised you?'

Luke stretches on the way out of the pub. 'I don't know; do you have a bunk bed Joe and I could sleep in?'

Chuckling, Bryn leads us to a chauffeur-driven minivan she's rented to take us to the cabin (she's such a good host).

Vancouver Island is a little drive out of the city of

Vancouver, including a ferry crossing which I'd love to say we were wide awake for and enjoying but actually I'm just sleepily watching the city lights melt away into the dark. Bryn is beside me, and the others have all drifted asleep by the time we reach the island, so I say to her quietly, 'Can I talk to you quickly, about ...' I nod my head towards Luke.

'Of course,' she says, leaning into me, her arm against mine, and it's just how we used to sit on her sofa on a weekend morning, half gossiping, half watching whatever random cooking show we could find on TV.

'Is it ... am I ...' I glance at him. His head is flopped against the window, his eyes closed, his eyelashes soft-looking, his arms flopped out to the side like he's fallen asleep giving blood. His breathing is deep and steady. Sleepy boy. 'I want your opinion; what would you think if he and I gave it another try?'

'I'd think it's awesome, of course,' she whispers.

I can't help the smile that sweeps over my face. I lean closer into her, a rush of love for my friend. 'You don't think it could cause problems, you know, for the group?'

'What are you talking about?'

'I'm talking about how last time, everything was amazing between the six of us, and then he and I got together and everything changed, and people got mad at us, and then each other, and then, well, you remember the rest.'

'I don't think history is going to repeat itself in that way.'

'You don't think it would … alter the dynamic? Irreparably?'

Bryn sits up and pulls me into a hug. 'Is this what you've been thinking the whole time we've not been friends? That you and Luke *finally* boning each other caused the whole fallout?'

I pull back and look at her. 'Didn't it?'

'No!'

Joss snorts in her sleep in the seat behind me, waking herself up. 'Are we there yet? What are we talking about?'

Bryn turns in her seat. 'Did you know Cali thinks she's the reason we all got the hump with each other for five years?'

'Vain, much?' Joss says, then winks a sleepy eye at me.

'Alright, we need to clear this up.' Bryn reaches over and shoves Luke awake, then back, lightly smacking the knees of both Joe and Sara. When everyone's alert and caught up, Bryn faces me, taking my hands in hers.

'You think everything was daisies and roses right up until the holiday, specifically, when you told us you and Luke had become a couple.'

'Right.'

'That is not the case.'

I glance at the others in turn, and they nod. 'It isn't?'

'I'm not saying we were arguing, but my God, we were a co-dependent little cohort in that house. Our lives were that friendship bubble, and *only* that friendship bubble. And it

313

was lovely, for a long time, but I think I speak for all of us when I say we'd come to a standstill in our lives, so keen were we not to change a thing. But actually, we were ready to grow and move forward, and that's not a bad thing. Even you.'

'I didn't want to grow,' I grumble.

'Then why did you finally make your move on Luke? Doesn't that tell you something?'

'Now hold on,' I say. 'He made a move on me … no … actually I did make the first move. Keep talking.'

'Hey, I initiated the first kiss,' Luke says, holding my gaze.

I smile at him, sweet thing. 'That's what you think.'

'Why do you think Joe and I started that business?' Joss interrupts.

'Which Sara and Bryn invested in,' chips in her brother.

' … And which then failed,' adds Joss. 'You don't think that caused some of the tension?'

'And I was applying for jobs outside of London,' Sara pipes up, rolling her shoulders. 'I would have moved out soon after the holiday anyway, even if what happened hadn't happened.'

Bryn nods. 'Same. I wanted more space. I might have stayed another year, perhaps, but no more. Of course, I wish we could have stayed friends, but I truly think we needed a bit of space from each other. Unfortunately, we let the tension rise too much, too fast, and that bit of space turned into a ridiculously long and petty silence.

But,' – she claps her hands together – 'we're here now, all together, and also, at your humble abode."

The car crunches to a stop, the headlights beaming through the dark at a structure I can only describe as the type of place Airbnb advertises on their main page. It's a gigantic cabin made of thick, gleaming wood, with billowing snow cascading over the lips of the roof and along the window ledges. Porch lights, surrounded by thousands of white Christmas lights, illuminate the front door, which has frosted glass panels and the biggest wreath I've ever seen. White ribbons tied onto the porch railings flutter in the soft night breeze.

'We're actually staying here?' I can't quite lift my jaw off the ground. The photos Bryn sent before we arrived didn't even begin to do this place justice.

'Yes please,' Bryn says.

I take a moment before following the others in, reaching for Luke's hand and holding him back. I'm dressed in the hugest of coats, the heaviest of boots, but I feel lighter than I have for many Christmases.

Chapter 44

Ember

'I believe you that it's paradise, but I can't see a thing,' Tonia says to me over a video call. I'm holding up my phone, trying to show her the brilliance of the view from my little cabin here in Jasper National Park, but the morning sun is dazzling directly at me, turning the snow into an iridescent carpet. 'Send me photos later, and get to the good part.'

I settle down on the rocking chair on my porch, coffee in hand, blanket on my legs. The air is crispy and crunchy-cold, the snow so deep it reaches in powdery drifts up the side of the cabin and is layered over the porch floor itself, but I'm breathing deep and slow here.

Tonia wants to hear about my kiss with Alex, for the third time. I already called from the train yesterday, and it was the first thing she asked me about this morning. I hunker down in my blanket, unable to keep the smile from my face, glowing in the sunshine.

'It was a really good kiss . . . ' I begin, rolling my head back at the memory, a smile playing on my lips like they're imagining hers exploring them. I might never see Alex again, but I won't forget how she made me feel. This smile isn't going away for a while.

I've decided to stay here in Jasper for another week. There's so much of the national park that I want to see. God, it's good to be out here in nature again, in a wide-open space, under the stars and the sun.

After I've hung up the call, I lace on my hiking boots, fill a bag with my travel flask and tons of snacks, and follow one of the winter trails towards Maligne Canyon, where I spend the best part of the day walking, crunching, stepping, a little sliding, and a lot of laying my eyes on frozen waterfall after turquoise frozen waterfall. At one of them, deep in the canyon, I remove a glove and run my hand over an icicle, which hangs like hair over the side of the rocks, surrounding me.

My mum and dad would have liked it here. They would have liked that I was here, soaking all of this in. I can picture Mum laughing in delight at the sight of the waterfalls. She always laughed when she saw something that made her smile, like the smile was trying to jump forward out of her and touch it.

I hope I can carry that on, find something every day that makes me smile so hard it tries to burst out of me.

Cali checked in earlier, which was nice of her. Like Alex, like Bryn, like all of them, she has come in and out of my life now and that's okay. I'm glad to have put any ill-feeling so very far away, because really, look at all of this. I inhale a lungful of big, clean mountain air. Sitting in thoughts of 'what if', not noticing all the amazing beauty the world has to offer, isn't how I'm going to live my life.

There's an awful lot of that amazing beauty still to see.

Chapter 45

Cali

One of the most beautiful things these eyes have ever seen, more beautiful than the Christmas lights over Regent Street, more beautiful than the sunrise glittering off the glass buildings in the City of London, is one of my best friends, on her wedding day, standing in the twinkling snow, under a big, blue Canadian sky.

The cabin we're all staying in has an out-house which is adorned in white ribbons for the wedding, the inside transformed into a reception room that wouldn't look out of place in an extremely fancy bridal magazine. In fact, I'm pretty sure their wedding photographer might work for an extremely fancy bridal magazine, because they keep talking about 'the issue' and I don't think they're referring to global warming, or that one of Ruby's cousins has put a tiny suit on the cat and snuck her into the ceremony.

And right now, the bride and bride, in their white-as-snow dresses, are having photos taken with a stunning mountain backdrop. Most guests are staying in the warm, but me and my friends – yes, it's early days, but I love that I can call them friends again – have donned coats over our wedding attire and are clasping crystal tumblers of steaming, spiced cider, our boots in the snow, enjoying watching Bryn in her new surroundings. Which, as great as our time at the townhouse was, this is clearly the place she's meant to be.

Joss sniffs at her dress. 'Do I smell like last night's alcohol?' she hisses, and we all say no to make her feel better.

Beside me, I spot Luke peeping at me.

'What?' I ask.

He is so bloody handsome in his suit. 'I very nearly didn't come to Canada.'

'What changed your mind?'

'I just wanted to see you again. Even if you hated me, even if you had another boyfriend whose name may or may not have been Luke, even if, actually, *you* hadn't turned up, I couldn't not take the chance of seeing you. You're like a magnet to me.'

I am pink with warmth despite the frostbite forming on every one of my toes. 'Well I'm glad you chose to come. Because Fake Luke would have made a terrible wedding date.'

'He can't dance?'

'No, it's not that ... he's just really partial to sleeping with the bridesmaids.'

I put my mittened hand into Luke's, my magnet. He and I have a lot to catch up, and the way we can't stop looking at each other, smiling at each other, talking like there's no tomorrow, I think we're going to enjoy every minute of it. And this time, neither of us plan to let it only last a week.

Speaking of bridesmaids ... Alex is looking lovely in her long, red-wine coloured dress. There's the smallest hint of sadness on her face while she's lost in thought, but then she catches my eye, does a small nod, and I see the sparkle return as she's pulled into the photos by Bryn and Ruby. She's going to be just fine, as will Ember.

I dropped Ember a message this morning, making sure she'd made it okay to Jasper, and she replied immediately to say everything was good, better than good, and she is so happy with her decision not to come as far as Vancouver.

A little later, Bryn and I flop down in two plush arm-chairs in front of a log fire. The sun is dipping in the sky, warm oranges and purples and pinks lighting up the scenery beyond the window. From this side of the cabin, we're facing a lake, and the snow-capped Mount Washington with lit-up ski trails looms across the water.

'How are you doing, beautiful bride?' I ask as she closes her eyes and leans her head back.

321

'So good, I've had the best day. Did you have fun?'

'It was . . . incredible. Better than that.'

'I'm so glad you all not only came but that we're finally all moving forward from that stupid fight. But like I said, it was never really about the fight.'

'We have spread our wings.' I nod. Even me, I think, now I've started making things happen for myself.

'Can you believe Sara has a daughter?' Bryn says.

'I can imagine she's just an awesome mum.' When Sara told us about Dina at breakfast this morning (Joss of course leaping in there with an 'I already knew'), it was a wake-up call that we hadn't made her feel part of our group enough that she felt the desire to tell us. I never want her to feel like that again. She might have moved on from us being her closest friends, but we're still her friends, and I, for one, want to see just how cool this little girl grows up to be. Just like her mum.

Bryn and I chat for a while, and she tells me how scary it was to make the move out to Canada, but it was something she'd always wanted. She tells me about how she met Ruby in Vancouver and it had been like Canada's way of telling her she'd made exactly the right decision. I describe in long, over-detailed detail what it was like going all the way across this incredible country on a train. And now feels like it might be the right time . . .

'I saw Ember recently, by the way.'

As soon as the words have left my mouth I feel like a

322

stupid plonker because why would I bring up Ember on her wedding day? This was exactly the type of thing I was trying to avoid by angling Ember away from coming to Vancouver in the first place! Maybe I am obsessed with forcing things. Too late now.

Thankfully, Bryn smiles wide, not even a hint of bad feeling on her face. 'That's awesome, how is she?'

'She seemed well.' I nod. And I force myself to leave it at that. Maybe sometime I'll fill her in on what really happened on this journey, but not today.

I can't imagine what the future holds, no matter how many scenarios I daydream up, so I took a risk coming out here. It was one hundred per cent worth it, because whether you need to forgive, or forget, or channel that Big City Energy or feel some perspective under a sky full of stars, it's fun to step out of dreamland and keep moving forward.

Acknowledgements

The train has left the station! Final destination!

A quick sweep about the carriages to say thanks to all the glimmering people that helped create this novel.

Thank you to my ever-awesome literary agent, Hannah, and my brillianttttttt editor, Bec, for Everything. You two are ace.

Thank you heaps and heaps to the rest of the extended Sphere team, including Frances, Jane, Hannah, Laura and Bryony. You are all golden.

Thank you Phil and Kodi, you're both my rocks and you keep me nice and warm while I'm in my head, writing, surrounded by imaginary snow-covered mountains.

Thank you Mum for being you, and thank you to my late dad who loved that I wrote.

Thank you to my brother and my family, thank you to my friends, thank you Canada for the inspo, thank you

Adam for the Vancouver Island suggestion, and thank you Ollie and Anita, who I promised I'd put in the acknowledgements, haha.

Thank you for coming with me on this journey, readers, big love, now off you go and please remember to take all your belongings with you.

(Leave the sweets, thanks.)

Author's note

In this novel, our characters are lucky enough to visit Canada's Jasper National Park. At the time of writing, the town of Jasper and the National Park have been tragically devastated by recent wildfires. My heart goes out to the community over there as they rebuild their lives, and we all look forward to the beauty of the area returning once again.

Will her dreams come true in the city that never sleeps?

On a magical trip to New York City, Ashling created a list of five ultimate goals. But now, ten years later, with four goals having crumbled before her, she realises she has only one viable dream left: move to New York City, before it's too late.

Armed with a ninety-day visa waiver, she's sure that a winter in the Big Apple will help her finally get her life on track. But, after arriving there with nowhere to live, Ashling realises that she may be in over her head, until she meets River ...

River is miserable. He's newly single, recently demoted and feeling entirely lost, but sensing Ashling could do with the help, he offers her his sofa bed. Despite their clashing personalities, outgoing Ashling finds herself growing closer to quiet, geeky River – but is he just shy or is there another reason he's holding back?

With snow falling on Fifth Avenue, can Ashling once again learn to follow her dreams – and maybe even her heart?

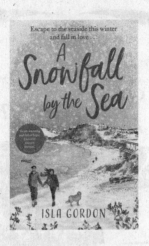

Escape to the seaside this winter and fall in love . . .

A Snowfall by the Sea

ISLA GORDON

A *heart-warming, feel-good festive romance* to settle down with this Christmas

Cleo loves winter in Wavebreak Bay. The tourists leave as the temperatures drop, the fairy lights go up and it really starts to feel like home again. It also happens to be the time of year that her best friend Eliot comes back from San Francisco.

Though the seasons change, not much else in Cleo's life does. She's in a people-pleasing rut, taking the worst shifts at the family restaurant, pet-sitting for her parents and making little time for herself. Cleo has spent so long thinking about everyone around her that she's lost sight of what *she* wants. And she wants Eliot. And she's decided that, this year, she's finally going to tell him.

But as the snow settles on Wavebreak Bay, Cleo's Christmas-for-two is disrupted by the arrival of her entire family – and more guests keep arriving. As Cleo works hard to make sure everyone else is having the most wonderful time of the year, will she finally pluck up the courage to stand up for herself . . . and to follow her heart?

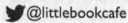